Always

Andy M Davidson

Elk Lake Publishing Inc.
PUBLISHING THE POSITIVE
Plymouth, Massachusetts
A Christian Company
ElkLakePublishingInc.com

Copyright Notice

Always

1st edition. Copyright © 2025 by Andy M Davidson. The information contained in this book is the intellectual property of Andy M Davidson and is governed by United States and International copyright laws. All rights reserved. No part of this publication, either text or image, may be used for any purpose other than personal use. Therefore, reproduction, modification, storage in a retrieval system, or retransmission, in any form or by any means, electronic, mechanical, or otherwise, for reasons other than personal use, except for brief quotations for reviews or articles and promotions, is strictly prohibited without prior written permission by the publisher.

NO AI TRAINING: Without in any way limiting Andy M Davidson and publisher's exclusive rights under copyright, any use of this publication to "train" generative artificial intelligence (AI) technologies to generate text is expressly prohibited. The author reserves all rights to license uses of this work for generative AI training and development of machine learning language models.

This is a work of fiction. Names, characters, businesses, places, events, locales, and incidents are either the products of the author's imagination or used in a fictitious manner. Any resemblance to actual persons, living or dead, or actual events is purely coincidental.

Scripture quotations are taken from the NEW INTERNATIONAL VERSION (NIV): Scriptures taken from THE HOLY BIBLE, NEW INTERNATIONAL VERSION ®. Copyright©1973, 1978, 1984, 2011 by Biblica, Inc.™. Used by permission of Zondervan

Cover and Interior Design: Kelly Artieri, Deb Haggerty
Editor(s): Sue A. Fairchild, Cristel Phelps, Deb Haggerty

PUBLISHED BY: Elk Lake Publishing, Inc., 35 Dogwood Drive, Plymouth, MA 02360, 2025

Always

Library Cataloging Data
Names: Davidson, Andy M (Andy M Davidson)
Always / Andy M Davidson
306 p. 23cm × 15cm (9in × 6 in.)
ISBN-13: 9798891344037 (paperback) | 9798891343207 (trade paperback) | 9798891343214 (e-book)
Key Words: Christian contemporary second chance romance; Christian love story later in life veteran coma; Mature characters contemporary romance Jesus; Faith-based romance finding love again later stage; Christian love and relationships romance over 50; Mature Christian relationship lost love clean; Christian fiction romance in midlife contemporary
Library of Congress Control Number: 2025937497 Fiction

Dedication

To my sister-in-law Clare, a true sister if there ever was one, whose body was ravaged by cancer, but whose heart was filled with love.

Acknowledgments

I must simply acknowledge God's grace in my life, who in these past three years especially has worked a patient miracle. He, who never gave up on me when I was lost in limerence, and who gently guided me back to true love. Limerence is but a misguided fanciful image of someone that only leads to confusion and heartache. But real love leads to peace, and God is real love. My prayer for all who read this fictional account is to seek God first, and all these things will be added unto you. The greatest of these is love.

To Clarice Gregoire James, the leader of our critique group. Not only did I value your criticism but was bolstered by your encouragement. After so many rewrites, I finally worked up the courage to send it to Elk Lake Publishing.

And to Deb Haggerty, who saw promise after so many rewrites, gave me a chance as not only a writer but someone who needed hope.

And to Sue Fairchild, with the patience that only our Lord can instill, took my disparities and inconsistencies and with her unfailing alchemy, worked to build my words into a real story.

Lastly to my readers, thank you. I am blessed by your presence, your thoughtful attention, and your love.

SIDE BY SIDE

See that sun in the morning,
Peeking over the hill?
I'll bet you're sure it *always* has and sure it *always* will.
That's how I feel about someone,
How somebody feels about me.
We're sure we love each other
That's the way we'll always be.
...
We'll be the same as we started
Just a-traveling along
Singing a song
Side by side.

—Harry M. Woods

February 2021

"Tonight, I end this madness. Tonight, I go home."

Sully overflowed Kat's colorful bowl with Friskies Seafood. He even filled a shallow plastic container with extra kitty litter, then fell to his knees and stroked her thick calico fur.

"That should hold till they find you. I'm ... I'm really sorry, Kat."

Sully grabbed the wooden kitchen chair and pulled himself up. Moments later, he walked out the door. The screen door slammed behind him.

He ran his weathered hand over his truck's hood. He loved the old truck. It wasn't just any GMC Sierra—Sierra wasn't just a brand, it was her name. But it was time. Maybe not Sierra's time but his.

Sully opened the door to the darkened cab whose light had long extinguished. "I just can't do this anymore."

There was no one left to hear him.

"Take me home, old girl." He turned the key to hear the starter click-click-click. Sully raised his clenched fist. "C'mon, start." He turned the key a second time.

As if the old truck heard him, Sierra's engine turned over, sucked in some gas, and rumbled to life.

"Yeah, Martha, I still get mad."

It'd been years since his deceased wife or anyone that mattered had heard him. His brother Stephen and sweet Jimmy from the Gulf War hadn't heard his bellowing for a long time now. But he still spoke to them.

Overgrown hemlocks swept downward and scraped at Sierra's side as she lumbered down his long drive to the highway. He could see his final end at the bottom of the valley on the old river bridge he'd never cross again.

"I just can't do this anymore."

Tears formed in the corners of his eyes, but he wouldn't let them fall any farther.

Soon, he turned onto the four-lane highway.

Wet snow lay on the shoulder of the road. Car tracks made slippery paths in both lanes. *Get over the crest. Push the pedal. See the stone wall. Aim the truck. Shut your eyes. Let go.* He'd hit the wall a thousand times in his mind. Tonight, he would finally hit the wall for real.

Sully winced as slush pellets from a rebuilt Humvee strafed Sierra.

Always.

He heard the word, and a familiar fragrance filled the cab as the Humvee slid by him.

Sully shook his hand. "Jerk." He drove on as a carousel of dark pictures clicked through his head.

His brother, his battle buddy, and his wife—all gone.

"Screw it. I end this madness tonight."

His heartrate rose with the needle on his speedometer. Now other cars got smacked from the slush from his tires as he passed them. *Who cares?* Sierra picked up speed as he crested the hill then shook slightly as they careened down the mountain. His focus narrowed while others honked.

Always

The bridge lay at the bottom of the long decline. *Bridge ... long decline ...* The metaphor wasn't lost on him. He envisioned the beginning, the climax ... the end.

Sierra slid as he swerved to miss a piece of truck tire and came close to a Fiat with a loud muffler in the lane next to him. *Don't take anyone with you, knucklehead.* He pushed even harder on the gas pedal. As he drove closer to the cluster of lights blinking in the distance, the line of cars slid to a halt.

Sully jammed on his brakes. When Sierra came to a shuddering, skidding stop, he breathed heavily, wiping sweat from his brow. *Coward, you can't even get this right.* His plan now foiled, he stared into the emptiness of the blackened gray sky. While he sat in the sea of traffic, he picked at a caramel he found between his seats. He swept the dust from his dash with an oily rag, but his hands still shook. He tried to fix the clock, but again, he failed. Sierra inched forward with the other vehicles until they arrived at the bottom of the hill.

Sully looked at the beehive of emergency lights, parts, and people on the side of the road. Someone else had beat him to the wall. *Nuts, that jerk ruined everything.*

Steam billowed from the converted Humvee's front end which now sat crumpled against the snowy concrete abutment. A cop stood with a clipboard next to a man in tight jeans cupping a cigarette. Plastic parts and a misshaped wheel lay littered around them.

"I knew that Humvee was trouble."

Sully didn't say "serves him right" out loud. Instead, he said a short prayer when the first responders slid a stretcher into the white and green ambulance. Brown hair spilled down one side of the gurney.

Always.

He heard her voice this time and smelled something familiar. A distant memory surfaced like a grainy black and white photo.

No, it can't be.

He swallowed his pain. He wouldn't let himself feel.

"Guess I'll be seeing you at the hospital," he mumbled.

Sully was a custodian for the local general hospital, but he had a mind for medicine from his time in Iraq. He knew this woman was in bad shape just from what he'd seen of her. He shook his head. *Someone isn't going home tonight.* He liked surprising people with his knowledge, liked having something on them—it was his joke. He had little else, unless Kat counted.

That knucklehead ruined everything.

After the bridge traffic began to move, he took a deep breath and increased his speed, now five miles under the limit. His hands shook ever so slightly as he drove into the night. Every time the grainy photo resurfaced, he shook his head and shouted, "NO."

But he had seen her hair.

Sully and Sierra ended their journey at the far edge of the hospital parking lot where he came out of his fog.

Well, I'm here now. Guess I'll go in.

He trudged through the slush toward the sliding glass doors of Mission Hospital. The western North Carolina hospital meant work, something to do, little more. He swallowed his ugly plan as he walked toward the stark white, sterile building, but his stomach remained in knots and his hands still trembled.

A medical resident jumped over puddles until one of his Birkenstock shoes stayed behind. "Aggh!"

"Evening, Doc." Sully bent down to pick up the wet, synthetic shoe. "Some weather."

Always

He handed the resident his shoe and moved on. The green and white ambulance sat cattycorner to the emergency department, the vehicle's doors open and its gurney missing.

Things missing or out of place always disturbed Sully. Maybe because so many things, so many people, had gone missing in his life. Death will do that. His brother, just a boy on a bike, hit by a speeding car. And Jimmy, his battle buddy, taken down by a sniper's bullet. Yet in Sully lay another missing memory, an incomplete time, an open wound that quietly festered.

At night, a vision would come to him. Always an angel. She walked with him in loneliness, held his hand in sadness, and even rejoiced in seldom triumphs. He couldn't shake her. In Iraq, she kept him safe. At night, she brought him sleep. She had brought him happiness in the past, but he'd given up. And now, any chance for happiness was gone. Just a memory kept him alive.

He squared his shoulders. *Just shut up and color*. That's what the Marines had told Sully when there wasn't anything to do but keep moving forward. As their corpsman, he had loved being called Doc by his Marines, but all he had loved was gone. Now, Sully just colored.

He rejoined the hospital with its bland, tiled walls. He shuddered as he hung his coat in the locker room, washed his hands, and combed the remaining hairs on his head. He rubbed his eyes, still watery, and his lips, still full. As a kid, he had tried to pull in his lips, but he had grown into them a long time ago. They were of little use to him now. No baby's head to kiss or a helpmate to caress. The longer he looked into the mirror inside his locker, the more he saw his father, and the less he saw himself. He stared for a moment longer. *Who are you, and what did you do with me?*

He slammed the locker shut and stepped into the bright hallway.

"Outta the way!"

He jumped back as a gurney sailed by with two saline bags swishing back and forth, suspended from a pole. A bloody sheet covered the accident victim. Her long brown hair dangled off the edge of the mobile bed as the medical resident and two wide-eyed attendants pushed past. A certain fragrance filled the air as they passed, rising above the Mr. Clean floors and sanitized attendants.

What was that fragrance?

"Second floor," one of them shouted at the elevator doors. "The OR."

Sully had seen the trip a hundred times before, but this time the medical personnel moved with a frantic pace. Maybe it was their inexperience, or maybe it was her condition.

"They usually change that sheet before moving them," Sully said to the closed elevator doors.

"Look out, old man." A man with a remarkable head of black hair with two gray shocks along his temples pushed by.

"Who you calling old?"

If he weren't at work, he would have stepped into the man's way and greeted him with his customary "Jerk." But tonight, he sensed the urgency as the man brushed Sully's shoulder, pushing him farther back. The man pounded on the elevator buttons then jumped into the next open door.

Sully rubbed his nose as if it had been caught in the closing doors, then headed for the stairs. *Stairs ... Exercise ... ugh.*

Always

The housekeeping supervisor looked up from her clipboard as he stepped out of the elevator. "It's about time. There's a line of blood on the floor from the elevator to the OR."

"Yes, mum."

Sully's "ma'am" sounded British. Somehow, he had picked up his habit in the military and never let go.

"Well?" She now held her clipboard on her hip.

"Yes, mum."

He jerked his yellow cart around and pushed his mop toward the trail of blood. He dropped his mop's tentacles into the fresh pail of water and twisted the handle as he lowered it into the press.

"Not too wet, not too dry."

He mopped back and forth down the hallway until he noticed bloody shoe prints leading into the waiting room. He walked in with his mop. A TV hung in the corner and lit the room with medical advisories and hospital announcements as he pushed his wet mop across the darkened floor.

"Hey, watch the Cucinellis." A man sat on a blue vinyl couch with an unlit cigarette stuck between two of his fingers.

Sully's eyes fell on the man's bloody, faded jeans, gaudy socks, and brown loafers. "Huh?"

"Brunello Cucinelli. The shoes, old man, the shoes. I had to walk around the outside of the hospital to find a dry way in."

"Oh, your socks must've distracted me." Sully couldn't help himself.

"These socks are Mario Breschianis. Probably cost more than your whole sock drawer."

Sully leaned on his mop in a darkened corner of the room. "Probably. I don't have a sock drawer. Sometimes, I don't even have socks."

A doctor in scrubs walked in, a surgical mask hanging around his neck. Glasses framed his piercing dark eyes, and his stethoscope lay on the collar of his long white coat.

"Mr. Jones, I'm Doctor Fenigrin."

Still seated, the man with remarkable hair turned toward the doctor. "Call me Jonesy, Doc."

"Okay, Jonesy." The doctor stared at his clipboard, his back to Sully, who stood motionless and unnoticed. "I see here you have temporary power of attorney. We sedated Ms. Mills and stopped all the external bleeding. We've cleaned her wounds."

With his neck stretched upward, Jonesy did not speak, move, or blink.

The doctor continued. "There appears to be a great deal of internal bleeding. One of our best surgeons is assessing the extent of those injuries to determine our course of action. We know her liver and kidneys have been affected and possibly her spleen. There are bone fragments from her broken ribs that will need to be removed. Once we get the bleeding under control, we'll take a closer look at her broken arm and leg—she'll need further operations. Then there's her cranium."

"Her head?" Jonesy jumped up and grabbed the doctor's arm. "What's wrong with her head?"

The doctor pulled away. "Her head must have slammed into the dashboard. Her skull is fractured. There is only so much room inside the skull, so the pressure created by her swelling brain will need to be addressed. We'll have to stabilize her and see if she survives this initial round. And there is the matter of the burns to her face and her right side—those will take time to heal as well."

The man's eyes widened. Despite an obvious tan, his face flushed. "What do you mean *if* she survives? What

Always

round? What is this, a prize fight? And what's wrong with her face?" He grabbed at the doctor's arm again, but this time the doctor did not pull away.

"I suppose I could have said *when* she endures this initial surgery." Dr. Fenigrin, not known for his bedside manners continued, "Sir, she is fighting for her life." He turned and headed out the door.

Sully stared from his corner. He was not prepared for this either. Since his wife died or "passed away," as people liked to tell him, he had tried his best to avoid such conflict.

"What are you staring at, old man?"

Sully looked into the man's face. "Ah, uh, your Mario Breschianis?" The tension had triggered his quirky sense of humor.

Jonesy looked at Sully, then down at his feet. When he looked up again, he shook his head, wagged his finger, and smirked.

"Here, let me help you," Sully offered. "You walked in blood and that can be murder on leather soles and stitching." He lay the mop head on the floor. "Just step on this and you should be able to wipe the blood off before it sets."

The man did what he was told. "Thanks."

Sully looked at the red streaks on his once clean mop, then said, "Sir, before I lost my wife, they just said, 'Believe, you gotta believe.' Well, I believed, but she's still gone. Anyway, you still don't have much of a choice. You just gotta believe she'll pull through."

Jonesy let out a breath, then began to pace. "Yeah, maybe you're right. Thing is, we were fighting. She caught me again and went ballistic. It's not like we're married. She doesn't get men." He looked back at Sully. "I mean we got needs, you know?"

Sully had boxed up his needs inside his little trailer, but he had longed for his angel to lift him from his misery.

"You listening, old man? Anyway, she punched me on the arm. Crazy, right?" Jonesy rubbed a hand over his tailored shirtsleeve. "So, yeah, I defended myself and that's when it happened."

"*It* happened?"

"Yeah—it—the accident, man, the accident. Are you even following me?"

"Yes, sir." Sully looked back down at his mop, feeling the rise of heat in his face. "I really should get back to my duties." He stepped back into the hall and wheeled his little yellow cart down the hall past his supervisor and away from Jonesy.

"Sully, I thought I told you to clean this up."

"Yes, mum."

"Honestly." She stood with her hands on her hips, watching him now to ensure he completed his task.

As he mopped, Sully kept thinking about the brown-haired woman. He wished he could squeeze out every ounce of blood from his mop and give it back to her. He tried not to hate Jonesy. He tried.

After he completed his usual rounds of emptying trash, dusting, and serpentine moping, he put his cleaning tools back in the closet. He wiped his brow and retrieved his tuna fish sandwich. He knew he'd get in trouble for taking an early break, but he needed new scenery.

He headed downstairs where young attendants talked sports, and doctors laughed with the nurses. He got his coffee and looked for a quiet place to land. People who normally work by themselves were forced to make small talk and endure insufferable pauses filled by loud chewers and sloppy coffee drinkers.

Always

Despite having cleaned up blood before, the scene remained on his mind. He found the loneliest table next to a darkened window. A pimply-faced first-year hung his waist-length white coat on the chair next to him. A doctor's status was known by the length of their coat. This was a newbie doing his internship, probably stuck on a rotation for which he was ill-prepared. But the coat had prominent blood stains. Sully watched him tear open a sugar pack, managing to get some into his Styrofoam cup. The rest landed on the table and his lap.

"Nuts." The intern sounded more like an adolescent.

"Rough night?" Sully regretted saying anything.

"Yeah, first night in the ER, and they wheel in this woman—just a little thing with her arm and leg going in the wrong directions and half her face burnt. Oh, the smell." He flushed.

Sully worried the intern would puke, and he would have to clean the mess.

"Sorry." The word sounded more like a question. Sully really didn't know what to say to this kid whose only worry was probably the stereo system in his secondhand BMW.

"Thanks, man. Joe." He stuck his hand out over Sully's tuna fish.

"Oh, ah, Sully." He shook the hand without looking. Sully was just as bad at shaking hands as he was at conversing.

"I don't know, man, I mean her burns stank, like burning the latrine barrels when I was deployed or something." He looked to Sully with tears in his eyes. "You ever smell that stuff? No, why would you."

"Persian Gulf, and a lot more too."

The intern nodded. "Well, this poor woman ... lacerations ... I think I saw her intestines."

"The burning oil fields were something you never forget," Sully continued, hoping not to hear more about the woman.

The two conversed like two kids pushing trucks around in the dirt, neither getting in each other's way. "I just kept thinking, lady, you could be my mom. Her head was cracked, and blood matted her hair. Here's the crazy thing, all I could do was stare at her brown hair, still parted down the middle, still flipped up like bangs on either side of her face. She looked …" The kid looked into Sully's face. "She looked like an angel."

"An angel?" Sully's attention went on full alert. "An angel, you say?"

"Yeah, man. What?"

"Um, nothing. An angel, huh? I knew an angel once."

June 1974

Danny shuddered as the Pocono breeze blew across his skinny frame. He shook violently after swinging on the rope and splashing in the spring-fed pond. He wished for a towel as he lay on his smelly T-shirt. The bluff gave him a good view of the entire pond and surrounding fields but offered little protection from the sun or the wind.

He fiddled with his prize possession—his newly minted class ring. He tried to read his book, "I Am Third" by Gayle Sayers. "God first, family second, I am third." People were always giving him books, but this one was about a football player, so this one he tried. He squinted to read the bright pages nearly washed out by the midday glare. He heard chatter in the distance before he caught sight of two figures laughing and running toward the pond.

Danny lay low in the weeds as he watched two girls in matching bikinis jumping off the dock doing cannonballs and can openers. They looked about the same size—one dark haired, the other light—both skinny like most girls their age. He rolled onto his back and went back to his book.

At sixteen, Danny—little for his age, young for his school year, and swift of tongue—didn't think like Gayle

Sayers. He was a definite first in his world of one. His skinny arms began to shake as he held the paperback in the air. He had no chest to speak of but did have a hint of abs and well-defined calf muscles.

He lowered his book and shut his eyes until he heard the girls giggling in the background. He peeked out over the weeds as they came up the bluff and stopped short.

"Hey, what do you want?" He stared at the one with dark brown bangs, which she flipped to either side.

"Nothing, just the rope."

"Well, can't you see it's over there?" Danny pointed while struggling to stand, clutching his smelly T-shirt against his reddened chest.

"Yeah, we see it," the light-haired girl said. As they walked away, he heard her say, "Why's he being such a jerk?"

"I dunno, but he is kinda cute," said the dark-haired girl.

They giggled and ran to the frayed rope, then took turns swinging over the pond.

Danny shook his head. *Dumb schoolgirls.* As he walked back toward the farmhouse, he heard a shriek and a splash followed by ridiculous laughing. *Jerk, huh? Kinda cute? Hmm.*

As he came back over the hill, he surveyed his uncle's farmhouse—plain, nothing unusual for the Poconos. The house formed a two-story L with a porch on the front that wrapped around on the inside of the L. The living room was in the front, the kitchen in the back with enough room for an oak pedestal table and four Amish-made chairs. The bathroom stood at the top of the stairs with its pedestal sink, toilet, and claw foot tub where his uncle had added a showerhead. Danny headed for the shower.

He pulled back the plastic curtain surrounding the tub. An external chrome pipe ran up from the faucet and ended in a small showerhead that put out an incredible force of

Always

water. He climbed over the edge of the tub and turned on the porcelain knobs before he lowered his head into the deluge.

Dark-hair girl said I was cute. Okay, kinda cute. Dogs are kinda cute ... well, not all dogs.

He could see her wet, dark hair flattened against her head and her dark eyes that had made him look away when she'd looked back at him. Her skinny bikini had revealed nothing but innocence. *She looked like ... like ... what's the word?*

The room had filled with steam when he pulled back the curtain again. He wiped the condensation from the mirror and looked at his reflection. *My hair covers my whole ear. Mom's crazy if she thinks I'm getting a haircut now. I can't believe she chased me around the house with scissors before I left.*

He plugged his hot comb into the one outlet on the side of the light above the mirror then worked with both hands to make the mop on his head manageable—curly in the back and flipped in the front just above his right eyebrow. *Wish I could part my hair down the middle. Glad I don't have one of those right-sided parts—how dumb.* The hot air blowing from his hot comb warmed his head.

With a towel wrapped around him, he headed down the hall.

"Boy, get some blue jeans on that body of yours. Auntie's about got dinner set." Whiskers, wrinkles, and errant hairs sticking out from his uncle's broken Dekalb cap told a story of hard work and disappointment. But Uncle Vern's watery eyes spoke of hope and a determination that he'd do it all again tomorrow. "And a shirt wouldn't hurt neither."

"Yessir."

Danny popped a Cat Stevens tape into his 8-track player. He had brought his music with him to stave off the boredom of the summer. He used to love his summers with his uncle and aunt in the mountains. Boating, archery, and guns used to be plenty enough to keep him occupied. Working the hay too. But he never really paid attention to the farm, and now he got up late, skipped feeding the chickens, ate, and went back to bed. He saw Aunt Clare shaking her head when he headed to the pond. He hardly ever helped her in the garden and no longer noticed the smell of fresh flowers or the mule in the paddock.

As he pulled a shirt from a drawer, he saw his uncle and aunt on the stairs through his open door.

"He'll be fine," he heard his aunt say. "He's in a phase, like his brother was."

"Stephen was a good boy," his uncle said. "Nothing like Danny."

"It hasn't been that long. Give him time."

Danny shut his door. Uncle Vern's comment stung. He lay on the overstuffed bed, buried his head into his feather pillow, and cried. His sides began to hurt, and his hands cramped from clutching his wet pillow, but he cried some more. *This sucks.*

Finally, Danny got up and looked at his face in the mirror, wrinkled and red from his crying. He wiped his tear-stained skin, then pulled out a bag from behind the dresser and spilled out dozens of sketches and watercolors onto his bed and floor. Deer were his favorite subject, but everything in nature was beauty to be captured at the end of an artist's stroke. He never felt as if he did. "Sticks, nothing but sticks," he'd say, remembering what Audubon, the naturalist and painter said in his youth.

"Dinner time, Danny," he heard Aunt Clare call from below.

Outside Uncle Vern rang the bell like every other night. *I wonder if he does that when no one's here.*

Always

Danny picked up the remaining pictures, shuffled them back into the bag, and put his collection behind the dresser before shuffling downstairs.

"Okay, okay, I'm here, I'm here." Danny sat down at the oak table now covered with a faded floral print and bowls of chicken, corn, and homemade applesauce. "Fried chicken, all right!" Danny exclaimed.

Aunt Clare nodded at Vern, who shrugged.

"Wait for grace, boy."

Three people folded their hands, two people closed their eyes, and one old man prayed.

"Father, we thank thee for these bountiful gifts we are about to receive. Amen."

Danny dug into the chicken, ate all his corn, and, of course, his applesauce. He had no idea how long it took to clean, core, peel, cut, and mash the apples to make the homemade sauce. He just knew there was nothing like homemade—nothing.

"Bill was by today," Auntie said.

Vern made a sound with his tongue. "What's he want now?"

"He wants to take Danny to the drive-in down in Canadensis."

Danny barely looked up from his chicken leg. "I hope you told him no."

"I told him you'd go." Auntie smoothed her apron.

Danny dropped his chicken leg onto his plate. "You what?" He raised his voice another octave, mimicking a skit he saw on *Saturday Night Live*. "Mr. Bill, oh no."

"Boy, what's got into you?" Uncle Vern chided. "You like Mr. Bill."

Danny picked up his chicken leg again. "He's a faker. And he's always getting up close to talk."

"Yeah, yeah, you're right." Vern slapped his knee. "Bill is a close talker, but he's our neighbor, and he always liked you."

"Well," Auntie added, "I told him yes. He'll be here at six-thirty. If you don't want to go, you tell 'im."

"Great."

Danny didn't say another word, just finished his dinner, and cleared his plate. He sat back down and ate some strawberry pie, all in silence. When he was done, he didn't clear his plate, just headed for the hall. Halfway to the porch, he heard his aunt call out to him.

"Let 'im be, Clare, he'll be fine," he heard his uncle tell her.

Danny slumped down on the porch glider. He could hear plates being cleared and water being run for the nightly wash and dry ritual. He imagined his aunt and uncle looking out the window as the sun began to set over the last hill. Danny had helped with the ritual a million times before, but it meant little to him now. He knew they'd both dry their hands on the same old tea towel painted with his brother Stephen's, his sister's, and his own little handprints. He knew they'd go out back and sit on the swing and watch the sun fade away.

The way Danny pushed back and forth on the rusty glider was more exercise than relaxation. He didn't know how to relax. He knew boring, and he knew distraction. He knew nothing of contentment that comes from doing nothing or the satisfaction from a job well done. He knew how to get up, how to eat, and how to lie back down again. And he knew how to hurt. Everything else was stupid. Books were stupid, people were stupid, school … stupid. Even his friends were stupid. There was stupid, there were fakers, and there was Danny.

Always

Uncle Vern is right. I'm no Stephen.

After a few minutes of lamenting, he saw a cloud of dust coming around the cinder-covered lane. He braced himself as Bill's orange VW station wagon stopped in front of him.

"Danny! It's been a long time. My, boy, you have grown."

Yeah, right. Why do they all have to say that? I'm the smallest in my class. There are girls taller than me.

"H-i. neighbor." Danny's greeting came out in two syllables as if he had just learned how to say the word.

The passenger door of Mr. Bill's car opened, the front seat pushed forward, and two girls wearing identical white pants piled out from the back seat.

He recognized them immediately. The dark-haired one wore a tight, blue, short-sleeved top. The light-haired one wore the same, but in red.

Do they always have to match? That is so corny. Eccchh.

Danny still sat on the glider when the one in blue stuck her hand in his face. "Hi, I'm MaryAnne, and this is my sister."

Next, the light-haired one stuck out her hand. "Hi, I'm Lynne, and I'm her sister."

He knew he should shake each one's hand. He knew that much. But he didn't know how to shake hands with a girl ... or with anyone for that matter. He thought about his limp handshake as the girls got back in the back seat, and he got in the front.

"Well, I see you met my nieces," said Mr. Bill. "Their family's staying with me for a while."

Danny was still thinking about the handshake when they cleared the gravel lane, sped toward town, and stopped at the old drive-in theater. *Shaking hands is stupid.*

Mr. Bill paid the man in the booth and drove past the sign that read "TONIGHT: Elliot Gould and Donald Sutherland partner up in *S.P.Y.S.*"

He drove around the lot to find the perfect spot and took three tries before he found one to his liking. "I'm going for popcorn, who wants some?"

"I do, I do!" MaryAnne exclaimed.

Lynne chimed in next. "Me too, me too!"

Mr. Bill took off for the concession stand, and Danny was stuck with the girls.

"Oh great!" MaryAnne said. "A double feature!"

"Do all of your sentences sound like they end in explanation points?" Danny smirked.

"Who are you, the grammar king?" Lynne asked.

"Lynne!" MaryAnne smacked her on the arm.

"See what I mean?" Danny's lip curled.

"We were just trying to be nice." MaryAnne sat back in her seat with a scowl.

Danny could see her in the rearview mirror looking out of the darkened window. Her flipped bangs pressed against the window.

She looks like ... what's the word?

"I'm sorry," Danny blurted.

"Huh? Oh, you're okay. I just like popcorn."

Mr. Bill came back with two boxes of popcorn and four sodas. Danny didn't say anything about the root beer being flat, and MaryAnne stopped exclaiming.

"Uncle Bill, we can't see. Can we get on the roof?"

"Sure, hon."

Danny got out of the car and watched the sisters' struggle. MaryAnne folded her hands together to make a boost for her sister's foot. On top of the car, Lynn tried to pull her sister up, but MaryAnne's legs flopped, so Danny grabbed her foot and pushed.

"Hey, thanks."

"Sure."

Always

Danny got back inside the car, slurped his root beer, and managed to stretch the popcorn until the movie finished.

"Whatcha think, Danny?" Bill asked as the credits rolled.

Stupid, that's what I think. But he had really been thinking about who was attached to the foot he had helped. "Okay, I guess."

The girls slid down the back of the car and got back in. Danny was certain MaryAnne paused to look at him with her deep brown eyes and thick eyebrows.

"We liked *S.P.Y.S.*, didn't we?" Lynne said. "Especially the song at the end."

The girls broke into song for the trip back to the farm. "We don't have a lot of money ... Maybe we're ragged and funny, but we'll travel along, singing our song, side by side."

Finally, Bill drove back down the gravel lane to the farmhouse.

"Well, this is your stop, Danny." Mr. Bill shifted the car into neutral.

Fakers.

MaryAnne looked up at him. Her brown eyes caught the little bit of light from overhead. "Did you have fun?"

"Yes, yes, I did. Do you want to get up front now?"

"No, we're fine," Lynne said.

"I will," said MaryAnne.

When she got out of the car, she stuck out her hand and again Danny fumbled to shake her hand. *What girl shakes hands?*

"I'm so sorry about your brother," she whispered.

Danny looked down at his feet. "Yeah, it's okay." *Geeze, I sound so lame. Why did she say that, anyway?*

As the car drove away, he lifted his hand to his face and inhaled. *What was that scent she wore?*

Aunt Clare met him at the screen door. "Was the movie fun?"

"Yeah, yes, it was fun."

He could see the surprised look on his aunt's face.

"Who was that in the back seat?"

Danny thought of MaryAnne's dark hair and eyes. "An angel," he mumbled.

"Who?"

Danny came out of his stupor. "I-I-I mean MaryAnne. MaryAnne was in the back seat."

An angel, that's the word.

February 2021

The roads were clear when Sully left for work the next day. As Sierra rolled down to the bridge, he noticed the tire marks that had veered off the edge and ended at the concrete abutment the day before. Pieces of bumper were all that remained at the scene.

Should have been me. Sully shook his head. *Coward. Suicide? Really?*

The memory of her long brown hair and a long-forgotten fragrance drove him now. *She's like an angel, the intern said. I knew an angel once.* Thoughts still revolved through his brain like an old slide projector. *It couldn't be her. It's been so long. Oh my, I gotta know. I just have to.*

He parked in his same space in the hospital parking lot and saw the same intern step in the same puddle from yesterday.

"Aghhh!"

"Evening, Doc." Sully felt like the sheep dog in the cartoon punching his time clock along with the wolf. He hung up his jacket, put his tuna fish sandwich in the fridge, and fixed his hair in the mirror before checking the assignment board.

Third Floor—Intensive Care.

Intensive Care meant too many machines to work around, everyone was tense, and everything had to be so perfect. He was always in the way when the bells went off, little lights flashed, and a computerized voice called out, "Code *whatever.*"

I hate that. Whose voice is that, anyway?

With each step, he pushed his toxic thoughts deeper into his head.

But the patient from the OR would be there. And Mr. Gucci with his gaudy socks.

He unlocked the janitor's closet to retrieve his cart. No one ever touched Sully's cart with the small American and POW flags. Sully gathered a few supplies on a rectangular plastic tray before he entered the locked ICU.

He lingered near the nurse's station. *What am I going to say? How's the angel doing?* He walked the aisle and peered into the glassed-in rooms on the perimeter. He saw a child with no hair and her mother, a teenager from a motorcycle accident, and an old man in for who knows what. *No angel.* He pretended to clean around the nurses' station, waiting for a sign.

The usual murmur about patient X and patient Y rose from the nurses. The pharmacist's aide came up to restock. Sully spied a gaggle of interns, and he recognized the intern from last night. There were only so many times he could lap the station, only so many times he could check the wastebaskets. He had begun to hope for some type of biohazardous spill when the mechanized doors opened and aides pushed a bed past him.

A piece of tape across the headboard read Mary Mills. *Not my angel.* Her head and much of her face was bandaged. They pushed her into room 3 where the attendants worked

Always

to raise her one leg in a wired medieval contraption. Both her legs and torso were covered with a white, knitted blanket. One of her arms was wrapped in a blue cast. She had tubes in her mouth and nose.

That can't feel good.

Sully's time as a navy corpsman with the Marines had taught him a fair amount of combat medicine. In war, she would have been labeled "EXPECTANT" as in "expected to die." In the Gulf War, he had taken the younger corpsman Jimmy under his wing. He had been willing to lay down his life for Jimmy but wasn't willing to let the other man do the same. Not on his watch. He never signed up to watch him die.

But war was war. His platoon, hungry for combat, had outreached their evac capabilities when they crossed into Iraq. Sully always felt he had made the wrong call when it came to life and death. It didn't matter what his commander told him, what medal they pinned on his chest, or how many times he'd heard from civilians "Thank you for your service."

Sully snapped back to reality as the PA—John—nudged a machine on wheels toward him.

"Here, move this down the hall and then come back for more."

He took the medical equipment with wires flopping everywhere and walked down the hallway. *John's a good piece of gear.* The term was Sully's highest compliment about the fortyish PA who had spent most of his life working in critical care. He had even been a custodian like Sully at one time before going back to college. John was Army Reserves, not Fleet Marine Force, but close enough. Sully really liked when John stood up to the attending residents. He liked that a lot.

"Hey, John, remember when you told off that young snot?" he'd asked him once.

"Now wait, Sully, it wasn't exactly like that," he'd said. Then he smiled, shook his head, and bowed away.

Now that's real leadership.

Sully took charge of the machine and wheeled it down the aisle. He hit the square button on the wall and pushed on past the doors to the medical equipment room. He was glad his ID was coded to open the room because he often forgot his keys. "They're not lost," he'd say, "They're right where I left 'em."

As he walked down the hallway to retrieve more items from John, someone in the waiting room caught his attention. He looked away, but not soon enough. Gucci waved him in. Sully opened the door, and the man lowered his phone against his thigh.

"Hey, old man, gotta sec? Come in here, would ya?"

He knew this man wouldn't accept no graciously. He wondered if he accepted anything graciously. But grace wasn't Sully's forte either.

Gucci raised the phone back to his ear but pointed a finger at Sully. "Just a sec, old man ... No, not you!" he screamed into his phone. "Look I've been a patron of your company since I was an officer. That's right, you are talking to a former officer ... National Guard. What's that got to do with anything? Ever hear of Kent State?"

This guy does a lot of pointing.

"Now look, don't you dare put me on hold again—" Gucci dropped his phone on the vinyl seat next to him. "Idiot." He turned toward Sully. "Say, old man, I just wanted to say I wasn't myself last night. I was worried sick, and I probably didn't come off right."

Always

Again, with the old man. Who does he think he is, anyway, Jay Gatsby? Gucci sounds like he's apologizing.

"So anyway, no hard feelings?" Gucci stuck out his hand.

Faker. Sully looked at the outstretched hand. He shook it—badly, but he shook it. *This guy knows how to apologize— he just can't do it well.*

"How *is* your wife, sir?"

"My wife? I don't have a wife. 'Course I never know what to call her. My girl? We're too grown for that. My lady friend? Too stuffy. True companion. I don't even know what that is. Fiancée? At my age? I suppose. I'm just really into her. Anyway, what did you ask?"

Sully sighed. "Sir, I asked how she was doing?"

"Oh, I'm not sure. They just wheeled her back from the OR. They relieved the pressure in her head, stopped the bleeding and something else."

"Oh." Sully shook his head as he looked at the coffee-stained floor.

"Yeah, she's been down there all day. It's tearing me up." Gucci took a flask from his back pocket. "Want some?"

Sully shook his head.

"Suit yourself."

The cell phone started talking before he could screw the top back on his flask.

"Hold." He covered the phone and looked at Sully. "I have to take this." As Sully left the room, he heard, "Now look, old man ..."

Sully hit the square button again and returned to the ICU. He stopped at each room, saying a quiet prayer over each, then stopped at room 3. He wasn't allowed inside while she was in there, so he said another prayer.

"Please God, save her life, and save her from that miserable jerk."

He walked around the counter where nurses, doctors, and attendants convened in twos and threes and then regrouped in different configurations before heading to their patients. A group of first-year medical students hovered around a small light board at the back. An attending doctor pointed out the highlights, the outliers, and the salient aspects of a series of x-rays and pictures.

"What about this?" asked a student with large spectacles and hair tightly pulled into a center part, ending in a small bun.

"Don't go there, newbie, not yet."

"But—"

"But nothing, follow your algorithm. Discipline, grasshopper, patience and discipline." The attending turned back to the light while the newbie shook her smirk away. "Now, where was I before the interruption ..."

His voice trailed as Sully went back to room 3. He folded his hands on the plastic handrail that circled the ICU and shut his eyes.

"Thought you already prayed."

Sully opened his eyes.

"John, I think this one needs another prayer. How's she doing?"

"Well, you mean for a brain that got bounced back and forth like a basketball inside a broken cranium? It's remarkable she's still breathing. Of course, technically, we're doing that for her. She coded today and again later in the OR. She may not look like much, but for now, you're looking at a minor miracle. So, yeah, she could use another prayer."

Sully turned back to the woman in room 3 as his past caught up to him.

Always

He saw himself kneel in the bloody sand on both knees as Jimmy's spit gurgled down the side of his mouth. *The sandbox. I hate this Gulf War.* Through the shooting, the yelling, and another bomb exploding, he heard nothing but a wheezing sound. He pulled away Jimmy's pack and harness to get to the body armor.

"Great, you left your armor plate behind, and you got yourself shot."

But he knew Jimmy did this so he could carry more medical supplies. Now his supplies were being used on Jimmy. He cut apart his charge's camouflage uniform.

"This is bad." He grabbed a dressing package from his med pack.

"Doc, what do want me to do?" asked a Marine.

"You remember your basic life support?" Sully threw a tourniquet at him. "Wrap this tourniquet right above his knee."

"Which one?"

"The one that isn't there anymore!" Sully threw a dressing pack at another Marine. "Cut this open. Now throw away the dressing. Cut the plastic package in a rectangle, and don't get your dirty fingers all over it."

Sully squirted water around the wound from his canteen and patted it off with a clean green T-shirt he had cut up the day before.

"Gimme—now." He took the plastic and gently taped down three sides over the half-dollar size hole in Jimmy's chest. He had stopped the bleeding and left an opening for air to escape.

"Way to go, Doc, you did it."

Sully focused on Jimmy's breathing.

"Nuts. Paradoxical breathing." In the middle of the screaming, shooting, and burning, he listened to Jimmy's chest. "Plural effusion ... pneumothorax."

"What's that?"

"He's got a collapsed lung."

The Marine outranked him by three stripes but now Sully was in charge.

"Gimme," he shouted again, snapping his fingers.

"Gimme wha—?"

"My med pack, bring it closer." He dug out another package. "Tear this apart, keep it clean."

He took the plastic tube, cut a slight angle with his Gerber, and slid it under the bandage and into his best friend's chest.

"What are you doing, Doc?"

"Shut up. Shut up and pray hard."

Blood and fluid flowed from the tube. He snapped a Heimlich valve on the end. He had already completed his body scan. He knew Jimmy had shards of glass and shrapnel in his torso, but other than his blown leg, the bleeding was minor. He knew his arm was busted, but it wasn't a compound so it would have to wait. The golden hour of survival was ticking away.

"Where's the sixty!" he screamed.

"On its way, Doc, on its way."

The Blackhawk wouldn't want to land if the landing zone was hot, but he figured the pilot wanted to save Marines as much as any corpsman. The rotor roared in front of him, and a stretcher attached to a smallish corpsman ran to him. The corpsman and a Marine carried Jimmy back to the bird. Sully kept two fingers on his friend's throat and squatted to feel his breath on his own face as best he could. He felt nothing ten meters from the open side of the HH-60M.

"Drop him, drop him here."

They did as they were told, and Sully began pumping Jimmy's chest. A PA ran from the helo hauling a defibrillator.

Always

"We got him from here, Doc." He pushed Sully back on his heels and placed two pads on Jimmy's chest without waiting for a pulse check.

"Clear." The PA shot him with over a thousand volts of electricity before they lifted him onto the helo.

"Don't die on me, don't you dare."

It was the last thing Sully would shout over the sound of the rotor wash to his only friend as he bowed away from the lifting helo. No tears, only sweat. Sweat and spit, what was left of it. He never saw him again.

"Hey, dude, Sully ... come back."

"What? I'm here." He looked up at John in the glare of the fluorescent hospital lights.

"Dude, you were giving CPR to the handrail. Take a break, man. The sandbox?"

"Yeah."

Still sweating, Sully headed to his cart and wobbled down to the cafeteria. His hands trembled as he grabbed his lunch bag out of the fridge, took a deep breath, and walked into the bustling dining room. Sully poured a cup of coffee, but there wasn't a quiet corner to be had. He set his kit downwind from the cackling of nurses. He recognized two of them from the ICU.

"How's your night going?" one nurse asked another.

"Okay so far, but they just brought back our patient in room 3, so things are a little tense."

"Tense for everyone but her husband," another nurse added. "What's with him, anyway?"

"Yeah, I know, but he sure can dress, and he smells good too."

"Really!" The first nurse shook her head. "Anyway, they had her in and out of the OR today. Her Traumatic Brain Injury resulted in increased ICP—intracranial pressure.

They were able to maintain cerebral perfusion with today's operation but are still unsure if they prevented a secondary cerebral ischemia. They think they got all the bone fragments, but complications can creep in."

"Huh?" the new nursing student asked leaning forward.

The nurse talked with her hands. "Basically, the brain's blood is now flowing normally. No leaks now, but secondary problems can surface, leaving her with significant neurological issues."

"Such as?"

She scratched her forehead. "They won't know until she wakes, but it could be anything. Her brain could have gone without blood, and a decreased amount of oxygen could result in problems with walking, sleeping, and retrograde amnesia."

Another nurse sat down, keeping Sully boxed in on three sides.

"Retrograde? That's when you don't remember anything before the accident, right?" asked one of the nurses.

"Yeah." Her hands waved in front of her face. "Normally, you wouldn't want to remember the accident, but with an injury this serious you could forget a lot more than that." The nurse picked at her food tray.

The nursing student cocked her head. "Really, like how to eat and drink?"

"No, that's procedural memory. I'm talking autographical memory." The nurse now pointed at the student. "She'll remember basic living skills, but she could forget days, weeks, even years in some cases."

Sully stopped eating his tuna fish and looked up. "What's autographical memory?"

"Well, it's personal memories, the ones that make you who you are, your personality, your secrets, your loves, likes, and hates. They could all be wiped out."

Always

Sully wiped his mouth. "Some memories I could do without," he replied.

The nurse smirked while another looked away, and one shook her head and rolled her eyes.

"Anyway, for nursing, it's vital to monitor ICP—intracranial pressure, hypoxemia, co2 changes in ph. Hypoxemia is—"

Sully interrupted, "Hypoxemia is a low concentration of oxygen. In the brain, it can cause hypovolemic shock and acute anemia."

"Very good." The nurse pointed her fork at Sully. "And that insufficient amount of blood supply could cause other organs to shut down."

"What then?" the nursing student asked.

Everyone looked at her, but it was Sully who answered. "Death, sweetie."

With that, the group broke up, leaving Sully to finish his tuna fish and coffee.

As he walked through ICU a little while later, Sully noticed Jonesy now sat by Ms. Mills in room 3 with a copy of *The Economist* in his lap and his cell phone in both hands.

Sully turned into the nurses' station.

John stood hunched over a computer screen as Sully grabbed a small trash can by his feet. "I thought you already cleaned here?"

"Um, not quite."

Sully looked over at a group of med students staring at more pictures. He could see red and flesh but not much more.

The attending spoke up. "So, what you see here are the results of the coup—the initial assault—and this one shows the—"

"What's that egg-shaped spot?" a student interrupted.

"That's a goose egg. You see it on the contrecoup side where the brain rebounded against the cranium. Temporal contusions present the greatest concern for brain herniation."

The attending shifted the pictures. "Williams, what do you see here?"

Sully looked at Williams who was at the back of the group and had yawned for a second time.

"Yes, sir, I see the back of a bunch of heads that are obscuring a better view of some pretty nasty blood clots."

The attending pointed at the picture. "Very funny. What's the problem here, and what's the solution?"

"The problem is blood clots compress the underlying brain tissue like an epidural hematoma. The solution? Time, medication, surgery. In this case, we don't have time, and medications would be ineffective, so removing them is our only option."

The other interns were now looking at Williams. Sully doubted if their smiles were genuine.

"Precisely. Golf claps, Willy. With a cranial compound fracture complicated by bone splinters, time is of the essence, and that is what we did."

"So, she's good?" asked a squeaky voice from the left side of the group.

"Who said that? Billingsly? Far from it, she's not out of the woods, not by a long shot. There's the risk of more bleeders, more clots, all of which means more pressure on the brain."

"VP."

"What ... who said that?" The attending saw Williams' hand go up in the back. "Talk to me, Willy."

"A VP, a ventriculoperitoneal shunt could alleviate the buildup of fluid and more blood that could likely congregate in the affected areas."

Always

"Willy here slept in a Holiday Inn Express last night." The attending shifted the pictures to a grainy x-ray. The group moved closer. Sully could hear mumbling.

"So here you see it, ladies and gentlemen. No magic, just modern medicine—a tube, smaller than the one on Billingsley's pet fish tank, his only friend, but basically the same thing."

The attending traced the curved line with the top of his pen. "The proximal catheter beginning in the lateral ventricles, leading around the back of the skull and terminating in the GI tract."

"What's the bulge behind her ear?"

"Why, that is her new double shunt reservoir valve. These two dots can control two shunts simultaneously, a little smaller but a lot more sophisticated than the valves under your kitchen sink."

Sully winced. Time for him to go. He walked past room 3 one more time. Jonesy looked up from the instruments next to Ms. Mills's bed and his eyes met Sully's.

"Old man, I say ..."

Sully sighed.

"If you could ... say a prayer for Mary tonight."

The old man nodded.

Ten minutes after the end of his shift, he was back on the road and less than a mile from home and off the interstate, away from the lights, the houses, the noise, the world. He turned up his gravel road toward his mobile home, flanked by arching pines and thick undergrowth. He turned off the truck by his front porch, and everything went dark. He liked the peace, and he liked the dark. Sully sat there for some time staring into the nothingness and bowed his head.

"God, take me. Please."

But thoughts of the patient in room 3 interrupted his selfish plea. *There's just something about her. I wish I knew.*

He bowed his head again. "God, save her, please."

June 1974

Aunt Clare stood at the stove. "Danny, you're up early, especially after your late movie."

"Yeah, well, Uncle Vern said he needed help bringing in some hay, and I didn't want to miss him."

Vern passed Danny in the doorway and took his seat at the table.

"Here, Danny, I made you some eggs," said his aunt.

Vern looked up. "I thought—"

"You hush now, Vern, yours is come'n." After setting down the plate in front of Danny, she got three more eggs from the rack on the wall and one by one, cracked them into her skillet.

Toast popped up, scrapple sizzled, and Danny grinned between bites. He could feel stares from two sets of eyes upon him, but he didn't look up.

Uncle Vern chewed on some scrapple. "The hay won't be dry until later, but I could use some help with the rake, Danny."

"Sure, whatever you need."

Vern's eyebrows raised as Clare slid the last of the eggs onto his plate.

"Eat up, Vern, if you want to keep up with Danny."

With a piece of butter bread in one hand and a fork in the other, he shoveled in his eggs.

After breakfast, the men left their dishes on the table and headed for the equipment shed.

"This here's a grease gun, take it."

Danny did as he was told but immediately regretted it. "Ugh." Danny looked at his hand. "It's all greasy."

"Yeah, it's greasy—it's a grease gun, ain't it? This here's a grease erg, these little nipples are all over the rake, from the hitch to the bars, to the teeth, to the wheels turning on the axle. They all need some of that there grease."

Danny searched for the little metal bumps. He pumped the handle on the one-foot cylinder and grease came out a thin rubber hose.

"Whatcha gawking at? Now put the hose on the grease ergs. Get started, you're gonna hafta get a little dirty to find all of 'em."

While Danny was pushing the end of the grease hose onto the first erg, he heard his uncle firing up the International tractor. The head of the grease gun hose popped off the erg, and grease squirted across his clean shirt.

"Ugh."

Danny looked up, but the sound of the old tractor had drowned out anything he said.

"Lift up the tongue, lift up the tongue!"

Vern had backed up the tractor and screamed at the top of his lungs before he cut the throttle.

"Lift up the tongue!"

Danny slid out from underneath the rake and grabbed the rake's hitch used to connect the rake to the tractor. *Doesn't look like a tongue.*

"I can't. It's heavy."

Always

"Well, sure it's heavy. Lift with your legs."

That was a phrase Danny had never understood. *My legs? What do they have to do with it?*

"I can't. This *tongue* is heavy," he said again as his weak hands and skinny arms tried to pull up the hitch.

"Lift it, boy!" Vern screamed.

Danny pulled again and the tongue jerked free from the mud. Vern backed up the tractor a few inches, and Danny dropped the weight of the hitch onto the bar and stuck the thick pin into the hole.

"Get the blocks, get the blocks!" Vern grabbed his DeKalb hat and pointed at the wheels.

Danny got down on his knees and pushed two pieces of railroad ties away from the wheels of the rake. Vern shifted into first gear and pulled the red rake from under the shed. The rake, like the tractor and most of his uncle's equipment, was more rust than red.

"The wheel, the wheel!" Danny screamed as he ran alongside the tractor, waving frantically.

Vern cut the throttle, shifted into neutral, and locked the double brakes.

"The wheel needs air," Danny yelled.

"Okay, okay, you don't need to yell at me," Vern replied, "besides, it's a tire."

"Well, you yelled at me."

Vern pointed a finger at his nephew's face. "Now look here, Danny. This is farm work—dangerous work. People can get hurt real bad. More kids are killed doing farm work than any other kind of work."

And yet you have your only nephew doing this work without any prior instruction?

"So, get this, good ..."

This is going to be good.

"When I'm yelling at you, I'm *not* really yelling at you."

Why am I not surprised by his wisdom?

"I'm just excited, understand?"

"Yessir."

"I mean it."

"I know you do." *That's the scary thing.* Danny went for the air pump. *Is everything on this farm heavy?*

He dragged it to the wheels, and Uncle Vern filled the tire with air.

"That gauge doesn't work." Danny tapped on the dial. "How do you know when you have enough?"

Uncle Vern kicked the tire. "Looks good to me." He handed the pump's hose back to Danny. "I'm going out to rake. You can grease the tetter and clean the barn floor where the old haymow used to be. Okay?"

"Okay. Just one thing. What's a tetter, and how do I know where the haymow used to be if it's not there anymore?"

"Well now, that's two things, ain't it?"

Vern smiled as Danny fought back a smirk.

"Must be that modern math they're teaching you young 'uns."

Now Danny smiled.

Vern pointed in the general direction of a piece of machinery that looked an awful lot like the rake, only smaller. "That there's the tetter. And the haymow is inside to the left of the barn doors. Sweep all the old hay down the hole for the steer. Any more questions?"

"What's a steer?"

Vern cocked his head at Danny who wasn't smiling.

"I'm just foolin', Uncle Vern, I know what a steer is. They look like horses, only fatter."

Always

Vern took a swipe at Danny's head. "Knock it off. And be careful in that barn. The floorboards ain't what they used to be."

Danny stepped back as his uncle mounted the tractor again and drove away, waving his hand in the blue sky. The diesel stack belched a black puff when he downshifted and soon his dusty yellow Dekalb cap disappeared over the hill—a sight that had been repeated countless times for countless years. Now, Danny was a part of it.

The farmland, along with the stream, the pond, the cinder road, and the century-old barn, cut into the side of a mountain. The homestead beat back erosion in a rainstorm, cold in the winter, and drought in the late summer. It even beat back time, but that took work—lots of work.

The farm wasn't perfect, but it was home. For Danny, home was something you could count on, and he counted on the farm in the summer. At home, people changed. His brother's death had changed everything.

Danny pushed home out of his head and pushed himself into his work the way he had watched his uncle do for so many years. Vern didn't talk much, but he could outwork any man half his age. *Guess that's how he deals with things. Just sweats it out.*

Danny returned to the tetter and strained to reach between the steel angle iron to get at the tiny grease ergs. Some were coated with old grease and camouflaged with hay shards. Just when he thought he had them all, he found another, then another. To be sure, he inspected his work—something he had never done before. He found two more then stood back to observe his work. *Nice.*

He hung up the grease gun. On his way to the barn to sweep hay, he noticed Aunt Clare collecting eggs and spreading feed for the chickens.

"How do you know where the eggs are?" he asked her.

Aunt Clare cocked an empty basket against her hip. "Well, just like you, these hens all have their place to roost at night unlike the Son of man."

There she goes with the religious stuff. "Why don't you pen them up, and then, you wouldn't have to look all over for the eggs?"

Aunt Clare straightened, holding another brown egg in one hand and her basket in the other.

"Then we'd have to feed them more, and the eggs wouldn't taste as good. And besides, what's the fun in that?" Auntie Clare gave him a big, toothy smile.

"You having fun?"

"Well, maybe fun isn't the right word." She placed another egg in her basket, then looked him over. "You done with everything your uncle asked you to do?"

"No, I still have to clean out the haymow."

"Best get to it then."

Danny headed to the barn. He loved the smell inside—the old wood and even the beams—rotted from termites but held together with oak pegs and tightly cut joints. He loved the still air. The walls were thin, the air was dusty, but inside, even though he could hear the outside world, once the doors were shut, nothing much mattered. The quiet reminded him of his attic back home.

The main doors were hinged on each side and held shut in the middle by a vertical 2x4 that ran the length of the door and wedged behind the top beam. Pushing the 2x4 to the side released both doors from the top beam. They swung open and unleashed sunlight that stretched across the roughhewn floor. Danny found a worn broom and a feed shovel to sweep the hay, rat poop, and an occasional snakeskin from the interior.

Always

He wasn't happy when his uncle caught two eight-foot black snakes and put them in the barn to eat the rats a few years ago. He'd rather have the rats, but the snakes didn't eat the grain. He continued to sweep, ever on the lookout, and stepped carefully wherever he put his foot. He tucked his pants into his socks and even wore gloves. Yet with everything to consider, he found a certain peace in the work. As much as he hated rats and snakes, he hated life more—his life or at least the one he'd been handed. *Son of man? Jesus, I know you're out there. I just wish I knew where.*

Hay dust stuck to his sweaty arms and neck as he worked. He coughed up more and blew hay seeds from his nose by pushing one finger against the side and blowing out the other. He had seen his uncle and aunt do that little trick before. "For when you don't have a hankie handy," Uncle Vern had told him.

He even surprised himself when he started to sing—first Jim Croce, then Simon and Garfunkel. Then he tried "We don't have a bunch of money. And maybe we're ragged and funny, but we'll travel along, singing our song, side by side."

"Hey, sounds good."

Danny turned to see MaryAnne standing in the sunlight. Her dark hair, round face, and thick eyebrows were even more inviting, even more striking in the bright light. Other girls plucked their eyebrows, highlighted their cheekbones, and painted their lips. Not this girl. She stood unique. Timeless. He thought her round face would look forever childlike, like a cherub. She stood as a classic black and white photo in a color Polaroid world. Danny was only sixteen, but he recognized beauty. He captured beauty in his watercolors, and now for a moment, beauty had captured him.

"Yeah, right, very funny, I can't sing."

"I'm serious."

"You really shouldn't sneak up on people like that."

"I wasn't sneaking, I was just—oh!"

MaryAnne's flip-flop folded under as she stepped forward, and her right leg buckled underneath her. Her left leg disappeared as she flopped to the floor.

"Argh, my leg … oh, it hurts. It hurts so bad."

Danny dropped his shovel and ran toward her. His foot broke through the floor as he drew near, though, so he pulled back, but MaryAnne sank farther.

"Oh, I'm falling!" she yelled.

"No, you're not." Danny reached forward slowly and slid his hands under her arms. "I got you. You're okay."

One of his gloves slipped off and fell on the concrete floor ten feet below. He pulled on her, but even though she was a little thing, he couldn't budge her. He paused to look at his glove and knew she wasn't okay.

Lift up the tongue … lift it!

Like his uncle told him, he tried again, using his legs to help. She moved a little, then a little more, and then a lot. Danny dragged her away from the rotted hole and fell over onto his backside, sucking air. MaryAnne ended up on all fours, crying. Danny lifted her to her feet, and she wrapped her arms around him and sobbed for a long minute. Danny could feel her ribs heaving and her tears soaking through his torn T-shirt. She felt fragile in his arms.

He buried his face in her hair while she cried. *My goodness, what hair.* He shut his eyes for a moment. When he opened his eyes, he saw his uncle.

"Uncle Vern!" He gently pushed MaryAnne away from him, but she held his arm around her waist.

"Well, what in tarnation?"

Always

"She fell, sir, she fell." Danny pointed to the hole.

"I can see that now."

"He rescued me, sir, h-h-he saved me." MaryAnne looked up at Danny as she wiped her eyes.

"I couldn't lift her, Uncle Vern, then I heard your voice."

Vern frowned. "I didn't say anything. I wasn't even here."

"I heard you say, 'Lift up the tongue, lift it!' and that's what I did. But she was heavier than that rusty, old rake."

"I am not." MaryAnne smacked his arm.

"Boy, you have a lot to learn about women. Come on, you two, let's get some lunch."

MaryAnne pulled away from Danny. "That's okay, Lynne and I are going swimming. I just stopped to see if Danny wanted to go."

"I still have work to do," he told her, looking at her scraped legs. "Are you going to be okay?"

"I will be if you're there."

Danny looked at his uncle with what he hoped was a pleading look.

Vern nodded. "Get yourself something to eat, then go swimming. The hay won't be dry 'til later."

MaryAnne smiled at Danny, then limped her way around the barn and down to the pond.

Vern grabbed Danny in a headlock and pushed him toward the house. "Come on, boy, what's gotten into you?"

Aunt Clare met them in the kitchen.

"Maw, we got ourselves a bona fide hero here. I tell you, bonafied." Vern smacked Danny on the shoulder.

Aunt Clare looked at her nephew as she put cold cuts, white bread, mayonnaise, and garden-fresh tomatoes on the table. Vern drank a glass of lemonade, and another, and poured a third.

"Now, Vern, slow down and give that boy some," Aunt Clare chided.

Vern poured another glass of lemonade and handed it to his nephew. "Tell her what happened, Danny."

They all ate as Danny told his story. When he was finished, his uncle said, "That isn't everything."

Danny frowned. "Yes, it is."

"It's not everything I saw." Vern tried to elbow his nephew, but Danny blocked him.

"Yes, it *is* everything, Uncle Vern."

"Okay, you two, no fighting at the table," Aunt Clare interrupted. "Here, Danny, take these peaches and the rest of the lemonade down to the pond. You've had quite enough, Vern."

Danny hustled into his cutoffs and grabbed another T-shirt and towel before running past the peaches and out the screen door that slammed behind him. He slowed when the girls looked up from the dock.

"Well, look who it is, Sir Lancelot."

"Stop it, Lynne." Danny dove into the water without looking at either of them. He swam almost ten feet to the bottom before surfacing.

Both MaryAnne and Lynne were bent over the dock looking into the water when Danny popped his head up and spat out pond water.

"Oh, gross," said Lynne before MaryAnne hit her on the thigh.

Danny climbed up the ladder and still didn't say a thing before doing a cannonball and splashing the girls.

When he surfaced, Lynne yelled, "Jerk."

MaryAnne scowled at her sister. "Lynne, am I going to have to hit you again?"

They pushed at each other until following Danny into the water with their own cannonballs. As they completed

Always

cannonball after cannonball, they didn't talk, not sentences anyway, just exclamations, shrieks, and more splashing.

When Lynn started singing "Side by Side," MaryAnne and Danny stared at her.

"What? You said he was singing it."

Danny turned to MaryAnne. "You told her that?"

"Well, you were, weren't you? Besides, it was cute."

Danny pushed MaryAnne to the edge as she squealed.

"No, don't you dare, Danny, you better not. I mean—"

Too late. MaryAnne went into the pond and came up spitting water. Somehow, she'd managed to get some leafy vegetation on her head too, and the other two laughed until she went back under.

When she came up, Danny untied the rowboat and stepped into it, grabbing up the oars lying inside.

"Wanna go?" he asked.

"Sure," said Lynne, moving forward to join him.

"I think he meant me, silly," MaryAnne said.

Danny smiled. "Well, do ya?"

"Where to?" asked MaryAnne.

"I dunno. We can't go far. It *is* just a pond."

MaryAnne climbed over the gunwale and into the boat, causing it to shake and her to fall on the seat.

Danny grinned.

"Don't make fun of me," she said

"I'm ... ah, laughing with you, not at you," he replied.

"I'm going back home." Lynne turned and walked away.

"Now, she's funny," Danny said as he began to row away from the dock.

"She's my little sister."

"I don't think she likes me."

MaryAnne laughed. "You don't think anyone likes you."

Danny rowed in silence. *How did she know that?* They circled around the edge of the pond and then again. He lost track of how many times. MaryAnne looked at the sumac and dogwood growing along the edge and dragged her hand in the cool water as he rowed round and round. When she looked at Danny, he simply stared into her eyes. An occasional bumblebee made music in the gentle air. A casual breeze did the same against the sun's warm rays.

Danny felt his pale skin growing hot as he rowed. If he was getting burnt, he didn't care. He gazed at MaryAnne's tan arms and legs. She had remarkable skin that would never burn, he thought, never wrinkle, never grow old with spots. It wouldn't stretch with age or grow weary from stress and succumb to gravity. She served no natural laws. To Danny, she almost wasn't real.

"I'm really sorry what I said last night … when I mentioned your brother," she finally said.

"That's okay."

"It was lame."

He shrugged. "Just a little, but I could tell you meant it. Most people when they say how sorry they are, they follow it with the word 'but.'"

"Huh?" MaryAnne twirled a piece of her dark hair around her finger.

Danny looked at his hands wrapped around the oars. "Like, we're sorry for your brother's death, *but* we can't help you. Or we're sorry the driver didn't have a license when he ran over your brother, *but* his father is a state representative. That kind of thing."

"I see."

MaryAnne said the words so softly, if they weren't in the middle of a quiet pond, he might not have heard her. It was the kind of "I see" that said so much more. The words said,

Always

I'll wait for you to talk. Just two words, but they said you can trust me.

Danny swallowed hard. "Yeah, it's been a year, so everyone thinks I should be better. I guess I am. I've been through denial, anger, and depression. I think that's the order. I even bargained with God, 'Save him and take me,' I said. But he didn't listen—he never does. So now, they tell me after a year I should accept it. I should move on."

"Who's they?"

"Oh, nobody and everybody. My parents don't say anything. So, I just scream quietly."

"How do you do that?"

Danny hit the water lightly with an oar. "I dunno, but it hurts. A lot."

The spring feeding the pond created a subtle current, unnoticed until a leaf, a twig, or the little rowboat drifted along. A light ripple fanned out from the stern and droplets fell from the quiet oars as the boat drifted down the middle of the pond.

"Do you miss him?"

Danny looked up into MaryAnne's eyes. He knew she could see his pain. He knew the truth wouldn't escape those large brown eyes, and he crumbled. Right there, in his cutoff jeans, and his hairless, skinny pale chest exposed for all the world, but where only one person could see him ... he crumbled. If he had melted, there'd be nothing but a dirty, syrupy mess. But he crumbled, and only the shadow of a boy remained.

This was the first time he cried, truly cried, for Stephen. His chest heaved with each sob. MaryAnne moved to sit next to him, and his tears wet her halter top that had dried in the sun. She pressed his head against her chest as tears rolled down both of their faces, formed together, and trickled away.

Their little wooden boat bumped up against the bank as they sat unnoticed by nature, alone in a place where suffering is felt, pain expunged, and people grow. A place where Danny wasn't over, past, or beyond it.

He couldn't explain this moment, he couldn't, but Danny felt secure leaning against MaryAnne.

The words weren't coming, not yet, just peace, like the breeze in the sunshine, and the harmless bee that's feared yet is one of the smallest in the food chain. Danny felt baptized in tears, exhausted in spirit.

He stood out of the boat, being careful to hold the side for MaryAnne to follow. Then he pulled the skiff out of the water and turned it over on a path choked with weeds. He stowed the oars under the seats so they wouldn't rot in the grass. As they walked back up the hill, their hands touched and slipped together. It was the first graceful moment in his ungainly existence. Neither spoke. For the first time in a year, Danny was no longer alone.

"I'll walk you home," he told her.

"We rode our bikes."

They turned the corner and saw Lynne on the porch glider. MaryAnne pulled on his hand and stepped back behind the corner. Danny's mouth gaped wide open in wonderment when she put her hand on the back of his neck and kissed him.

When MaryAnne pulled back, he said, "I'm sor—"

Then she kissed him harder.

"I have to go," she whispered when she finally let him go.

"No, you don't."

"No, I really do. My dad's taking us waterskiing tomorrow." She smiled. "If you want to go, be at our house by ten. Okay?"

Always

Danny nodded. "Sure, what do I bring?"

"Nothing, just what you're wearing, silly. You do know how to ski, don't you?"

"Um, sure I do."

"See you tomorrow," she whispered in his ear before kissing him on the cheek then walking away toward her sister.

Danny watched the girls get on their bikes and pedal away. He didn't move until long after the dark brown ponytail disappeared beyond the last hill.

He was still holding his cheek when Uncle Vern brushed by him on the steps.

"Boy, what's gotten into you?"

February 2021

Sully worked when most slept and slept when the rest of the world worked. He liked it that way—a world of his making.

The sun faded over the next hill as he slowed Sierra down out of respect when he came down the hill to the bridge. A lime green jeep was parked on the side, and a man walked in a large arc around pieces of wreckage. *Gucci.* Sully pulled over and stared for a moment before getting out. He noticed Gucci's Sorrel boots with white wool around the edges and his Eddie Bauer down jacket.

"Mr. Jones?"

"Thought I'd see you here," Gucci said while still walking around the jeep.

"You did?"

Jonesy stopped and smiled at him. "No, just kidding, old man. Something, isn't it? You're driving along, coming back from an awesome ski trip, and your life changes in an instant." He snapped his fingers. "In an instant, everything that mattered doesn't. The only thing is what's in front of you and the person beside you."

Sully fidgeted with his keys in his pocket. "It's a frightening thing to face your mortality, Mr. Jones."

"Well, if I tell you something, I don't want to hear about it ever again, understand?" Gucci turned to face him, just a foot of space separated the two.

"I'm not sure I do, sir."

Gucci lowered his head. "When we hit the wall, I wet myself. Right there on my fine Corinthian leather." Gucci frowned. "What is Corinthian, anyway? A place or something?"

Sully took his hand from his pockets and touched Gucci's shoulder. "Sir, I've been in combat. Voiding on yourself was a common occurrence. Sometimes we laughed about it—gallows humor and all that. In the real world, we can't laugh. But let me tell you something. Your body was preparing for trauma. You didn't need that urine, did you?

Gucci shook his head. "It kinda felt good."

Sully laughed. "Now, that's funny. I, ah, I gotta get to work."

He turned back to Sierra and drove her to the hospital. As he parked, he let out a sigh. *Familiar territory.*

Sully went through his routine of hanging up his coat, visiting the time clock, the fridge, the work board, and finally the mirror to check himself. He wasn't a vain man, just disciplined. In the military, he learned to check himself before proceeding. Doing so kept him out of trouble, kept him alive.

He had been thinking about Mary Mills all day, more so after seeing Gucci. As he walked closer to the ICU with his kit, his thoughts grew louder, his steps quicker. He smiled when he saw her. Her bandages were different today. She had a smaller head dressing, and he could see more of her thick hair. Sully thought he could smell the long locks too. He spied the tube in her mouth bringing air, the tube down her nose bringing her nourishment, the saline bag bringing

Always

her hydration, and the morphine bag bringing her peace. There was a new dressing on the side of her face too, still obscuring her profile. But her arm was still in a cast and her leg still elevated.

That's gonna hurt for a long time. Stiff and sore. Muscles atrophied. A good candidate for PT someday, no doubt.

"Sully."

He turned to see his PA friend. "Hey, John."

"I see you're checking in on your gal."

Sully ignored the insinuation. "When will she wake up?"

"They induced a coma after her first series of operations. Today, the burn docs did their excruciating, painstaking work."

Sully shook his head. He knew burns. *The worst pain imaginable.*

"Well, then, I guess it's good that she's asleep. Not everyone gets that choice." Sully drifted back to the Gulf.

The Humvee in front of him didn't get far. As it was enveloped in a ball of fire, it careened off the sandy road.

"Lemme out, lemme out." Sully rolled out the back of his Humvee.

In front of him, the platoon sergeant, the CO, and two grunts were trapped inside theirs. The flames weren't high, just hot with amazing color. A heat he'd never experienced before, even in the desert. He shielded his face by twisting his brain bucket and ducking his chin under his body armor. His M27 bounced against his hip. His plastic eye-pro glasses shielded his eyes but felt like they were melting into his face.

He had seen the accident, but he really couldn't explain it—not in words anyway. The lead armored 18-ton truck had passed by the culvert without a hitch, but the command vehicle now lay on its side, one of the wheels spinning, one already melting.

Sully had been in the third vehicle.

"IED, IED!" someone cried out.

"Got it," Sully screamed.

"Get back, Doc. Get back!"

Sully knew the protocol. There could be a secondary device. There could be a second explosion when the gas tank caught, and Sully knew it would. But he pressed forward. He folded his hands under his arms—his gloves wouldn't protect him—and crept forward, completely vulnerable. He was close enough to hear the screaming and the smell. Oh, the smell. It flared his nostrils and stuck to the inside of his nasal cavity. The stench would never go away.

He could hear the first lieutenant, and he made his way to the front where the driver was kicking at the windshield. Sully used the butt of his M27 to crack the reinforced glass further. A leg broke through.

At once Sully's flak jacket was up against his chin, and he was moving backward. His master sergeant had him by the scruff of his neck and had yanked him back.

"Lemme go. Lemme go, Top."

"Too late."

Top dropped Sully in a ditch and covered him with his own body as the Humvee blew. Pieces of glass and metal and sand pelted them like hail.

"NO!" Sully cried, "No." He couldn't look.

"Hey, man, hey."

Sully felt John's hand rubbing his back.

"It's okay. It's okay."

Sully moved away from his soothing hand. "Yeah, yeah, sure it is."

"You've been doing a lot of that lately."

Always

Sully shrugged.

"You know you ought to see a—"

"I know, I know."

"I mean it, dude."

Sully wasn't angry at John's kibitzing. Anyone else would have been different, but John was right. He really needed to see someone.

"I will." Sully took a deep breath. "I will."

He used his sweaty palms to push his cart to the next window, the next, and the next until he stood around the other side of the wing where he noticed two of the nurses from yesterday.

"Ladies." He nodded.

"Sully," said the one.

"How's your gal, Sully?" asked the other.

Why do people keep saying that? My gal?

"I hear she's had another rough day. I don't know how many more rough days she can take. Who's the new doc?" Sully nodded to a little man with oversized pants and glasses standing near the nurses' station.

"That's Dr. Smeltzer, a burn specialist."

Sully turned to listen in on Dr. Smeltzer and another doc's conversation.

"Room 3, Ms. Mills. We had her down for a debridement."

"Another?" the second doc asked.

Smeltzer pointed at the picture on the tablet in his hands. "And it won't be the last. She's got deep tissue burns on her face and side. They can get worse, even grow deeper. Good news, they're less than five percent. Bad news, it's the face and her ear. The ear is incredibly susceptible to infection."

"Third or second degree?"

"Third, but we now call that a full thickness burn, involving her epidermis, dermis, and into the fat. Did you see that leathery looking skin? That's the hallmark of a full thickness burn. We removed that. Then down along her side, we split the skin to give it room to heal and allow it to drain properly. Now she looks like a hot cross bun."

Sully winced but stepped closer to the two docs. He focused on his cleaning tray, acting as though he were looking for something.

"Her side was cooked white and dry. Her nerve endings were fried, so it's not as painful as it looks. We had to do the debridement to determine the degree, so we took off most of her blisters."

Sully couldn't help himself. "I thought you should leave the blisters?"

The doctor looked up at him and narrowed his eyes at the custodian. "Maybe out in the field, but in the hospital, you want to remove all the blisters bigger than a quarter in size so the skin can start to heal itself."

Sully squinted. "Interesting, wouldn't that open her up for more infection?"

The doctor sighed deeply as he scratched his head. "Look, it could, but plasma and cellular tissue need to escape. We coated it with Silvadene then wrapped it with some flexnet to keep it draining and finally covered it with elastic wrap."

Sully pretended to empty a trashcan between the two docs who never moved, the one never even looked his way. Then he looked at the picture on Smeltzer's tablet.

Sully pointed at the tablet. "We used Silvadene in the field. The silver ions worked great on second- and third-degree burns."

Dr. Smeltzer raised his eyebrows but nodded. "It's still a great bactericidal, but it will have to be changed otherwise pseudoeschar will form."

Always

"What's that on her face?"

Smeltzer shrugged. "That's a new biosynthetic cellulose. We put it over the topical ointment."

"More Silvadine?"

The burn doctor shook his head before answering. "Not near the eyes. We used Geramycin. The ear is tricky, you can easily debride too much, so we use the Sulfamylon to penetrate deeply to attack the bacteria. Someone will have to change it twice a day until we do the skin graft." The doctor sneered. "Interested?"

"No way." Sully couldn't help himself. He had to ask. "She gonna make it?"

The burn doc paused. "Well, her age—fifty-nine—plus five percent for the burns gives her a sixty-four, but you also got to add in seventeen for the inhalation that damaged her lungs. I'd say they were lucky to intubate and, well ... she's lucky to be alive. She's a fighter, for sure."

"They used to tell us in FMS"—Sully looked up from the tablet to the doc—"Field Medical School, 'Airway, airway, airway.'"

Sixty-four plus seventeen equals eighty-one. That gives her a nineteen percent chance of survival. And that doesn't even account for her other trauma.

"Hey, Sully, is it? If you're interested, I'm presenting her for the third shift providers' brown-bag. Just slip in the back. No one will notice." The burn doc looked back and forth between the other doc and Sully. "No one notices the janitor."

Sully turned to walk away. Gucci had just come through the double doors with his cellphone glued to his ear.

"Mr. Jones," called a nurse. Sully saw her point to his cell phone while shaking her head.

"Oh, sorry, Nurse ... Ratchet, was it?" Jonesy put away his cell phone and headed straight to room 3.

That guy's got style.

Jonesy walked into Mary's room and came out immediately. "What's with these new bandages?"

"Well, that's my call," said Dr. Smeltzer, walking toward him. "Mr. Jones, let's step into her room. I'll walk you through it."

The door shut behind them and after a few minutes, Gucci opened the door and called out, "Hey, old man, come in here. We've got a cleanup on aisle three."

Sully looked around, then pointed to himself. "Me?"

Gucci smirked. "You see any other old man?"

Sully knew he was not allowed in an ICU room and certainly not with a patient, her family, and her doctor.

"It's okay, Sully," said Dr. Smeltzer from behind Gucci. "I could use your help."

Nurses stopped what they were doing, attendings interrupted their talking, and interns gaped at the man everybody else was now gaping at—Sully.

"Ooo-kay."

Sully walked in the room like he was the chief of surgery on a routine consult. There was a spilled coke on the floor that apparently Jonesy had tucked in his too-small pocket.

He started the cleanup when Smeltzer tapped him on the shoulder. "I was explaining to Mr. Jones the criteria for transferring Ms. Mills to a burn center in eastern North Carolina when he, well—"

"I blew a gasket, old man."

Sully knelt to wipe up the spill with a rag while the men continued their conversation.

"Anyway, as I was saying, Ms. Mills has deep partial thickness burns on five percent of her body and face including full thickness burns and inhalation burns, all of which are criteria for moving her to the burn center. That's when you interrupted me and got, well—"

"Ballistic. I went ballistic."

"Anyway, sir, counterbalancing all this is Ms. Mills's multiple organ issues, her broken limbs, and especially her TBI, that surpass her burns for risk of mortality."

"So, you're telling me she's gonna die."

Sully stood, damp rag in hand. "No, Mr. Jones." He looked to Smeltzer who nodded for him to continue. "She has injuries in lots of areas, you know that. And each of them is significant. And yes, together, they seem overwhelming right now. Normally, she would be in a burn center but it's half a state away, so with everything else going on, she's going to stay right here."

Jonesy rubbed his knuckles over his jaw. "Oh. I thought he wanted to move her out because she didn't have long to live."

"Mr. Jones—" Sully stopped as he looked down at the woman lying still in the bed. This was the first time he'd had a good look at Mary in room 3. He could see the exposed side of her face. He could see her hair that even now had a small flip near her forehead. He saw her skin—what it used to look like. He imagined her fragrance. He filled his nostrils. "Mr. Jones—"

"Yes, old man. Yes?"

"Mary ... MaryAnne is not going to die."

Dr. Smeltzer grabbed Sully's arm. He had said too much. "Mr. Jones, she still has a long way to go, she's not out of the woods, but we are optimistic."

Jonesy relaxed into the one chair in the room. Sully didn't move, still fixed on MaryAnne. With his hands clasped together and his head bowed, he barely blinked.

"In summary," Dr. Smeltzer said, letting go of Sully's arm, he began to read, "Ms. Mills came to the hospital with multiple traumas but intubated with exterior bleeding under control. With bilateral breath sounds, she was placed on a vent, pedal pulse present, GSA 5T, pupils 5m, and sluggish. Heart Rate 140, BP 110 over 36 with a TBSA of five percent second- and third-degree burns."

"TBS what?" Gucci frowned.

"Sir, are you getting all this?"

"Doctor." Now it was Sully's turn, although he couldn't look away from the patient to address them. "I think Mr. Jones has got enough for now."

Dr. Smeltzer nodded and walked out of the room. Sully turned away from the bed to follow but stopped in the doorway.

"Mr. Jones, one more thing. Please, I'm not Nick Carraway, and you are not the Great Gatsby. Call me Sully. Please."

"Certainly ... Sully. And for the record I'm not *Gucci*. Everyone calls me Jonesy."

The old man smiled. *How did he know?* He collected his cart and headed for his tuna fish sandwich and brown bag lunch.

Sully entered the room a little while later just as Dr. Smeltzer took the podium with a small clicker in his hand for his brown-bag presentation on Ms. Mills.

A few people shifted their chairs to make room for the custodian with his tuna fish, coffee, and one napkin. Sully sat on a plastic chair next to a table and the door. He folded his stubby fingers across his belly and looked at the screen,

Always

but he really didn't hear much of the lecture. His mind was a half century behind.

MaryAnne, after forty some years, you are still ... what's the word ... angelic.

June 1974

"So, you're going waterskiing at Wallenpaupack, are you?"

"Um-hum." Danny slurped down the last of his milk and Cheerios while Uncle Vern and Aunt Clare cleared the table.

"We got most of the hay in yesterday, so I guess your auntie and me can get the rest without you. You know how to water ski, don't you?" Uncle Vern asked.

"Uh-uh," he said through his mouth full of toast and the last of his orange juice.

"You don't? Well, it's easy. Just like life, you gotta know when to hold on and when to let go."

Danny frowned. "Isn't that poker, Uncle Vern?"

"Oh, you let him be, Vern." Aunt Clare looked over her shoulder at her two men.

"Thanks, Aunt Clare, love you." Danny wiped his mouth with his forearm, kissed his aunt on the cheek, and bolted through the back door. With a towel, book, and flip-flops in his backpack, he jumped on his rusty red bike and pedaled down the lane. *Waterskiing like life? Sounds more like gambling.*

He arrived at Mr. Bill's house, panting. Sweat soaked his muscle shirt and cutoff jeans. Mr. Bill was hitching his boat to the back of his truck, while another man lashed a small plastic sailboat to the top of a station wagon.

Oh no, that must be MaryAnne's father.

"Danny," Mr. Bill said, "this is my brother, Bob."

Bob wrapped his hand around Danny's. "Mr. Becker to you. Nice to finally meet you, son. I've heard a lot about you."

Danny's hand went limp. *What had MaryAnne told him?*

MaryAnne, Lynne, and a young boy barged out the front door. The boy got knocked to his knees by a German shepherd who barked and bared his teeth at the edge of the porch.

"Max! Max, get back," MaryAnne cried as she grabbed his collar. "Bad dog, bad. She won't hurt you, Danny."

"I can see that." Danny had backed up to the boat.

"Come over here. Let him sniff you." MaryAnne took Danny's hand and let Max smell it until he stopped snarling. "Pet him," she encouraged.

Slowly Danny patted the still sniffing shepherd.

"Rub his ears. He likes that." Danny obeyed, and MaryAnne let go of her dog. "Max is just a big baby."

Danny said, "A big baby with even bigger teeth."

"You'll be fine. Hey, you can ride with us."

"Danny's riding with your uncle, honey." Mr. Becker wrapped his huge arms around his oldest daughter. "Isn't that right, Danny?"

"Yes, Mr. Becker." Danny replied with the courtesy of a primary schooler. Her father had yet to learn Danny's sarcasm.

MaryAnne had her arm on the younger boy's shoulder who carried a small fishing rod and tackle box. "This is my little brother, Mikey."

Mikey had long, light-brown hair with natural highlights that went everywhere but looked right—the combination of everything good between his older sisters.

"You fish?" Danny asked.

Always

"Yeah. Do you?"

"A little. Maybe we could do some today."

Both Mikey and MaryAnne smiled.

"Let's go, everybody." Mr. Bill waved from his truck.

A woman backed out of the front door and turned around. *Whoa, she's beautiful.* Danny stared at her long, dark hair, matching brown eyes, and the one-piece bathing suit partially covered by cutoff jean shorts and a checkered shirt. A bandana wove its way through her hair. She was MaryAnne filled out and all grown up.

Mr. Bill pinched Danny and whispered, "Don't stare, son. Ain't polite."

Danny shook his head and got in the pickup before Mrs. Becker walked any closer. The pickup truck towing the boat and the station wagon with the sailboat on top took off for Wallenpaupack.

After a time, Danny looked up from his book, *Of Mice and Men*, to stare at the scenery. "Where are we, Mr. Bill?"

"Almost there, but I need gas. Can you pump while I run to the bathroom?" The truck, trailer, and car pulled next to the gas pumps. The small office next to the pumps was only big enough for a counter. A bottle Coke machine stood outside.

Mr. Becker shot Danny a look as his girls ran for the bathroom, and he began pumping gas. A few minutes later, as Danny was putting the nozzle back into the pump, MaryAnne approached him from behind.

"Hey."

"Hey."

"I like your sunglasses."

"Yours too."

"Sorry about my dad. Heard he insisted you call him Mr. Becker." She rolled her eyes. "He's just being funny."

Danny shoved his hands into his pockets. "Funny, huh? Is that what you call it?"

"Yeah, funny."

Danny shrugged.

"It's just how he is and ... well, that's just how I love him." MaryAnne stomped back to her station wagon and sat in the back seat while waiting for everyone to return.

What did I say?

Mr. Bill came out of the station tucking his shirt into his cargo shorts. "Let's get going, whadda ya say?"

"Sure, Mr. Bill."

As Mr. Bill turned the ignition key, he glanced at Danny. "You okay?"

"Sure." Danny stared out the window.

"You know anything about Wallenpaupack?" Mr. Bill didn't wait for a reply. "It's a man-made lake. But to build it, they wiped out whole towns. Divers can see some of the remains of houses and old trucks at the bottom. But today, we're going skiing, not diving. Ever been?"

Danny didn't say anything, he just stared out the window.

"Anyway, it's easy. You lock your knees, don't pull on the rope, but don't let the rope pull you over. Just let the boat do all the work, and you'll pop up in no time. And don't worry if it takes you a few tries. But listen, most important is if you start to fall, let go of the rope."

Of course, I'm gonna let go, why wouldn't I?

"You'd be surprised." It was as if Mr. Bill could read his mind. "You'd be surprised what people forget when they are falling at thirty miles an hour."

Danny swallowed hard as he saw the entrance to the marina. The two men parked their vehicles and waited for the girls and Danny to get out. Outside the truck, he stood

Always

by as the two brothers backed the motorboat down the ramp. Mrs. Becker and MaryAnne took the two lines and guided the boat to the side.

The men unloaded the plastic Sunflower sailboat from the top of the station wagon next and pushed it in the water. Mr. Becker raised the mast and sail while Danny and Mikey carried the cooler to the motorboat.

"I'll see you at our favorite beach," Mr. Becker yelled.

The Johnson 70 outboard gave it her all to haul six people and a day's load of fun as they set out toward their preferred spot. Along the way, Mr. Bill fantailed a heavy dose of "Hello!" at his brother who vehemently shook his fist. Danny realized he was laughing the loudest at Mr. Becker when Mrs. Becker looked over at him.

She didn't talk much. She didn't have to. Her quiet beauty wielded great power. He tried to say something to her, but the words got stuck in his throat.

A few minutes later, Mr. Bill beached his boat on a little island in the middle of the lake. The beach was magical, something out of a Stevenson novel. Danny sat on the dry sand with the cool water nipping at his toes for a bit before rising to show Mikey how to wet some bread and knead it into dough bait.

While the girls water skied, he and Mikey caught sunnies at will. Mr. Bill had started a small grill when Mr. Becker finally showed up.

"Just in time for lunch, Bob," his brother called.

"I didn't miss anything, did I?" He looked at Danny and Mikey.

"Danny and I have been fishing," his son said. "He showed me how to catch sunnies."

Soon, Danny sat down with a double paper plate loaded down with a hamburger, hot dog, and German potato salad.

He couldn't tell Mrs. Becker he didn't like potato salad when she told him she'd made it herself. MaryAnne sat close to him with her own plate full of food. They said little and gazed at the water—and occasionally each other—as they ate.

After a few bites of his hot dog, she wiped some mustard from his face.

"Careful," he said, eyes widening, "people are watching."

"Stop it." She punched at his ribs.

"Who hasn't skied yet?" asked Mr. Bill when they'd all had their fill.

"Danny hasn't," MaryAnne offered.

He shot a look at her that said *Thanks*.

"Well, let's go then," said Mr. Bill, moving toward his boat. "MaryAnne, you come with and be the lookout for the skier."

Mr. Bill pushed the nose of the boat around to face the water while MaryAnne climbed in with her dad.

Mr. Becker sat behind the wheel and turned the key. "This one's mine, Bill," he shouted over the noise of the two-stroke engine.

Danny waded into the water with Mrs. Becker. She helped him keep his balance while he leaned back to put on the wooden skis and tried his best not to bump into her.

Mr. Bill waded into the water next to him. "Just keep your tips up and the rope between them. Lock your legs, and don't bend forward but don't pull back too much either. Give the thumbs up when the rope gets tight, and the boat starts to pull on you. Got it?" Mr. Bill swam to the boat and climbed in the back.

Mrs. Becker held Danny's life jacket from behind, while Danny held onto the handle of the ski rope between his knees. His head, his knees, and the skis were the only

Always

things out of the water. When the boat took off, the last thing he saw was MaryAnne watching him from the back of the boat. His skis flopped from one side to the other as the rope picked up speed in the water then snapped taught and jerked the handle out of Danny's hands. Mr. Becker just shook his head and drove the boat in a circle back to Danny. Mr. Becker had to make a second pass so Danny could grab the rope behind him and pull the handle in front. Now they were lined up for another try. He was already worn out and started to shiver when the rope grew taut, and he finally gave the thumbs up.

Mr. Bill called from the back of the boat, "Remember, let go if you fall."

Suddenly, the boat jerked him out of his skis, plowing him underwater for ten feet, then pulled him up to catch his breath before he finally let go and landed face first with a mouth full of lake water.

"You're pulling too fast, Bob, you're pulling too fast!" shouted Mr. Bill.

Mr. Becker circled the boat back around behind Danny again. MaryAnne had collected the skis from the side of the boat and pushed them back into the water. Her look told him everything—he was in trouble.

"All right, let's try it again," Mr. Becker shouted.

He's trying to kill me.

Mr. Becker smiled before pushing the throttle forward. Danny pointed his skis, leaned back, locked his knees, and shot up another thumb. He was jerked back into a black hole underwater at what felt like the speed of light. He screamed out loud at the top of his lungs before surfacing.

"You're trying to kill the boy," Mr. Bill shouted at his brother. "You're going too fast, Bob." He walked to the back of the boat and shouted, "Danny, want to try again?"

Danny looked at him but said nothing, hoping someone would call the whole thing off.

"Danny?"

He looked at MaryAnne before saying, "I guess."

Mr. Bill took the boat's helm and circled around him. Danny knew the routine by now. He was getting good at putting on his skis underwater, at least. He lifted his thumb, and this time, the boat lifted him at the right speed. He stared at his hands and the tips of his skis. He could hear MaryAnne yelling but didn't look up.

They had told him the boat would leave a wake. Outside the wake would be fast and rough. Inside the wake was like the porch glider. Danny glided into the sweet spot the boat left behind. They circled back, and he heard Mrs. Becker, Lynne, and Mikey cheering him on. He grew brave and waved like a skier on *The Jackie Gleason Show*. But he didn't realize how tight the boat was turning, and he ended up outside the wake. His skis went airborne, and he hit the water face first. He popped up quickly.

Mr. Bill turned the boat back and came up next to him.

"Go again?"

Danny shook his head. "No, I'll let someone else have a turn."

After only a few minutes on the skis, he felt spent. He'd fallen just a short distance from the shoreline and could walk back most of the way. MaryAnne dove off the side of the boat and headed to the shore with him.

He flopped down on his towel while Mikey and the others slalomed and did their stunts. MaryAnne brought over two plums, handing one to him then dropping down onto the sand beside him.

"You're good," she said.

"Yeah, right. You're better."

Always

"Don't say that."

"Why not, you are."

"I know. Just don't say it." She bit into her plum, and he watched a moment as juice ran down her chin.

"Do you think we could take your dad's sailboat out?"

She turned to him with wide eyes. "Do you know how to sail?"

"No, but a few minutes ago, I didn't know how to ski." He smiled.

"Good point."

The two pushed the yellow boat with the sunflower on the sail into the water until they felt a breeze. When they got in, Danny pulled in the boom and the sail filled with just enough air to get them started.

"We're sailing!" MaryAnne cried.

"This, I like." He pointed the boat toward the wind, and the yellow sunflower heeled over as the two smiled.

He filled his lungs with air, then pulled again on the line, but this time the boom swung across the boat, knocking MaryAnne into the lake. She came up sputtering.

"You did that on purpose," she accused.

He panicked, unsure how to bring the boat back around to her. "No, honest, I didn't."

MaryAnne knew how to swim and made it back to the boat.

"I am so sorry," he said as he helped her up over the side. "I feel awful, are you okay?"

MaryAnne started laughing and couldn't stop. "I'm f-f-fine. It's f-f-funny."

Danny shook his head at her silly nature. *Who are you?*

MaryAnne looked to the beach where everyone was now standing looking back at them. "Oh, boy," she said.

With the paddle, some wind, and some luck, they got the boat headed back to the beach.

"Who said you could take my boat out?" Mr. Becker said as he helped pull the boat to shore.

"It was my idea, Dad, I thought it'd be okay."

"Do you know how to sail, Danny?"

"Better than I ski." Danny grinned and everyone laughed. Everyone but Mr. Becker.

Mrs. Becker moved closer. "Let me take a look at your head, young lady."

"Oh, Mom, it's just a bump. Do you always have to be a nurse?"

"Yes, and a mom, too."

Mrs. Becker gently ran her fingers across MaryAnne's hairline and then looked into her eyes. "Your eyes aren't dilated. Do you remember what happened?"

MaryAnne brushed her mother's hand aside. "Yeah, Mom."

"What time is it?"

"Time to go," said Mr. Becker.

"Well, that's for sure," said Mr. Bill.

Danny looked toward the horizon. The sun had dropped behind the mountaintop pine trees, casting orange, purple, and colors yet to be named across the water. The world had melted into itself and turned upside down—sky was water and water sky.

The crew loaded up the motorboat while Mr. Becker tied the sailboat to the stern. Everyone took a seat—the brothers in front, Lynn and her mother behind them. Danny, MaryAnne, and Mikey sat at the stern. Danny looked back one more time at the beach before searching for the dock in the distance.

The lake air blowing his hair back, the boat speeding to the ramp, and MaryAnne slipping her hand under his ... nothing else mattered now. Not her father, not drinking

Always

lake water, or fumbling with his weak handshake. His world had heeled over then righted itself.

Life became perfect. One moment seemed like forever. *What's that feeling?* Something he had never felt. *Peace.*

Back on shore, Danny helped the men return the motorboat to the trailer and helped Mr. Becker lash down his sailboat.

"Sir, thank you for letting us use your boat."

Mr. Becker nodded.

"Please don't be mad at MaryAnne. It was my idea."

"Oh, trust me, son, I'm not mad at MaryAnne. I just want you to know I'm here. I'm here, and I'm not going away."

"Me neither." Danny startled himself with this revelation. He wasn't trying to be snippy. Confident, maybe—another new feeling. He looked her father in the eye then walked away.

"Hey, Bob, what do say you ride with me in the truck? We don't get enough time to talk." Mr. Bill put his hand on his brother's shoulder and guided him away from the other car.

"Kids, get in the station wagon," called Mrs. Becker.

"Mom's driving! I got shotgun," shouted Mikey.

"No, I do," countered Lynne.

"Mikey, let's let Lynne ride up front this time." Mrs. Becker smiled ever so slightly at Danny and MaryAnne.

Mikey sat at one window in the backseat, and Danny sat at the other with MaryAnne in the middle. This time Danny reached for her hand. No one else noticed her smile or that she really wasn't saying much of anything on the way back—no exclamations, no chatter.

"So, what did everybody like today?" Mrs. Becker asked the quiet group.

One by one, her children took their turn.

Man, this is a real family. I've heard of those.

"How about you, Danny? What was your favorite part?"

Lynne turned around, and MaryAnne turned as well to hear his answer.

"Well, I don't know if you know this or not but, this was my first time waterskiing."

"Oh no, we had no idea," said Mrs. Becker, glancing up at him in the rearview mirror with a smile.

Everyone laughed.

"And while I'm being honest, it was my first time sailing too."

"Really!" exclaimed Mrs. Becker.

Again, everybody laughed.

"But I'd have to say …" Danny looked at MaryAnne. "I really liked catching all those sunnies. How 'bout it, Mikey?"

"Yeah!" Mikey thrust his fist into the air, and MaryAnne pouted until Danny squeezed her hand.

When they got back to Mr. Bill's, Danny helped unhitch the boat. Then, Mr. Bill loaded Danny's bike in the back of the truck and told him to jump in.

"It's dusk, and you're tired. I don't want anything to happen."

Danny thanked Mr. and Mrs. Becker, then Mikey, and he even thanked Lynne, then MaryAnne.

"You are welcome," MaryAnne replied as she held out her hand.

He shook it formally, and they smiled together. Danny bit his lip, turned, and got in the truck.

They drove in silence until Mr. Bill stopped the truck when they got to the farm. "Did you have fun?"

"I had the best time ever."

Mr. Bill leaned against the open window frame. "Well, that's good. We all like you, even Bob."

Always

"You'd never know it, Mr. Bill."

"Let's just say, he's—"

"Old fashioned," Danny prompted.

"I was going to say traditional. You gotta remember, MaryAnne is his oldest. And you really don't know what that's like."

Danny shifted in his seat. He wasn't used to talking to adults. Not like an adult, anyway.

Mr. Bill put his hand on Danny's shoulder. "So, I'm going to say this for your own good. She's young. She's innocent, and she's naïve."

She didn't seem all that naïve when she kissed me yesterday.

"So please, be kind and respectful, and whatever you do, remember, she's also my first niece."

"Yessir."

"Danny, I can't imagine what it would be like if I lost Bob, and so I don't know what it's like for you to lose Stephen. But maybe God's putting someone in your life. None of us want you to blow it. Right?" His hand squeezed Danny's shoulder.

"Yessir."

Danny got out of the truck and retrieved his bike which he leaned against a porch post before waving goodbye to Mr. Bill and opening the farmhouse door. He brushed past Uncle Vern on the stairs, causing the older man to lean against the wall.

"Boy, what's gotten into you?"

Danny didn't stop until he got to his room and pulled out his watercolors. He scribbled a few pencil lines before he wetted his brush and painted a little sailboat with two young lovers against a setting sun.

When he was done, he looked at the painting and smiled.

Then he fell asleep on top of his bed, still in his cutoffs and T-shirt.

March 2021

Make the bed, load the dishwasher, clear the counters, feed Kat. Nuts, I'm a cat person. Least I'm not that old man in the big truck without a scratch in the bed who can't park because his lap dog is licking his face. Not yet.

He used to think about dying and would wake up each morning disappointed. Today, he woke up happy. But he knew the axe would eventually fall. It always did. He went through his list of disappointments starting with getting cut from the Little League in 1968. He thought about his brother Stephen. Then about Jimmy and about his wife passing, and then he thought about himself. All disappointments.

But today, he thought about MaryAnne, about what could be.

You're crazy, old man. "Old man" sounded different when he said it. More like a Hemingway old man than a Fitzgerald old man. Grizzled. The kind of *The Old Man and the Sea* that's earned through years of toil, not a momentary Gatsby formality.

He couldn't shake the feeling of happiness now, although he tried. He drove happy, punched-in happy, and checked the work board happy.

Then, he saw the small note: *Sullivan—my office.*

Happiness left, and familiarity returned. *I knew this couldn't last.* Worry, even disaster would have creeped back in if there were more floors to climb before he arrived at his supervisor's desk.

He found her on the phone, so he sat down on a padded bench that made him feel like he was in the principal's office again. He bit his lip.

"Sully," she said after hanging up. "You're making quite a name for yourself."

"Excuse me?"

"You've been one of my best—quiet, dependable, no trouble except your occasionally misplaced manners. I'm not sure of your game, but now I'm getting emails from the chief of surgery, our lawyer, and this Mr. Jones. Somehow, he's got power of attorney. What's with him?"

"I don't know what you want me to do, mum."

"All I want you to do is your job, but now I get this." She waved a note from the chief surgeon then read, "Make this happen."

The axe ... I knew this happiness couldn't last.

She handed Sully an embossed card tucked inside a small gold-lined envelope.

> To whomever holds the keys,
> Please allow Mr. Sullivan of housekeeping the opportunity to visit Ms. Mary Mills on a regular basis. While she is in a coma, I am told human contact is important, but due to my work, I have been called away to attend other matters.
> Respectfully,
> I.M. Jones
> JJ&T LLC

Sully's hands rested in on each thigh. "I don't understand."

"Frankly, me neither. But it's been written into Ms. Mills's doctor's orders that you are to visit her regularly

Always

with no restrictions." Sully's supervisor shifted in her seat. "But here's *my* restriction—see to it your work does not suffer."

He nodded. "Yes, mum."

Sully turned to the door as a little smile expanded to include a tear in his eye. He shook his head and left.

This is an axe I like. I like it a lot.

Sully grabbed his little, yellow cart, made sure his flags were unfurled, and went to work. He felt like eyes were upon him, and he grew suspicious with every new hello. But he kept his head low and tried his best to be just as ornery as he'd had any other shift. Yet he couldn't contain his excitement. His feet felt light, and his work bordered on a near pleasure. He embraced this newfound lease. New wine in old skin. Joy unleashed in dried sinew and bone.

"God," he finally said out loud, "Thank you."

At his break, he struggled to pace himself, left his tuna fish in the fridge, washed his hands like a TV surgeon, fixed his hair, and headed back upstairs. He so wanted to read his new charge's chart, but he knew that he would be overplaying the hand dealt him. Instead, he put on a hospital gown and slowly made his way into room 3. Breathing intentionally, he pulled up a heavy metal padded chair and sat.

Sully remained silent for a long time. *Where to begin?* He saw her as awake, her deep eyes that sparkled at night, still adolescent, still innocent. He transformed back to an age of vulnerable invulnerability, an age of paradoxes and challenged paradigms.

"Hey."

Hey, he heard her say in reply.

"It's me, Danny." He hadn't said his real name for a very long time.

I know, silly.

"So, you remember me?"

I remember everything.

"Not everything."

Ah-huh.

He laughed, and so did she, more of a giggle, though.

"MaryAnne, how I've missed you. I never forgot you, ever. Never forgot our kiss, our moment in the barn, the corner of the house, our maiden voyage on the SS *Sunflower*. I was just a kid. And I'm so sorry."

His eyes welled up. He hadn't expected this emotion. He retrieved his checkered handkerchief from his back pocket.

Why the tears, Danny?

"You know I was always a baby."

Oh, pooh, I know nothing of the sort. Take my hand.

Sully reached for her hand, but it was Danny who felt life pulsating through her fingers into his dried heart.

You were brave when I was weak, real when the world wanted you quiet, and sweet, my sweet boy, even when my father was harsh. But you were never a baby. Not to me.

"Well, MaryAnne, or is it just Mary now? You always knew what to say to me. You were always so kind."

It's MaryAnne with an e, always has been, no matter what they say.

"Yeah, people call me Sully now, but I'm still that pimply faced Danny."

Oh, stop. I remember you being cute, not pimply faced. And I remember those lips too.

"Well." Danny looked up to see if anyone was watching, if anyone could hear. "I remember being young. Man, you were so young, wide-eyed, and so innocent. That hasn't changed."

Always

Are you looking at me? Young? Wide-eyed? And after they toyed with the inside of my head, I don't know what I am, Danny. That's why I need you. You are still my Sir Lancelot.

Danny looked around again before saying, "Don't take this the wrong way, I mean, I'm really not a creepy, old man, but when I told you I never forgot you, I really meant I never stopped thinking about you." Danny's voice quivered. "You would come to me at the strangest times. For years, I focused on family, on my wife Martha, on my career, but just every once in a while, you would seep in. In a dream sometimes. In a breeze, other times. I loved my wife, but I gave her such a difficult time. I'm still moody, I get hurt easy, and I can be ugly. I hurt her, and yet she forgave me. So, in a way, I'm grateful you and I were apart, grateful I didn't hurt you."

Danny paused then took a deep breath. He could hear a quiet woosh from the machines and a murmur outside the room.

"After my brother Stephen ... I wanted to hide in my cocoon. But with you, love broke through. When Jimmy, well, when Jimmy never got off the HM-60 alive, a part ... a big part of me never left him. Never will. You didn't know Jimmy."

Danny now had his head in his hands, and he sobbed. He didn't look up for fear that someone on the other side of the window would see him lift his handkerchief to his face.

But I do know him. I can't explain it—this state I'm in or where I'm at or where I've been. But I know things. Maybe when I wake up, I could tell you, I don't know. Danny, I have a confession ... I'm scared, really, really scared. I was scared sliding down that highway. I pulled on Jonesy's arm as we slid off the side of the road. "The wall," I screamed, "the wall." I was on my side. Oh, the heat. Then, I thought you were there. No, it was Jimmy. He was in a camouflaged uniform and helmet. There was a patch and a tube in his chest. "I'm Jimmy, ma'am, you're going to be okay," he said. "I'm sending Danny, he's a better corpsman than I'll ever be." It's all so mixed, all so crazy. But Danny ... I'm so scared."

Electronic beeps sounded, and a bell started ringing. Sully looked up and saw flashing red and orange lights. The door slid open, and two doctors and a nurse rushed in. Sully got pushed to the back.

Don't go, Danny, don't go.

"You—out now!" the nurse bellowed.

Perplexed, he looked at MaryAnne.

Danny, please stay.

"Now, Sully!"

He backed out and sidestepped to the observation window by her bed, pressing his hand against it. "I'm here, and this time, I'm never leaving ... never." He felt an arm on his shoulder that tried to pull him away, but he resisted.

"Sully?"

"John." He glanced at his PA friend. "MaryAnne told me to stay."

John frowned. "Sully?"

Sully smiled. "Dude, I'm good."

"Convince me. What's the date?"

"March 1991. Got anything easier?"

John's hand on his arm tightened. "Don't play with me, man. What's the date?"

"Oh, yeah, um ... March 2021."

"Close enough." John let go of his arm.

As they talked, a doctor punched buttons on the computer next to MaryAnne's bed. Another shot a syringe into a port on her wrist. The nurse wrote down the time and recorded numbers on a clipboard. They stopped to

Always

watch how MaryAnne would respond. Moments ticked by. MaryAnne's breathing returned to normal. Her color improved and all but one nurse slowly filed out of her room.

Sully went back in. "Did I do that?"

The nurse turned. "No, no way. I don't know what you did, but you didn't hurt her. You can't."

"Are you sure?"

"Sully, Mr. Jones may have requested you here, but many of us believe you are good for her. I don't know how. Some things in medicine can't be explained. I believe in miracles, and I believe you are good medicine."

The nurse closed the door on her way back to the nurses' station.

Danny fell into his plastic seat and reached for MaryAnne's hand.

"Now, where were we?" he asked.

Ha! You're still funny, that's for certain. Maybe we could talk about something else. I'm feeling a little out of sorts.

"Gee, I don't know why. Let me see …"

Tell me about your family.

"My parents passed away a few years back. Somehow Stephen, Mom, Dad, Jimmy, Martha—she was my wife—they're more alive to me now than ever. Anyway, I remember your sister and your little brother. And your parents and Mr. Bill. 'Oooh, Mr. Bill.'" Danny used his high-pitched *Saturday Night Live* voice. He chuckled. "I haven't done Mr. Bill in a long while."

Do you still paint?

"Oh, heavens no. Really, it wasn't the same after I came back from the Gulf War. After all that sand with nothing but shades of brown, the bright colors here made me wince. I tried every once in a while when the mood hit, but I gave that up after Martha died."

You should paint. You were good.

"Yeah, right." Danny smirked. "I don't even know where my paints are."

He squirmed in his seat, certain his talent was taken because he hadn't used it. He had painted what had come from his heart—an artist's heart.

My uncle Bill still lives in the Poconos, I think. I haven't seen him for a long time. Mom is still alive, growing in grace, growing old in stunning beauty.

"I'm sure."

I always knew you had a crush on her.

"Now, you stop it." Sully could feel his neck getting red. He shifted in his chair. "Anyway, after 9/11, I enlisted in the navy. They wanted me to go the officer track, but I liked working for a living and ended up retiring as a chief. That job ruined me, but I miss it, and I'd do it all over again. Well, most of it. I was bored, though, so I got this part-time job at the hospital after Martha—"

Don't you have a job to do now?

"Yeah, I'm doing it. You sound like my supervisor, but I should get to some of my other duties before I punch out. Same time tomorrow?"

I'm not going anywhere.

"You better not. I can't lose you again."

Sully put back his chair, went to her bed, and squeezed her hand lightly. She might have squeezed back—he couldn't be sure. Maybe she smiled behind all the tubes. He felt sixteen again.

"See y'all," he called and waved to the nurses' station.

Everyone stopped and stared. He pushed the big square button then held the door for a group of interns who also paused to stare.

"Have a good shift, team ICU," he said to the group.

"Was that Sully, the guy you warned me about?" he heard a newbie ask the attending.

Always

Sully smiled as he went through the ICU doors into the hallway and danced his cart to the elevator. He had a song in his head he couldn't recognize right away, but by the time he put his cart back he was singing more of it.

> See that sun in the morning,
> Peeking over the hill?
> I'll bet you're sure it always has and sure it always will.
> That's how I feel about someone,
> How somebody feels about me.
> We're sure we love each other
> That's the way we'll always be.

He tipped his battered navy ball cap to his supervisor as the glass doors slid open for him. He moved with lightened purpose toward his rusty steed and picked back up on his song.

> We'll be the same as we started
> Just a-traveling along
> Singing a song
> Side by side.

He arrived home, not knowing how, which was not unusual for him as he'd traveled the distance so often. Sierra could do the trip without him. But today he was startled to see his trailer with the broken screen door, rusty metal steps, and the grain shovel-turned-snow shovel laying in the yard. *I really should do something with this place.* The mess hadn't bothered him before, now he saw decay.

He went inside, opened a tin of food for Kat, and fell into his velour TV chair. He pulled the lever back and nodded off to *Good Morning Carolina* with Kat purring on top of his chest.

I really should do something with this place. But not today.

July 1974

    A week had passed since Danny last saw MaryAnne and the absence was killing him. To pass the time, he brought in more hay and sang songs on the back of the hay wagon, confident his uncle couldn't hear over the broken exhaust stack on his old International. Danny smiled as the old couple worked in tandem without saying a word except an occasional, "Hey, watch it," followed by a grunt.

    They gathered hay like their ancestors.

    His aunt, in her sixties, gathered the row of cut hay in bunches with a wide rake with wooden fingers. She had made five-foot-high mounds that looked like one of the little pig's homes before the wolf came puffing along.

    Uncle Vern came along on the tractor towing a flatbed hay wagon while Aunt Clare and Danny carefully forked the hay onto the wagon. They positioned the hay so it laid over the one-foot-high wagon sides. The wagon was narrow enough and the strands of hay were long enough so the ends of the hay met in the middle of the wagon.

    "Careful, Danny," warned his uncle, "it's gotta make it down the side of the mountain without spilling."

    No ropes or straps were used, just Aunt Clare who climbed to the middle and plopped down in her long skirt, old blouse, and a bandana tied around her head. Her weight held down the ends of the hay. She motioned Danny to do the same. He could feel her strength when she pulled him up to the top.

"Ya know, Aunt Clare, some people bale hay with equipment into neat little squares and pile them high in wagons with sides," Danny said.

"Then where would we sit?" Aunt Clare put one arm around him and used the other to drink spring water out of a round, metal thermos.

Yup, this is home. Something Danny counted on and was sure would always be there. As the tractor and wagon made their way to the barn, he shut his eyes and lay in his aunt Clare's arms like a little boy.

"Hello, ma'am."

"Hello, lass."

Danny opened one eye then straightened. "Hello, lass," he repeated when he saw MaryAnne dressed in a flannel shirt, jeans, a baseball cap, and cowboy boots standing near the barn.

Wow, she even makes flannel look good.

"You need any help?" she asked.

"We got it—"

"Sure, we do, lass," Aunt Clare interrupted. "I need a break, anyway." She scooted down off the trailer and went into the house while Uncle Vern pushed the rear of the hay wagon with the tractor. Danny guided the front of the wagon next the growing haymow.

"How do you know how to do that?" MaryAnne asked him.

"Se-easy,"

"Do you remember how to fork off the hay into the mow, so it lays right and gets the air it needs?" Uncle Vern asked.

Always

"Yessir."

"Well, get it right. Get it wrong, and you'll burn the whole barn down." Vern headed for the house.

"What's that mean?" MaryAnne asked.

Danny already had a fork and was back on top of the wagon. "If the hay is forked all at once, it will be too tight—air won't be able to dry it. It could heat up and spontaneously combust—not good."

He started forking the hay onto the mow while MaryAnne broomed the loose hay that missed over to the side. Danny noticed she slowed her work when her hair fell in front of her face, and she began to breathe heavily. She dropped her canvas gloves and held her hand. Danny winced when he saw her broken blister, but she didn't complain. He hopped down and took her hands in his, feeling their child-like softness. He wondered if this could be her first ever blister. He lightly kissed the wound, then pulled her to lay down with him in the middle of the mow. They stared up at the timbered roof beams.

"Look at that bark, wouldja?" Danny pointed out a hundred-year-old beam with some loose bark.

"I hope I still have my bark when I'm a hundred," MaryAnne said.

"Somehow, I think you will."

"How about you, what do you want when you're a hundred?" she asked.

"A coffin."

"I'm serious."

"Me too."

She slapped his shoulder. "Well, you're not funny."

"Okay, serious?" Danny's voice became measured. "When I'm a hundred ... I want you."

They stopped looking at the beams and turned their eyes to each other. A strand of Timothy hay lay in MaryAnne's hair, and Danny shook off his glove to gently return the strand to the hay mow. As she looked at him, all he could see were her brown eyes sparkling beneath her thick brown eyebrows. He put his hand on the back of her neck, leaned in, hoping he'd find her lips. He did.

When he opened his eyes, she was gazing back at him.

"What?" he whispered.

"Nothing."

"What nothing?"

"I said, nothing." Her voice was defiant but not believable.

"What were you thinking?" he probed.

"Just … just maybe what it'd be like to be here with you in a hundred years."

The picture brought up a wealth of unknown joy in his heart and he laughed.

"I'm serious," she said.

"I know … me too." He pulled her closer. "I promise, wherever you are in a hundred years, I'll find you."

The stillness of the barn was broken by a car pulling into the gravel driveway. Car doors opened and slammed shut. MaryAnne popped up and put her face to a slatted opening in the wall.

"Oh no, my dad. I forgot. I gotta go. Oh no, oh no."

She slid down the side of the haymow, followed by Danny. Her father, Aunt Clare, and Uncle Vern looked their way as they walked into the light.

Danny tried to take her hand, but she shook him off. *What's her problem? We weren't doing anything wrong.*

Her father's hands squeezed his hips. "MaryAnne."

"Daddy, I am so sorry. What time is it?"

Always

"Six-thirty."

"Did I miss Mom's birthday?"

"Not dinner, not the cake ... yet."

"I am so sorry. Bye, everyone, bye."

MaryAnne hurried to her father's car while Danny stood there with his thumbs pulling at his front pants pockets.

"Mr. Becker—"

MaryAnne's father turned away from Danny to address his grandparents. "Goodbye, folks." Then, with a curt nod, Mr. Becker got in his car with MaryAnne and drove away, kicking up driveway stones.

Uncle Vern looked at Danny and shook his head.

Danny's eyes welled up with tears, but he walked away before the waterworks could roll down his face. He wanted to be held by Aunt Clare but shook off his boyish thought. *I'm a boy, not a man. I'm not eighteen, but I know what I want.* He walked down to the pond and sat on the dock. Another song came to mind, but this time he heard Otis Reading instead of Alice Cooper. He was only sixteen, but he felt a hundred and just knew he would keep his promise.

The sun changing colors gave him a thought. *Oh, man, that's crazy. But it might work.*

When he got back to the house there was a wax-paper covered dish of meatloaf and mashed potatoes in the fridge. He didn't care that the food was now cold. He ate and washed the meal down with even colder milk as the thought came back to him.

Yeah, man, do it.

He rushed upstairs and pulled a satchel of drawings and watercolors from behind his dresser. He thumbed through the pile until he came upon the little, yellow sailboat with a backdrop of sunset purples and blues. The sail in his painting was full, the boat heeled over, and two people, male and female, sat on the gunwale holding the main line and the rudder. He grabbed a black felt marker and scribbled a beard onto the man. Next, he took down a small picture from his wall, measured it, and used his X-Acto knife to replace the picture in the frame with his own art. Downstairs he grabbed the newspaper and wrapped it around the frame with baler twine.

A few minutes later, he dropped his bike at the Beckers' house. He pulled at a piece of Timothy hay growing in the front garden and slid it under the baling twine. What others would see as a weed, Danny saw as art. His present was now complete. He saw the family singing "Happy Birthday," and Mrs. Becker blowing out candles through the dining room window. He had to ring twice before Mr. Bill answered the door.

"Danny! Come in, come in. You're all sweaty."

"I-I-I have something for Mrs. Becker." He breathed heavily, gulping air.

"Of course you do. Anne, someone's here to see you."

Danny followed Mr. Bill into the dining room where the chatter and laughter stopped upon seeing their visitor.

"Oh, Danny," said Mrs. Becker. "It's so nice to see you. Would you like some cake?"

"Danny has something for you, Anne." Mr. Bill pushed Danny toward her.

"Interesting choice of decorating," said Mr. Becker, eyeing Danny and his newspaper package.

"Oh, it's just lovely," Lynne said.

"Mom, open it," said Mikey.

Danny noticed MaryAnne had not said a word but simply watched him with wide eyes.

Always

When Mrs. Becker tore off the paper, she stopped, her own eyes now wide. Danny stood motionless as the room grew quiet. Mrs. Becker ran her finger across the little painting as if she were painting it herself.

MaryAnne shuffled past her sister and brother to get a look.

"Mom, that's you, your black hair." She pointed. "That's you and Dad in the *Sunflower*."

"Let me see that," said Mr. Becker, reaching for the picture.

Danny couldn't tell if he was mad or curious, so he assumed the worst.

"Look at that. Is my beard that dark?" Mr. Becker swiped a hand over the hair on his chin.

"Oh, Dad," said Lynne, rolling her eyes. "I didn't know Danny was an artist."

"Me neither," said MaryAnne. "Me neither."

Everyone looked at Danny, but no one else's opinion mattered in that moment—only MaryAnne's. Danny had never shown his art to anyone before.

But it was Mrs. Becker who stood, wrapped her arms around Danny, and pressed her red lips onto his cheek. He could feel her chest against him, and he did his best to remain calm as she pinned his arms to his sides.

He was ever so thankful that eternity ended when Mikey called out, "Break it up, break it up."

Everyone laughed when MaryAnne wiped the lipstick from his face and slipped her hand into his.

"I thought you were mad at me," he said.

"No, never. That was nice what you did for my mom."

"The Timothy strand is for you," he whispered. "Our secret."

MaryAnne punched him in the shoulder.

"Hey, careful, MaryAnne, that's his drawing arm," said Mr. Bill. "Did he ever paint you a picture?"

"I didn't even know he could paint a picture."

Danny and Mikey stuffed themselves with cake and homemade ice cream while Mrs. Becker unwrapped the rest of her gifts—some sort of pottery from Mikey, jewelry from Mr. Becker, and a blouse from her girls. But after the gifts were opened, it was his painting she went back to as she walked from room to room, looking for a place to hang it. She took down other pictures, plates, and prints until she found the right spot by the overstuffed chair.

"There, so every time we come up here, I can look at it in the evening when I'm done with my day and want remember our summer fun full of happy thoughts. What do you call it, Danny?"

"You just named it," he said. "'Happy Thoughts.'"

"Yes, that's it." She smiled. "'Happy Thoughts.'"

MaryAnne smiled too. For Danny, she'd been glowing since earlier in the haymow. Sure, she'd lost her shine when her father had showed up, but now she'd regained every bit and more. Now, she beamed.

Danny stayed to play Clue with Mikey, Lynne, and MaryAnne. Lynne brought out a box of Cheez-Its and fought over them with her sister. They lost track of the time which was becoming a theme with them.

Eventually, the phone rang, and he heard Mr. Becker reassuring his grandparents he was fine, and they would be bringing him home after he finished his game. When Danny heard that, he intentionally flubbed his guess of who the murderer was to extend their game. But on the next round MaryAnne figured that Professor Plum had used the pipe wrench in the library. All that was left was the cleanup.

"Danny, you ready."

Always

Mr. Becker's statement was not a question.

"Yes, Mr. Becker," he replied in his best Eddie Haskell voice.

They got into Mr. Bill's truck with Danny's bike in the back. Neither Mr. Becker nor Danny were heavy conversationalists.

When he saw the lights of his farmhouse, Mr. Becker remarked, "I hear you like lacrosse."

"Yessir."

"Well, we shall play sometime." Again, not a question.

Least with lacrosse, he can't drown me.

"Sure."

"Well, here we are." Mr. Becker squashed the brake with his foot but didn't put the truck into park.

"Yes, here we are."

The cab light turned on when Danny opened the door, and he had one leg hanging out the side when Mr. Becker reached across the bench seat and grabbed his forearm. Danny saw the porch light come on and his uncle's shadow.

"About my daughter."

Oh man, here we go. Don't kill me. No, that would really be crazy—not in front of my uncle.

"She likes you."

Danny nodded.

"So, ah … we like you too."

Danny nodded again and freed his arm.

"What I mean to say is … I got my eye on you. And you two stay out of the barn, ya hear?"

Danny nodded a third time, then jumped out of the cab, shut the door, and strained for all he was worth to lift his bike over the side. He could have climbed in the back, but that would have taken way too much time, and he valued living far more.

Danny felt a twinge in his wrists as he leveraged his bike and bounced it on the ground before banging two times on the side of the bed and leaning toward the open window.

"Thank you for the ride, sir. And sir, thank you for your approval. I really like her too. I won't screw it up, I mean. Goodnight."

Uncle Vern met him at the door as Mr. Becker's truck barreled down the gravel driveway.

"I noticed that picture of the pond laying on your bed. Any idea where the frame got to?"

"Oh, yeah, I should have asked you about that. I guess I gave it to Mrs. Becker."

"You guess? Well, whatever was inside, I'm sure she liked it." Uncle Vern held the door for him. "Everything go all right with you and Mr. Becker?"

"Fine, he's a little scary, but I think he's like Max their dog, his bark is worse than his bite." Danny started up the stairs.

"How about you and MaryAnne?" Uncle Vern jabbed his elbow in the air. If Danny had been next to him, he would have felt the poke in his side for sure.

"Fine, Uncle Vern, just fine."

Uncle Vern put his hands on his hips. "What, you're not going to tell me anything? What's the fun in that?"

Danny bounded up the stairs and headed for his room. He gathered his pictures and put them behind the dresser again, got undressed, then sank deep in his bed.

This has got to be the best day of my life. Just then he remembered ... *Oh no, I sure hope Mrs. Becker never takes "Happy Thoughts" out of the frame and sees "Me and MaryAnne" written on the back of her picture.*

Danny turned out the light, rolled over, and screamed into his pillow. "Oh no, Mr. Bill!"

March 2021

He used to relish being in his own world, away from people, disappointment, and death, but now Sully longed to be at the hospital. Away from her, the quiet unnerved him. He went for walks now and often broke the boredom by eating at a diner in town. At first it was just coffee, then a sticky bun, then lunch. And then, he started to talk to people, which felt very strange. One morning he told a trucker about sailing with MaryAnne, making hay with MaryAnne, and when he ran out of stories, he just talked about MaryAnne.

The trucker had simply gotten up from his stool, reached for his chained wallet, and paid his bill before turning and saying, "You have a good day, sir."

Man, I told him my life story, and I don't even know his name.

Sully went home and started digging through closets, filing cabinets, and dressers for his artwork. Not finding any, he lay on his bed staring at the ceiling. He rolled onto his side and stared at his dresser, recalling how he had hidden his work behind a similar one. But when he got up and pushed the dresser aside, all he found was an old sock and a dime.

He stumbled into the hallway and stopped under a cord dangling from the ceiling. Years before, Sully had built a new roof over his trailer when he got tired of patching holes with tar. The new roof had left a small storage area. Sully pulled down the collapsible stairs now and pulled on the light string at the top.

He hadn't been up there in years. Navy plaques and winter clothes waited behind clear, thin plastic. After rummaging for a lost amount of time, he spied a leather suitcase underneath a small mountain of cardboard boxes. He knew right away this was what he was searching for. He pushed the boxes to the side and kneeled in front of an almost forgotten life.

He used to paint in the attic at the farmhouse because it was the only timeless place where he could be free. His trailer attic was too small for art, and he was too bitter. He had shut away his supplies in the old leather case and tried to forget them under layers of dust—dust and time.

As he lifted the lid, its corroded hinges gave way, and the lid slid behind the suitcase. Sully picked up the green nylon parachute bag within and worked at the zipper until it surrendered his paintings. Hands trembling, his breath grew shallow. One by one, he surrounded himself with his old friends—a deer lying peacefully in a gentle snowfall, squirrels playing, ducks floating, a mountain lion poised atop a massive rock formation, mountain plants, fawns nestled under hemlocks, and baby cardinals nested in a massively old oak.

He ran his finger lightly across many of them, just as Mrs. Becker had done so long ago. His heart cried quietly as a gentle warmth enveloped him. His old world in front of him woke up tired eyes, sore muscles, and fingers fattened from abuse, age, and arthritis.

Always

"Sticks, all of them, sticks," he muttered. "But you're my sticks, and I missed you."

He gathered them, careful not to tear an edge or forget even the littlest painting. He put them back into their bag with his paints, brushes, tape, and pallet, then picked up the parachute bag and walked hunched over to his world below.

Sully cleared the kitchen table where northern light spilled through the window. After taping down one of his cheaper watercolor papers, he retrieved a bowl of water and a little sponge from beneath the sink. *This should work just fine.* He drew a horizon line that could develop into a couple of mountains. *Maybe snake a stream and a few ducks for interest. Oh, and some happy trees.* Sully laughed out loud and looked at Kat who stretched his neck in his direction. He took out three colors, dried and cracked. But they woke up with a little water rubbed from his brush.

He stared at the white in front of him. An eighteen by twenty-four-inch blank space, but it looked like eighteen by twenty-four miles. He nuked a cup of chai with a spot of honey and creme. Still, blank space stared back at him. He could hear his clock radio ticking away each second.

I used to get lost in this blank world. I could bring color and life to dead paper. Time suspended. Now time is all I think about. I guess you took this from me, too, God. I guess I deserve this.

His blank paper cut deeper than any mirror in which all he could see were bloodshot eyes and a few remaining hairs atop his head. He used to see beauty and peace on these blank pages—at least when he was done. But now he saw so much more. Now he saw the nothingness his life had become.

Sully didn't go back to the diner that night. He heated up some fish sticks and stirred some iced tea from a tiny packet. He glanced at the table with the square, white paper taped across its top but distracted himself with British TV, Kat, and more tea.

That night he dreamed of getting sucked into an immense white whirlpool. He reached for the edge but neither Martha, Jimmy, nor Stephen could reach him. He awoke sweating.

MaryAnne, where are you?

"Thank God," he said the next day when the sun finally dropped, and he got in Sierra and headed back to work.

"Sully! Nice to see you back," his pal John greeted.

"Ah, thanks, glad somebody is."

Sully leaned on his wet mop, a little, yellow "wet floor" sign propped up next to him.

"Watch your paws. I don't want to get your New Balance's wet."

"Yeah, thanks, but your reputation with harassing young doctors' Birkenstocks is well-known."

"Ha! You heard about that? I get a little over-enthusiastic about cleanliness and some young intern gets all entitled. Go figure." Sully wrung his mop and slid it back and forth over the floor again. "I'll be up to see you in a bit. Say, how's room 3?"

"Lots happening there. Dr. Smeltzer grafted skin to her neck and face. The heavy facial bandages are gone, but her thighs are wrapped from where they took the graft. It's not pretty, but she's showing potential. Also, Ortho completed their surgeries. Her kneecap is wired, and while she still has a brace, the medieval contraption for her leg is gone."

Always

Sully didn't look up from his mopping. "I suppose she's still in a coma?"

John reached for his mop, making it stop swishing. "There's news on that front as well. Her head wrap is still there, but she's breathing on her own. They cut her coma drugs."

Sully looked up at John. "Is she ... awake?"

"No, she's not." John put his hand on his shoulder. "I'm sorry. Now, it's up to her."

"When? How long?"

"No one knows. Days, weeks ... months."

The truth sent a chill through him.

John dropped his hand, and they both went back to work. Sully scrubbed ferociously down the hall, ran his cart back to the closet, and took extra-long readying himself. He grabbed a Mylar balloon he had purchased from the hospital's gift shop earlier from his locker and headed to room 3.

Upstairs, he gave a boyish wave to the crowd behind the nurses' counter and walked into MaryAnne's room.

"Happy birthday to you, happy birthday to you, happy birthday to MaryAnne with an e, happy birthday to you. Here's a balloon. It's silly."

Still in a coma, her eyes shut, her lips never moved.

Oh, you remembered my birthday. It's sweet.

"I confess I saw the date when I peeked in your chart last week. There are flowers from your guy at the station, but they're not allowed in your room. Normally, they'd go to the waiting room, but apparently, they're pretty special."

Orchids, right? I hate orchids but Jonesy loves them.

Sully smiled. "Yeah, well, the nurses seem to like them."

I'm sorry. It's just that every time we had a fight or he acted like a jerk, he'd make a phone call, and orchids would show up at my door.

"I've noticed apologies are not his strong suit."

A red light flickered on one machine, while another made a whooshing sound. Sully looked up at the nurses' station where everyone was busy working or talking or both.

"Anyway, how about you?"

Oh, I'm just a human pin cushion. Strangers come in and either take or give and then leave without a word, not an introduction, not even a thank you.

Sully patted her hand. "You know you're in a coma, don't you?"

I'm still alive, sort of, so they could at least be polite.

The red light continued to flicker.

"Gee, MaryAnne, please don't take this wrong, you can be whatever, you've certainly deserved the right, but you sound pretty angry. It's okay, I just don't remember angry MaryAnne. I remember grateful MaryAnne."

Sully, still seated, reached for her hand.

I know. You're right. I just don't feel it today. You must think I'm horrible. I'm grateful to be alive, grateful you are here, and I'm grateful for everyone working so hard for me. I am.

"Like I said, to me you can be whatever you need to be. I'm here for you."

It's really Jonesy I'm mad at. Again, he sends flowers. I know he works hard, and we've had plenty of birthdays, but this one's different. Anyway, I love the balloon.

"It has a teddy bear on it. I know it's been a while, but I remember you told me you had a collection." Sully got up to position the ballon in the corner of the room.

Oh, I almost forgot that. What else have I forgotten? They say I can wake up when I want to, and then, I can get out of here.

"So, what's holding you back?"

Getting out of here. It's safe here.

"You could be anywhere, anywhere in the world and you want to be here? In a hospital? With hospital puree pumped into your stomach?"

Isn't this where you'd rather be?

Sully leaned back in his chair. "Well played, but only because you're here. Thing is, you're asleep, or something, so it's not real, and I'd really like to see you for real."

Don't you see me? My ear, my burns, even the shape of my head? I'm a freak now. There are no secrets here. I'm hideous. They had to shave a big chunk of hair to operate on my head. They've taken my spleen, part of my liver, even some of my intestine. There's nothing else to give, and there's nothing left to see. I'm not sure if I want to wake up if I have to witness pitiful stares and the silence of strangers.

"That's not true." Sully leaned in close to whisper.

It is. What else is there?

"Your eyes. I want to see your eyes, just one more time. I bet they are still beautiful." Sully stared at MaryAnne's injuries but only saw beauty. His eyes began to water.

What was it you said? Well played.

Sully sighed. "I mean it MaryAnne. I want to see your eyes, just one more time. I've seen my share of a lot of bad injuries—missing legs, blindness, really bad burns. Somehow burns really do a number on people—it messes with their minds. They get depressed. It's a huge loss." Sully rubbed the back of his neck. "You know I've changed a little too."

You're so right. I'm angry, and maybe I'm depressed. I've never been either. Dealing with Jonesy, in the shadows all these years, I've acted like the happy one. But this is the worst thing ever for me. I'm falling apart.

"No. No, you're not. Don't do that. That's self-pity and that's not you. You are strong and ..." Sully leaned in and whispered into her good ear, "And you are my angel." He sat back. "Even the paramedic who brought you in at your worst said you were angelic. And when he told me that, before I knew it was you ... I knew it was you."

I'll think about it.

Sully shifted in his chair. The thin padding wasn't built for comfort. "Okay, change of subject. I got out my watercolors. They're in rough condition. I taped down some cold-press on the kitchen table, drew a horizon line and wetted it down."

And?

"And nothing."

Sully looked away, noticing for the first time that there were no pictures on the walls in the ICU.

Nothing?

"I just stared at the white paper. It felt like a hole, a whirlpool sucking me under. I even had some colors out and a brush in my hand."

It'll come.

"No, I think it's gone for good. Use it or lose it. I don't deserve a talent I've wasted."

Now who's feeling sorry for themselves?

"Ouch, that hurts." He smiled and squeezed her hand. "Guess I can't complain about pain to you."

Nope, I have the market on pain, and these rooms are only big enough for one patient at a time. Just bow your head and breathe. Maybe you're just missing your muse.

"You may have something there. Anyone come to mind?"

Well, yes, yes ... I do, but she will have to wait.

"Okay, next topic." Sully shifted again in his seat. It was okay to be optimistic for MaryAnne, but he was uncomfortable

Always

with hope. With hope comes disappointment. "Tell me about your days. Any visitors?"

Nope. It's just me these days. I was married for a time, but he turned out to be an abusive jerk. I just couldn't take it anymore, so I mustered all the courage I had and walked out. Jonesy was my divorce lawyer, and well, he doesn't take no for an answer.

"Somehow, I'm not surprised. He's a force of nature, for sure."

Good news is you're here. Despite the jerks in my life. You came back. After you jilted me.

Sully got up and paced around the room, examining each piece of medical equipment and lightly punching the teddy bear balloon. Finally, he turned to face MaryAnne. "You know, you jilted me."

I jilted you? That's not how I remember it.

"What happened to us, MaryAnne with an e?" Sully had stood up, but Danny sat down. "Here you are, stuck with tubes pumping stuff in and out of you. And here I am, potbellied, nearly bald, and mopping other people's floors. How did this happen? And to top it off, you lost your 'e'—lost the whole second half of your name, in fact. We were so young with so much to live for. We thought nothing could go wrong. We were together, and that's all that mattered." Sully shook his head. "When did life get so complicated?"

She lay in silence. The hustle of the nurses' station remained a distant din. Miles away. They were alone in their own world. They could have been lying in the hay mow or on the sunny hill of flowers, maybe in the rowboat or the SS *Sunflower* or even in a room full of partygoers. Where ever they were together, no one else was there, no one else mattered. It's simply how it had always been. *Always.*

Sully knew her parents had recognized their world and longed for it themselves, most couples do. But their connection scared her father and bothered her sister. A bubble had formed around Danny and MaryAnne that blocked the world and included only each other. Just holding each other's hands or looking into each other's eyes was enough to be transported to a world of two—no ... one. Together, they were a world of one.

They'd been so young, not married. They'd never lived together, raised a family together, or suffered loss together. They had been brought together for just a twinkling of an eye, maybe for just as long as it takes a shooting star to go from one side of the universe to the other. Two kids who consummated their love with a simple kiss and little more. Nothing more was needed. No one else knew. They weren't bound together before man, just each other and God.

"I suppose I should go and finish my duties."

Duty first.

"Something like that."

Sully got up to leave but held onto her hand. It seemed she was holding on to his. He lay her hand down on the edge of the bed and pulled the thin white blanket further up to keep her warm. He recalled how they had huddled together years before to ward off hypothermia. He turned to go, stared out the window, motionless, hearing only his own breathing and the machines.

"Fred?"

"Yeah?" He was still staring out the window.

"Fred."

He turned to her open eyes and fell back into her soul. "Wilma, you remember Bedrock."

Lights on the machines began to pulse. A high-pitched beep rang out.

Always

He didn't bother with the chair. He reached for her outstretched hand and went to one knee.

"You are ... angelic." Sully looked through the window and across to the nurses' station. A swarm emerged from its hive and converged on room 3. Nurses pushed him to the side. Almost trampled upon, he backed up.

"Fred," her raspy voice called out.

The nurses backed him up beside a quiet machine, tucked in the corner where he would not be dislodged. But they could still see each other—in their world.

"Ms. Mills, Ms. Mills, welcome back!" a nurse gently exclaimed. "You are in a hospital in North Carolina. You were in a car accident, and you were unconscious. There is more to tell but not right now. Mr. Jones will be so glad to see you."

MaryAnne stared at her Danny. He was certain he saw a teardrop form and trickle down the side of her full alabaster cheek.

"Fred."

July 1974

Danny grabbed his art satchel before he bounded down the stairs and into the kitchen as the morning sun streamed across the hallway floor. His aunt stood by the sink; his uncle sat at the weathered oak table.

"You want to ride the old mule? It's been a while, and well, you never showed much interest before." His uncle shoved a piece of toast coated in dippy egg into his mouth.

"If you think it'll be all right. MaryAnne is coming over with her horse."

Aunt Clare turned from the sink. "I think it's a fine thing. Let the boy have some fun, Vern."

"Betsy's getting ornery in her advanced years. Can't say she'd enjoy a trail ride, but I suspect it'd do her some good to get out of the pasture for a while. She's surefooted, but she's just as obstinate, so you gotta be firm." Vern pointed his fork at Danny. "Mules are half horse with an attitude. What do you expect from an animal that can't even reproduce? They'll work all day for a carrot, but they gotta think they are boss, even though they feel better following. If not, they'll lay down and expect you to carry them home just to teach you a lesson."

"Yessir." Danny reached for the Cheerios and a glass bottle of whole milk.

"What's that you got in that bag?"

Danny pushed his satchel under his chair. "Oh nothing—just some stuff I want to show MaryAnne."

"Do you have your pocketknife?"

Danny put a spoon into his cereal bowl. "Don't own one."

"You're sixteen and you don't own a pocketknife?" His uncle stood and walked over to the kitchen's junk drawer where he pulled out a yellow knife with a bear head on one side and "BSA" stamped on the other side. He handed the blade to Danny. "Here, this was Stephen's. He left it here. I was going to give it to you when you made Eagle Scout."

Aunt Clare now rested her hand on her husband's shoulder.

Danny stared at the offering before clipping it to his pocket, unable to say a word. He felt connected to Stephen in a new way as he felt the weight of the knife on his trousers.

"I hope her horse gets along with Betsy," Vern said, returning to his eggs. "Not many do. Betsy thinks she's just as good as any horse even if her sway back and scraggly mane makes her look like she's a hoof away from the glue factory. Do you know what breed she's riding?"

Danny wiped a drop of milk from his chin before replying. "I think she said she was a gelding."

"Do you know what a gelding is?" Danny remained silent, knowing his uncle's tone meant he'd said something wrong. When he didn't reply, Vern tapped his finger on the table. "Let's just say, *she* can't be a gelding and geldings can't be stallions. Got it?"

Always

"Leave the boy finish his cereal," said his aunt.

"I'm just trying to school him on the birds and the bees, it could be a long ride." Vern air-elbowed Danny just as a whinny came from the paddock. "Sounds like your little friend's likely here."

Danny stood. "Gotta go—"

"Stop right there, young man," Aunt Clare ordered. "Take these sandwiches and thermos. You have your rain slicker?"

Danny scrunched up his face. "Aw, I don't think—"

"Go upstairs now and get it." Aunt Clare pointed to the stairs. "Thunderstorms can come up pretty quick in the mountains."

Danny obeyed and was back out the door to the barn and paddock a few minutes later with his arms full. He stopped short when he saw MaryAnne patting the white blaze on her horse's chestnut face. The horse's dark stockings gave way to its trimmed hooves. Betsy looked even older beside this beautiful animal. MaryAnne's jeans were tucked into her boots, and her floppy sweater draped over her jeans. Her hair was braided in pigtails which made her look even younger, if that was possible.

"Wow, your horse sure is purdy." He tried to sound like John Wayne.

"He's a Morgan," said MaryAnne.

"Oh, I thought he was a gelding."

MaryAnne shook her head and smiled.

Danny knew he was missing something but didn't want to seem dumb. He retrieved a blanket out of the tack room, then threw it across Betsy's back.

"Aren't you going to brush her first?"

"Yeah, sure," Danny stuttered, "I was just seeing how it fit."

Danny grabbed a horse brush out of a dusty closet, then slipped his hand under the leather strap and held tight to the wooden brush as he stroked Betsy's back in a circular motion.

"Not like that, you're not waxing her." MaryAnne took the brush from him and began stroking his horse from front to back. "Have you ridden before?"

"More than I've skied," he admitted. "Mostly county fairs. I prefer a spirited pony."

MaryAnne shook her head again as she worked. Uncle Vern wandered in a few minutes later, and Danny tried to look as though he was helping. His uncle brought Betsy's saddle out of the tack room and lowered it onto the mare's back.

"Look here." He motioned for Danny to come closer. "This is her cinch strap. It's what keeps you and her saddle on her back, so watch how I tighten it. It'll come loose as you ride so you'll want to redo it after lunch too."

He reached underneath and took the long strap from the other side, fed it through a large silver ring, and kneed Betsy hard in the ribs.

Danny grabbed hold of his uncle's arm. "Uncle Vern!"

"You gotta do that to make her let out her air. That way you can get the strap tight."

He crossed the strap next, fed it back through the ring, and slipped it under the cross section to form a simple knot.

"There now, this is so you can undo it. It won't knot up on you and it'll hold you when you need it to."

Danny nodded then got a bridle out of the closet.

"That one's for a horse." Vern took the bridle from Danny and returned with a different one. "This here's a mule bridle. It doesn't use a bit, and see, Betsy doesn't like bits or stuff around her ears. This one puts pressure on her

Always

nose. Just a quick tug on the reins, and I mean quick, and she'll go left or right. Too much and she'll lay down. Too little and she'll stand like a statue all day long. Snap your heels into her side and she goes, and pull 'er back to slow down or stop. But ..."

He stopped to look up after he had the bridle fastened, and Danny tried to take it all in.

"Most important, after pulling back, let go. She'll ignore you if you're too soft, but she'll fight you off if you don't let go."

This isn't like sailing at all, unless I was sailing a walrus.

His uncle held the stirrup. "Now, put your foot in here."

Danny grabbed the right stirrup.

"Not that side, son," Vern whispered. "Over here."

"Oh, right, I forgot." He started around Betsy's backside to her left, but Vern pulled on his arm.

"This way." He guided Danny around to the front of the beast. "Betsy doesn't like when someone walks behind her, and watch her mouth, she has a wicked bite."

Sailboats don't buck, and they don't bite either. A quiet float around the pond sounds pretty good compared to this.

But unlike waterskiing, Danny was up on Betsy the first time he tried, and his uncle handed him the reins.

MaryAnne waited patiently on her Morgan.

"Now let MaryAnne go first," Vern told him. "Betsy's used to following. As long as she sees another animal's rump, she'll feel safe."

Danny looked up at MaryAnne.

MaryAnne nodded. "Ready?" she asked.

Her eyes looked even bigger now as she sat atop her beautiful horse. Danny wasn't sure if what he was feeling in his gut was fear or breakfast. He figured it was likely both. He nodded back, and MaryAnne turned her horse without even using her reins, just a nudge of a knee and a shifting of her weight, and they were headed down the path toward the mountain. MaryAnne clicked her tongue and began rising off the saddle in rhythm to her horse's trot. Even her braids were in sync.

Danny bounced behind, jarring his teeth, dislodging his hat, and causing him to lean forward to grab around Betsy's withers. *How does MaryAnne ride like that? This really hurts.*

MaryAnne looked at him and laughed. "It's called posting," she yelled. "Try rising up and down so Betsy doesn't bounce you off."

Danny started to get the hang of it as they reached the farm lane.

MaryAnne yelled again, "Now squeeze your knees into Betsy like me." When she did, her horse began to canter. Betsy followed suit which caused his jarring ride to ease. *Oh, much better.*

Despite Betsy's age, condition, and breeding, she caught up to MaryAnne and started to pass.

MaryAnne looked at Danny with wide eyes.

Am I doing something wrong?

Up ahead, he saw how the road's shoulder had been washed out on the right. A slip would mean an ugly tumble. Then, he saw the postal truck coming around the hillside. He quickly pulled on the reins.

Betsy swung her head from side to side until Danny remembered to let up. *Just a quick tug.* But letting go was hard while he was staring down a ton of truck. Yet, Betsy slowed and reclaimed her proper position as he did so.

"Sorry," he yelled to MaryAnne who looked back and waved.

Always

After the truck passed, they turned the bend and crossed the road, heading up a steep bank to get on a narrow, barely marked trail. The yellow blazes painted on the young trees were all but washed out.

"Do you know where you're going?" he yelled.

Again, MaryAnne turned and waved.

Danny's satchel drooped from his saddle horn, lower than when he'd started. MaryAnne's small backpack had pulled away from her horn as the trail got steeper too.

Now I can see why Uncle Vern was so concerned about the cinch strap.

Danny could feel Betsy's heavy breathing as they neared the top of the ridge, and the trail grew wider.

"It should get easier from what I remember," said MaryAnne.

"You're quite a horse woman."

She smiled. "You're not so bad yourself."

Danny knew she was just being kind, but her comment made him feel good. *She can't help but make people feel good.* Danny started whistling "Side by Side," and MaryAnne joined in with the words.

> Don't know what's coming tomorrow
> Maybe it's trouble and sorrow
> But we'll travel the road sharin' our load
> Side by side

Danny hadn't done this much grinning in a long time, and after a while, his face started to hurt.

The sun shone, but the breeze on the ridge and the shaded trees cooled the trail. Up ahead, he saw a wooden sign pointing the way to a lean-to shelter.

"Could be a good place to stop and give the horses a break," offered MaryAnne.

"Go for it, Kemosabe."

"Huh?"

"What Tonto used to say to the Lone Ranger."

"Tonto used to say, 'Go for it'?"

"Sure ... in so many words." Danny remembered to get off the left side of Betsy when he saw MaryAnne dismount.

The trail dwindled down to a narrow, muddy trough as they walked. They tied the animals to saplings before exploring the three-sided shelter, privy, and cold spring.

"Man, you'd think I never had water before, this tastes so good," Danny exclaimed as he scooped some of the coldness into his mouth.

The woods, or maybe the horse ride, had loosened him up. He felt free, as unfiltered as the natural spring he drank from.

"MaryAnne, I'm happy."

"Me too." She stood from the spring and smiled.

"I don't think you understand. Maybe people who are always happy can't understand. But like the spring water, I feel like I'm drinking something I've never tasted before. I'm drinking water for the first time." Danny's eyes grew watery. "The watercolor I gave your mom? That was the first time I ever saw my art through somebody else's eyes. It was the only happy picture I had, because, well, it was the only time I ever felt happy in my life."

MaryAnne frowned. "The only time?"

"This whole week—the only time I can remember—at least since Stephen."

MaryAnne sat down on a rock outside the shelter, then took Danny's hand as he sat down next to her.

"Right now, I'm so happy I could bust. People say that, but I mean it. I'm afraid I really could burst. Maybe not break up in a million pieces but ... yeah, I'm afraid something's gonna happen, and I'll just fall apart."

Always

MaryAnne lay her head on his shoulder and began to cry.

"Hey, don't do that," he said, brushing his hand across her cheek. "Now I've made you sad."

"It just hurts to hear your sadness."

"Then I'll stop."

MaryAnne looked into his eyes and wiped away her tears. "No, no, no, don't stop telling me. But maybe for today, stop the sadness. Didn't you say you were happy? Then be happy. Be that happiness. Just live it today. 'K? I mean God dressed these little flowers for us."

"God, right. 'K. But now I'm hungry. Posting will do that, you know."

Danny stood and took his satchel off Betsy's saddle horn, pulling out the paper bag with chicken salad sandwiches and small bags of chips.

"Hope you like chicken salad," Danny said as he went to the picnic table next to the fire pit which was strewn with garbage.

"I love chicken salad." MaryAnne dumped the contents of her backpack on the wooden table. "Mom made me bring Dad's poncho. I have water and fruit too."

"Not surprised." Danny smirked.

After they ate and drank from the same thermos, MaryAnne took off her sweater and stretched out on a flat-hewn log in the one spot of sunlight. The pin oaks overhead cast twinkling shadows all around her as if she were floating on a pond.

Danny dug to the bottom of his satchel and pulled out his sketch pad made of cold-press watercolor paper. He sketched MaryAnne's silhouette with a fine-tipped pencil, adding the pin oak's shadows, the pond, and Betsy in the distance. MaryAnne's Morgan was better looking, but

Betsy had character that could only come from being an aged work mule. He liked the contrast she offered to the otherwise serene setting. He couldn't explain it, but Betsy was just as beautiful as any pure breed.

After pouring some water into the thermos's cup, he used his wide brush to get his paper wet then mixed some sap green with burnt sienna and created a wash of leaves and light. After waiting for that bit to dry—waiting was the hardest part of watercolor painting—he took his number six brush and painted his muse.

He loved watercolor, for what it showed and for what it didn't, and how the eye fills in the rest. The art lover becomes part of the painting. Danny was a lover of art—but for him the real beauty was in a simple life. As he painted, he became so enthralled that he became part of his own created scene in the world he had splashed in front of him.

MaryAnne turned slowly as he worked, then smiled and stretched her arms to heaven.

How does she manage to look so serene ... my angel?

"How long was I asleep?" she asked.

"Few hours."

"No way." She sat up, wide-eyed.

"You were really snoring."

"No way."

"Scared Betsy."

"Stop it." She threw her sweater at him.

"Okay, but you were out for almost an hour." He threw the sweater back.

"I'm sorry. I didn't know I was tired. It's just so peaceful here."

He nodded. "I could have sat here another hour just watching you sleep."

Danny handed her the thermos. She took a swig and water dribbled down the side of her mouth. She wiped her lips with the back of her wrist and shrugged her shoulders unapologetically.

"Guess we should get going."

Danny started washing his brushes with the water left in his cup.

"What's that?"

MaryAnne walked toward his painting resting on a rock in the sun.

"Nothing." He rushed to snatch it out of reach. "Nothing. It's not done."

"Let me see."

Danny held it by his side.

"I told you, it's not done."

MaryAnne lurched for the painting, but Danny held it behind him. Every time she reached, he turned the opposite way. He could smell her hair as her braids hit his face.

"Stop it, Danny."

"You stop it."

"Please let me see it?"

"Okay." He gave in. He knew he would.

MaryAnne's mouth gaped as she took in the painting. "You painted me."

"Oh?" He frowned and looked at his work. "I thought I was painting an angel."

Danny stood close, so close, only paper and pigment lay between them.

"What do you call it?"

"Serenity."

"I want it."

She looked up at him, past her eyelashes and into his eyes.

"Then you shall not be denied, my lady."

"My Lancelot. You're my renaissance man."

He could feel her breath as he reached for her hands and lowered their picture. Their lips met, perfectly matched. They might have stayed there forever, frozen in time like a fairytale, but Betsy started whinnying.

The startled couple looked to see their rides jerking at the saplings holding them back.

"Easy, girl, easy." Danny raised both hands as Betsy's teeth gleamed.

"Don't do that." MaryAnne rushed to pull down his arms. "They're scared. You'll only scare them more."

"Scared of what?" Danny turned to the sound of a black bear growling and snarling. The beast stood massive. "Uh-oh."

Two bear cubs had stumbled to the other side of the horses and were tearing through the garbage in the fire ring.

"The horses are between the mother and cubs," MaryAnne yelled.

Danny could see the whites of the horse's eyes as they jerked free of their leads. The Morgan reared on its hind legs before running down the trail with Betsy, followed by the mother bear in pursuit. The cubs scampered off when Danny yelled and ran toward them.

"What are we going to do now?" asked MaryAnne.

"Looks like we're walking. I'm more afraid for the horses. A bear can outrun a horse, especially on its own turf. Hopefully, she'll give up and go get her cubs," replied Danny.

They gathered up the remnants of their day—the art supplies, their leftover food stuffs, and MaryAnne's painting—and put them in the torn satchel.

"This way." MaryAnne pointed and the couple walked.

Always

Rocks and roots were plentiful on the worn trail. Branches overhead kept them sheltered from the light that seemed to be fading. The wind blew, shaking pine needles off the hemlocks.

"Is it getting late?"

"I don't think so, why?" asked Danny.

"It's getting dark, isn't it?"

"It's the woods. It's always a little dark."

"This dark?" MaryAnne looked up at the green canopy. "I think a storm is coming."

"Naw, don't—"

Thunder cracked and lightning hit something nearby, then rain peppered the trees. Soon, the deluge was coming down in sheets. Where there once was trail, now was a river.

July 1974

Rain dripped off Danny's face. "How did this happen so fast?" he asked, trying to make his way while watching out for MaryAnne ahead of him.

"That's the mountains, I guess." As she looked back at Danny, her foot got caught under a root and her other foot slid off the side off a rock, upending her into a muddy mess. "AGGHH, my ankle."

"Lemme see." Danny slushed his way to her but with the rain and her boots, there was little to see. "Let's see if you can walk on it." He helped her to her feet.

"Oh no, oh no," she said in between breaths. She put her arm on Danny's shoulder, and he put his arm around her waist. She barely put her weight down but cried out each time.

"This isn't working," he grumbled.

Up ahead, they were able to duck under an outcropping of boulders.

"Thank you, Ice Age," Danny muttered. "You know, for dropping these rocks off for us."

MaryAnne tried to smile while Danny pulled out the poncho Aunt Clare had insisted he pack in his satchel. Together they huddled, wrapped in thin vinyl on the one dry spot while the trees bent, leaves left their homes, and rainwater gushed down the trail in front of them.

"My ankle is throbbing," MaryAnne said.

He could feel her shivering as he focused on trying to control his own body to little avail.

"This is all my fault." Danny hung his head.

"Stop it." MaryAnne punched him in the side so hard it hurt. But he didn't show it—messaged received.

Be strong, be strong for her. Then fake it if you're scared. There's no time for self-pity. Danny started to take a mental inventory. *We have two ponchos, a little water, fruit ... but we're not hungry. We have some pencils, art masking fluid, watercolor paper, some wooden matches, and a candle I use for art. My pocketknife—good ole' Uncle Vern—and my satchel. We're wet, and we're cold. We won't make it back by dark. The trail is unnavigable now, and it'll get worse in the dark.*

They shivered together—cold, wet, forlorn. Minutes ticked by and little was said between the two. No telling what time it was when Danny heard humming. Then singing.

> Oh, we ain't got a barrel of money
> Maybe we're ragged and funny
> But we'll travel along singing a song
> Side by side

He kissed her wet forehead. When she buried her trembling fingers under his shirt, Danny joined in.

> Through all kinds of weather
> What if the sky should fall
> As long as we're together
> It doesn't matter at all

As the rain subsided, it took most of the light with it.

"What now? We need to get back," insisted MaryAnne.

Always

"We can't, not with your ankle. It's almost dark. We could end up somewhere worse." Danny pulled her closer. "You know what I mean. I've been thinking. We can start a fire, cover the rock opening with the poncho, and if we dry out, we'll be fine.

"Danny, I can't feel my fingers."

"Okay, angel, let's get moving. If we sit here wet, we get hypothermia. If we get hypothermia, we—"

MaryAnne put a finger against his lips. "Okay, got it."

They didn't venture far before they found bits of dead wood. MaryAnne hopped on one foot and held onto a dead branch.

"It's all wet, it'll never light."

"I gotta plan, just bring it back to Bedrock."

"Bedrock?"

"You know, the Flintstones, Wilma."

"You have watched way too much television."

They talked and sang as they worked, not because they were happy but because they were afraid of losing each other in the blackened woods.

"Here you go, Fred. I found some dry stuff lying under a bunch of branches and leaves and stuff."

You're hopping on one foot, and still you won't give up.

Danny used his pocketknife to make a series of cuts into small branches. The bark curled as he cut. Next, he made a bed out of some of the dry pine needles they'd been sitting on.

"You ever do this before?" she asked.

"Cub Scouts."

"Does it work?"

He shrugged. "It was a long time ago."

Danny took his watercolor paper and tore up the sheets. He held up *Serenity* and looked at MaryAnne. Her look answered him, and he lay it aside. He took his masking fluid, smashed the bottle with a rock, and dripped the liquid across the paper.

"It contains natural latex that'll act like an accelerant." MaryAnne frowned at him.

"Pyromania is sort of a recreational hobby for me."

"I see that. How many matches do we have?"

"Three." His first strike went out as fast as it lit. "Arggh."

MaryAnne prayed next to him as he tried again. The second match took most of the striker surface with it, but the flame stayed long enough for Danny to get it to the edge of the paper coated with masking fluid. He waved the fire gently, but when he blew on it, the paper was reduced to a blackened smolder.

"I can't ... I can't do this." He sat back on his heels and sighed.

"You can pray with me," MaryAnne encouraged.

Together they bowed their heads. They were silent until MaryAnne started the Lord's Prayer, and Danny followed. They said amen together.

"Hey, what about the candle?" she asked.

"Of course!" Danny replied.

She held onto the candle as he struck the match on the last of the striker. Together they blocked the outside world. She leaned the candle into the flame, and it took.

"It's working!" she exclaimed.

Danny just smiled.

Next, he held the paper over the candle. Then, with the patience of Job, they lowered the flaming paper into the pine needles where it lit.

MaryAnne quickly grabbed a stick cut with curly bark. He did the same and they held them in the flame which was already dying. As much as Danny wanted to pile on leaves, needles, and branches, their fledgling embers needed to breathe and take their place in the world. MaryAnne blew on the smolder. The little flame spread as they each added branches at the right time and blew just the right amount of air. Their lives depended upon the right air, the right heat, the right moment.

As MaryAnne kept adding firewood, Danny dragged a log to the edge of the fire to dry out. As it caught and burned down, he moved more of the log into the hot flame. When the fire had fully taken hold, they took off each other's boots and socks and rubbed each other's feet.

Danny started having other thoughts now that the threat of imminent doom had passed. He thought about Uncle Vern who had elbowed him when he'd said he and MaryAnne could be in the woods a long time.

Knock it off, Danny ... just focus. Remember, her life depends on it.

With the fire came warmth and hope. They warmed themselves while building up the flames and the blaze returned the favor. Danny used his poncho to drape in front of the entrance, as it began raining again. The poncho kept the rain and some of the cold out. He wedged rocks and sticks to keep it standing and tight against the ground. There was enough space for the smoke to escape, but not much. Their eyes burned and their lungs ached from the smoke, but they were warming. Summer nights in the mountains can be cold, but wet cold was unlivable.

Despite the fire, they were still soaked and still cold. Both Danny and MaryAnne shivered together. He knew it would only get colder, reaching the coldest just before dawn.

"We have to do something. I'm dying." MaryAnne's voice quivered.

"Don't say that," Danny said, pulling her closer. "Say you're cold, or say you're wet, but don't say that."

"I can't feel anything—my fingers, my toes. I can hardly see straight or barely move 'em, I'm so wet. I'm sorry." MaryAnne's teeth stopped chattering, and her eyes glazed over.

"I'm sorry too. I'm sorry I yelled at you, and I'm sorry for getting you into this mess."

Danny knew about hypothermia. He knew when teeth stopped chattering it was a sign of the body shutting down in a last attempt to save itself. Her condition was becoming severe. Soon, she might think she was hot— that's when people die from exposure. Some of her words were unintelligible now, but it was the distant look in her eyes that scared him the most.

"We need to get our clothes dry—wet makes everything twice as bad. You need warmth. I remember that from scouts. Any ideas?" He knew but wanted to keep her talking.

"Well, on PBS my dad and I saw an outdoors show where they took off their clothes to use their body heat to stay warm. If we did that, then our clothes would dry out and maybe we could—"

"Okay," Danny said quickly.

I just wish she hadn't mentioned her dad.

"—make a sleeping bag."

Danny was already taking off his shirt, followed by MaryAnne who took off her wool sweater, then her T-shirt. He took off his jeans and hung them on a stick in front of the fire. He did his best not to watch MaryAnne do the same. They wrapped her father's large poncho around them from head to feet. Danny began to shiver more as they embraced each other, gently lowering themselves to their knees, then on their sides on the bed of dry pine needles.

Always

Their shadows danced against the rocks, the golden embers casting a hazy light across their faces. She looked up into his eyes and took his hands. Her eyes were now deeper, clearer. She guided his hands up to the middle of her back. He could feel the line of her backbone where it met the back of her bra. They gazed into each other's eyes ... Danny's emotion trapped in his heart.

It took a moment, maybe two, before he fumbled with the clip and unfastened it. He looked into her eyes again, her trusting dark eyes.

But Danny clipped the ends of her bra back together then held her head between his hands. "Someday." He took off his class ring and slipped it onto her ring finger where it flopped to one side. She looked up as he stared into her dark eyes. "Someday," she said.

With nothing more than their underwear between them, they kissed softly and pulled each other even closer. Each buried themselves in the other's wet hair and as they rubbed warmth into each other's body. MaryAnne prayed and fiddled with her new ring.

Soon, they drifted asleep. Hours passed before they stirred again.

MaryAnne reached out to feel her sweater. "It's damp but it's better than it was."

"So are you," Danny said, "Wool is a good insulator. When it's damp, it can still insulate."

He added wood to the hot coals while she put on her now dried socks. He noticed her ankle was swollen and now black and blue. As he watched, she took out her braids and combed through her hair with her fingers.

"This will be wild in the morning."

"Oh boy, I get to see your wake-up look."

"Maybe I should warn you now." She smiled.

Danny cut the neck out of her sweater with his brother's pocketknife and smiled when he looked at the bear's head and the letters BSA embossed on the side. With a lot less grace than a circus act, they wiggled into the body of her sweater together. Their cotton jeans were still wet and would not help them.

"Do you think we'll live to a hundred?" she asked.

"I promise." Danny sighed. "We'll live to tomorrow."

They lay down again, wrapped in their poncho cocoon and prayed for daylight.

Danny was the first to wake. His eyes burned, and he smelled of wet, burnt wood. He wiggled his toes and fingers and knew they had been spared. There was little else he could move without involving MaryAnne.

Instead, he went to God.

I know I don't pray much, and when I do, it isn't to thank you, so don't think I'm any different just because I'm talking to you. But thank you, God—for her, not me. Thank you.

He stroked her wild hair. When his fingers caught, she opened her eyes and smiled.

"I slept great," he said, smiling back at her.

"Yeah, me too."

"Did ya?"

MaryAnne just laughed.

Outside a dog barked, and they looked at each other with wild eyes.

"It's Max. My family!"

At once they both started clawing at clothes and gyrating until they contorted themselves out of their makeshift bedroll and into their T-shirts. Putting on their dirty jeans in the confined stone palace was equally trying.

Always

They both heard the calls in the distance.

"MaryAnne ... Danny ... MaryAnne!"

"Hurry, hurry, it's my dad," she cried.

"Hush, or they'll hear us."

"So now you don't want to be found?"

"Not like this, and not by your dad!"

As they buttoned their pants and almost fastened their belts, MaryAnne's German shepherd broke in, bringing the vinyl poncho down around them.

"Okay boy, okay," MaryAnne squealed as Max licked her first then Danny. "Oh, I am so glad to see you!"

"Max, I didn't think you liked me," Danny said, petting the dog on the head.

"Maybe because my smell is all over you."

"Whatever. I like it. I like it a lot."

Danny got on all fours as he looked down the trail. Mr. Becker and Mrs. Becker came walking up the trail, and behind them came Uncle Vern. The young couple both tried to stand but fell back down, wrapped up in poncho and Max's kisses. They laughed when they tried again, and then, MaryAnne's mother was upon them, hugging them both. She kissed Danny on the cheek, this time leaving no lipstick, and set to hugging her lost daughter.

"I knew it. I just knew it." Vern slapped Danny's shoulder with his Dekalb hat. "When we found the mule standing on the road last night with her saddle hanging under her belly, I said 'It's okay. Danny was a boy scout. He'll know what to do.'"

"I used Stephen's knife," Danny told him. "We got a fire started and dried out our clothes, and ... and..."

"Mom, Dad," MaryAnne broke in, "let me introduce you to Fred—my hero."

Mr. Becker remained silent and motionless.

MaryAnne kissed Danny on his cheek as her mother had done. "How 'bout it, Fred?"

Danny noticed Mr. Becker's stoic stance and felt a wave of nervousness. "Well, MaryAnne is exaggerating a bit. If it weren't for her, we'd never have made it, and I'd-a jumped off these rocks rather than living under them. Right, Wilma?"

"Let's go, young lady." Mr. Becker now moved to his daughter.

Danny dropped his head. *That can't be good.*

She and Danny gathered what was left and put their stuff into their bags. MaryAnne handed her painting to her parents as Max sniffed her cut sweater lying by the fire. Danny bent over and softly scooped it into MaryAnne's backpack. Vern elbowed Danny, who shot back the fiercest of looks.

Mrs. Becker noticed MaryAnne's limping, as she tried to put her boot on over her bruised ankle. "What's wrong with your ankle?"

"I don't know. Maybe I broke it."

"Let me see."

Mrs. Becker, ever the nurse, pressed into all the tender spots causing her daughter to yelp.

"It's not broken, but it's a bad sprain, for sure."

Mr. Becker reached out to lift MaryAnne into his arms.

"I can walk, Dad," she said.

"You're not walking anywhere," her dad replied. She reached her arms around his neck while he reached behind for her legs, and together, they stood. "We've done this before, but you were a bit smaller then."

Vern led the way down the trail followed by Danny and MaryAnne in her father's arms while Max ran back and forth chasing errant squirrels. MaryAnne and her mother

Always

chattered as they walked. The adrenaline of being rescued wore off long before they reached the farm. Mr. Becker grew tired as they walked but refused Danny's offer to help. Aunt Clare met them at the door, with a huge pot of oatmeal and hot chocolate simmering on the stove.

Aunt Clare found an ace bandage from the bathroom and two bags of frozen peas in the freezer and gave them to Mrs. Becker who wrapped them around MaryAnne's ankle. She sat on a chair at the table with her ankle propped up on Danny's seat. Mr. Becker stared out the window while the once-stranded hikers ate.

After they ate, exhaustion overtook the group.

Aunt Clare spoke up first. "Well, I just knew you'd be all right. I told Vern, I did, they're up on that mountain, under one of those big boulders. Danny will know what to do. He was a Boy Scout. But your uncle—"

"Okay, Ma, okay," Vern interrupted.

"We should be going," said Mr. Becker, standing from his seat at the table.

"Are you sure I couldn't talk you into more coffee?" Aunt Clare turned to grab the kettle.

"No, we're leaving ... today."

"What do you mean leaving?" MaryAnne asked, frowning.

"We talked it over last night and realized we've stayed long enough. Maybe too long."

Mrs. Becker stared at her husband. "Your father talked it over."

MaryAnne looked at Danny with wide eyes. "That's crazy. We have another week."

"We're going." Mr. Becker walked toward the door.

She reached out a hand to stop him. "I'm not."

Danny stood and grabbed her hand.

"It's okay, MaryAnne. We'll write. You have to go. I get it."

He turned to her parents. Mrs. Becker's face was pained, but Mr. Becker's was stern.

"Can I come over before you leave to say goodbye?"

"We'll be on the road after lunch. We'll wait 'til two."

"Thank you, sir."

Mr. and Mrs. Becker, followed by MaryAnne hobbling next to and supported by Danny, walked out to their car. No one said a thing as the Becker family and their dog got in their car and drove away. Danny turned and headed up the stairs before Aunt Clare could reach out to him. He heard her sob but refused to turn.

In his room, Danny buried his face into his pillow and cried. Sheer will got him to the shower a few moments later to wash away dirt, soot, and ash. If he stood there forever, it wouldn't erase the hole in his heart which had now grown larger. After washing down his tears and dirt, he made his way back to his room, where he fell onto his bed. Danny shut his eyes, hoping he wouldn't wake up.

But he did. The alarm clock's red numbers glowed. He couldn't believe his eyes. 1:20. He had only forty minutes to see MaryAnne before her family left. For the second time in the day, he jammed his legs into a pair of jeans, put on his socks, grabbed his sneakers and a T-shirt, and ran down the stairs.

"Where's Uncle Vern?" he called. "Where's Uncle Vern?"

His aunt looked up from her needlepoint. "Honey, he took the truck to town. Why?"

"I need a ride to the Becker's. I need a ride."

Always

He ran outside. With his sneakers and T-shirt barely on, he jumped on his bike.

Danny pedaled with everything he had. As he came around the mountain, he saw the house with Mr. Bill's truck and boat, but he didn't see the station wagon that had held the *Sunflower*.

Mr. Bill came out as Danny leapt from his bike that rolled a few more feet into the lattice bordering the porch.

"Where is she?" Danny cried. "Where is she?"

Mr. Bill reached out to grab his shoulder. "Gone, Danny."

"What time is it?

"2:15."

"No ... no, no!"

"It wouldn't have mattered, son, they left a half hour ago. Bob said he needed to get on the road."

"Sure, he did." Danny sat on the step with his head in his hands. "Sure, he did."

Mr. Bill went back into the house and came out with an envelope.

"She left this for you, son. I'm real sorry. I know you two really like each other. Probably doesn't help, but she didn't stop crying the whole time. Even the envelope is stained with tears."

Mr. Bill was right—that fact didn't help. Imagining MaryAnne in pain only made Danny feel worse. They'd had just two weeks together, but it was the only time he had felt like a real person since Stephen had died. He had walked through much of his young life asleep, but she had awakened him. Something had been stirred, and now, nothing could be put back in its place.

Mr. Bill also handed him his class ring. "It was on top of the envelope." Then he left Danny alone with his thoughts.

Danny stared at the envelope with a sunflower inked over the flap. Underneath it, MaryAnne had written, "I'm not an artist." He pressed his class ring into his palm so tightly it hurt, then shoved it into his pants pocket.

He turned the letter over and made what could have been a faint smile. She'd written "Fred" on the front, underneath, "Bedrock," and in the corner, "Wilma."

Danny turned the envelope over and over without opening it. He looked at it, then he stared at the mountain wishing he was still cold, wet, shivering, and lying next to her.

But he got up, tucked the envelope in his back pocket, and rode off.

March 2021

Sully stood by the nurses' station, hands trembling. He'd been ushered out of Mary's room even as she'd screamed, "Fred, bring him back, Fred."

John walked up to him now. "It's okay, Sully. They're giving her some fentanyl to calm her down. She was agitated and confused. The neurologist says she may be suffering from retrograde amnesia."

"She doesn't remember anything before the accident, right?"

John nodded. "Yeah, but it's worse than that. He thinks she might have a severe case. She may not remember years of her life. They're thinking this Fred character is someone from her past, maybe even before her first marriage."

Sully squirmed, unsure how much he should say. *No, I can trust John.*

"They said seeing you made her more confused, and well, she thinks you're Fred. Crazy, huh?"

"Yeah ... crazy. Uh, do you think I could see her, maybe sort it out for her?"

John leaned against the nurses' station's counter. "You can't. Doctor's orders. Her fiancé's been notified. He's flying in overnight, and there will be a case review tomorrow. Then, hopefully, we'll know more. Go home, Sully, get some rest." John smacked him on the shoulder. "I'll see you tomorrow night."

Sully didn't trust the higher-ups any more now than in the Gulf. He knew he couldn't outrun the friendly fire from an Air Force A-10 then, and he couldn't beat the hospital now. Sully headed home.

The next day, Sully parked Sierra and strode with heightened haste toward the elevator to the executive suite. He thought about his summons earlier. A secretary for the chief surgeon had called, asking him to come to the case conference about Mary. He didn't know why he'd been summoned. Perhaps they were going to fire him.

This gig was only a part-time job anyway. I can find another. But MaryAnne? I can't let her go, not again. I'll die before I do that. I've already died too many times to this world.

As he waited for the elevator to open its doors, he worried about what he'd say. *"Hello, gentlemen. I'm Fred, and Mary is Wilma. We slept together under a rock when we were sixteen- but nothing happened. Honest."*

They would think he was crazy for sure. Maybe they'd think he had amnesia.

The elevator dinged and the doors opened onto an outer room with a desk and woman sitting behind it.

"Mr. Sullivan? I'm Rachael. I spoke to you this morning on the phone?" He nodded. "Come this way. They're expecting you."

Sully followed her down the hallway to a glass-enclosed conference room where he saw a half dozen white coats and suits sitting at one end of a long mahogany table at least

Always

the width of his trailer. They stopped their conversation and looked his way as he turned the knob and entered. He recognized John, his PA buddy, Jonesy, and Smeltzer, the burn specialist, but others were unfamiliar.

"Mr. Sullivan, we've been expecting you," a man in a white coat and salt-and-pepper hair said, standing and holding out his hand in introduction. "I'm Dr. Armstrong, the chief surgeon."

"Sit next to me, Sully." Jonesy patted the plush office chair next to him.

Sully took in the man's tailored, three-piece suit with a glittering chain connecting the front pockets of his vest. He tried not to stare. The man's white, collared shirt and cuffs contrasted with its blue pinstriped body. *Gucci, no doubt.* He could smell his cologne too. He was sure, in fact, that everyone could smell it. Even Rachael, who had returned to her desk.

"It's highly unusual to have someone from housekeeping at such a meeting," Dr. Armstrong began.

Jonesy scratched his chin. "Look, Sam, I wanted Mr. Sully here, and Bob, your esteemed counsel, obliged me. Thing is, from what I hear, he's been with my Mary more than anyone in this room."

Sully shifted uncomfortably in his seat.

"I asked for him to be here. He's been my eyes and ears while I was away, and no offense ladies and gentlemen, but he's the only one I really trust to tell me the truth. And around all you medical types, he's the only one I can understand."

Polite chuckles traveled around the table. Sully sat silent, stoic, unwavering.

"Mr. Sullivan, maybe you could tell," the chief surgeon continued, "but we've been convening here for some time before you arrived and have worked out a preliminary treatment plan." The chief pointed toward Jonesy. "Mr. Jones here has medical power of attorney, and until Ms. Mills's cognitive deficits clear, that is how it will remain. As with all our patients, particularly those who are high risk, we like to consult all parties involved."

High risk? Martha had been high risk, and you didn't convene, as you put it, with me. Don't you mean high visibility? The ones with money?

Dr. Armstrong nodded to another man who introduced himself to Sully as the neurologist.

"To recap, the neuro evaluation indicates Ms. Mills has significant deficits in her temporal lobe resulting from a lack of blood delivering oxygen which has caused impairments to the hippocampal formations. Her retrograde amnesia is pervasive—she's lost decades of memory. She is fully capable of operating, let's say, a computer or cell phone, but she couldn't recognize any of the pictures we showed her from her current life and couldn't tell us any memories associated with those objects or people. She initially said something about Fred and Wilma Flintstone, but it's believed these random memories to be associated with her childhood."

He turned to Sully.

"We don't know why she called you Fred, maybe simply because you are a heavyset male. Possibly because of your time spent with her while she was in a coma. She may have formed an attachment in her preconscious functioning. That's an area we know little about. At any rate, she hasn't mentioned those names again since we showed her pictures of the cartoons. Did you talk about such things while she was unconscious?" he asked. "Maybe those moments somehow seeped in and are now causing delirium."

Always

No kidding, she doesn't want to talk to you eggheads. Geeze, you doctors. Why not quit poking and prodding her and just hold her hand? Sounds like you're looking for someone to blame when the man responsible is sitting right next to me in his finely tailored suit.

Sully cleared his throat and looked at his folded hands. "I'm just a janitor."

"I see. So then—"

"But I will say this." Sully paused again, willing his words to be slow and measured. He knew their opinion of him would be made in this moment, so he made use of every syllable, the quiet between each word, and his deliberate focus on each member. "She's scared, real scared. One minute, she's careening down an icy road, and the next, she's surrounded by a herd of white coats with pen lights. Maybe if y'all held her hand and just sat with her, maybe then you'd get the answers you think you need. But like I said, I'm just a janitor."

"Well said, old man," said Jonesy, patting him on the shoulder. "That's why you're here. I want this man assigned to my Mary's care."

"Well, hold on a second, Mr. Jones," said Dr. Armstrong. "Your Mary has been transferred to a step-down unit now that she's awake and breathing on her own, but she is going to need extensive therapy, for everything from her limbs to her limbic system. Her emotional memory, I mean. This is the work for professionals."

Jonesy stood and pounded on the glossy mahogany table with his ringed fingers. "How long—days, months, years? She doesn't even know who I am! When do I get my Mary back?"

The chief surgeon cringed with every rap on his very expensive boardroom furniture.

143

"Mr. Jones," the neurologist countered. "Sir, you may never get Mary back."

Jonesy slumped back into his leather chair.

He looks so small, defeated. Is that how I looked when they told me about my Martha?

The neurologist held out his hands, palms up. "Sir, we just don't know. There is a window of, say, six months, for some a year, but with Ms. Mills's age, I expect ninety percent of the progress she makes will be in the next six months. She may have to be trained how to walk again, how to eat, even. Good news, though, she knows how to do those things. But with all the trauma, burns, muscle loss ... her balance and her dexterity have yet to be determined."

"And sir," Dr. Smeltzer, the burn specialist added, "she will continue to require work to her skin grafts which come at yet more emotional expense."

A woman at the end of the table raised her hand. "Mr. Jones, I'm the neuropsychologist assigned to Ms. Mills. You can expect periods of depression, punctuated with anger and intense anxiety." The neuropsychologist pushed back in her chair.

"Okay, okay, I get it," Jonesy said, brushing his hand through his hair. "Y'all don't need to pile on. How much do you think a fella can take, anyway?"

Even now all he thinks about is himself.

"Look, I'm not the smartest person in the room. I never am." Jonesy sat up in this chair again. "So, I surround myself with thousand-pound brains. But lots of time you brainiacs make the difficult way too complex. I'm sticking to what I said." He pointed at Sully. "I expect this man to be assigned to her treatment team."

The lawyer and chief surgeon threw up their hands.

Always

"I have a suggestion." *My buddy, John.* "What if Sully makes a temporary lateral transfer to nursing services as a nursing tech where he can be assigned to physical therapy? He could transport the patient to and from PT. He could be tasked by the therapists to help her with her exercises and provide encouragement."

"Sully?" Dr. Smeltzer asked.

"Yes, Sully," John countered. "He knows what it's like to struggle, and he knows what it's like to lose someone. He used to be a navy corpsman. I got a feeling Mary is not someone he wants to lose."

John doesn't know how right he is. Sully had been paying rapt attention but now he went into an even higher level of alert as if he was in the Tactical Operations Center being briefed for an assault.

We're about to run the gauntlet all over again.

Jonesy nodded in agreement. Others shook their heads.

After looking around the room, Dr. Armstrong looked at his watch and asked, "Consensus?" After hearing nothing further, he slapped the table. "Consensus! Thanks, John. Make it happen. It was your idea." He got up and left the room.

John wagged his finger at Sully who shrugged. *Did I do that?*

"So, what now?" asked Sully outside the boardroom.

"I don't know." John laughed. "You're just a janitor, and I'm just a PA. Look, I'll talk to your super. You probably don't need to be there. I'm sure she'll want to blame you. I'll talk to the head of physical therapy too—our kids do daycare together. Then, we'll let them sort it out."

"When?"

"Maybe tomorrow, possibly."

"How about now?"

Sully didn't wait for John to answer. He headed to the hospital's gift store where he bought a bouquet of tulips and headed for MaryAnne's room.

"Sully!" Jonesy yelled. "I'm holding the elevator for you. You coming or what?"

Sully shook his head, remembering how Jonesy didn't have any regard for him the last time the two took an elevator. Now, his heart beat faster the closer they got to MaryAnne's new room.

This is nuts. I'm on my way to see my first love who still thinks we are dating. I have flowers in my hand, and I'm standing in the elevator next to her fiancé.

As they approached her room, he could see the TV was on with no sound. A plastic pitcher and slippers wrapped in plastic sat on a skinny table with wheels next to MaryAnne's bed. In the corner was a forgotten wheelchair. Next to it sat the kind of chair that could stretch into a poorly configured bed.

There were no machines, no tubes this time, but her head was wrapped, and her face had a new dressing. Her arm and leg were still in casts too. A large calendar hung on the wall with today's date marked by a big red X. Orchids covered every free space including the windowsill. MaryAnne stared at the ceiling as the nurse's aide filled the cream-colored pitcher with water.

"Now drink, hun. It will help your skin and just about everything else."

"Everything except my catheter."

"Oh, they told you about that, did they?"

Jonesy and Sully stood in the doorway, waiting. The nurse bustled over to them and pulled Mr. Jones by the arm. Sully could tell he was clearly annoyed, but he was always annoyed.

Always

"Mr. Jones, your fiancée ..." she began. "I don't know how to say this, but your fiancée doesn't know who you are."

"I know that. That's why I'm here."

The nurse reached out her hands. "You don't understand. It would be a tremendous shock to her. She wouldn't know how to handle the conflict. You see, deep down, those memories are there, but right now she can't access them. So, in her mind it's not that you don't exist, it's more like you *can't* exist. Seeing you is a non sequitur she is unable to process."

Jonesy scratched his head. "I don't know about all this psychobabble." He waved her away. "I just know she needed me in that crash, and I know she needs me now." He turned to Sully. "What do you think?"

Sully stared at the floor and shrugged. Jonesy grabbed him by the sleeve, pulling him into the room with him.

"My Fred," MaryAnne said looking at Sully.

Sully's lips moved but nothing came out. *Wilma.* He raised the tulips to eye level.

"It is you," she said.

Sully had a lump in his throat. He just nodded.

"But who is this?" MaryAnne frowned at Gucci standing next to him in his expensive suit and overpowering cologne.

"Mary, it's me, Jonesy." He rushed to her side. "Honey, look here, I brought these pictures."

Jones pulled out a stack of snapshots from the inside of his coat pocket and began to spread them out on her bed.

MaryAnne picked up the first picture—one of her kissing Jonesy. A look of terror stretched across her face before she dropped the photo and held her hand to her mouth.

She began shouting, "Get him out of here!" She raised her bed sheet to her face which caused the photos to spill about the room. "Get him out of here!" she screamed louder.

"But honey, I'm Jonesy, your fiancé. I had these orchids flown in from Shenzen Nongke ... China, babe!"

"I hate orchids!"

Sully touched Jonesy's arm. He jerked back, then looked at the tulips, looked at Sully, and cocked his head. He stared at him for a cold second before hustling out of the room and down the hall.

MaryAnne cried. Sully moved her tissue box closer.

"My Lancelot," she said, drying her eyes.

"MaryAnne," he said softly. "Hi."

"Hi." So much in such a little word. She smiled as best she could.

"So, you remember me?"

"Of course, I remember you."

"Do you know my real name?"

MaryAnne studied his face. "Come closer." She touched his cheeks, cupped his chin in her hand, then traced along his neck and onto his shoulder. Sully closed his eyes, loving the feel of her touch after all these years.

"Danny, of course, but I called you Fred, once, and you ... you called me Wilma. Why is that?"

He opened his eyes and straightened. "We have lots to talk about, MaryAnne. Or do you prefer Mary?"

"It's MaryAnne with an e. I hate the name Mary, but everyone here wants to call me that. Who was that man, anyway?"

"Like I said, we have lots to talk about."

"Danny, I know I'm not sixteen anymore. Sixteen-year-olds don't have hands like this." She held out her hands to show him. "I'm not crazy, am I?"

"No, you're not. You're blessed. You lived through a horrible accident. You're a survivor. And when you woke up, so did I. A long time ago, you prayed for me." Danny's

Always

eyes filled with tears. "And now I'm praying for you. But you've been in a coma for a while now, and you've forgotten things, lots of things."

"Like that horrid man?" Her forehead wrinkled.

"Um, yeah, he isn't so bad once you get to know him."

"That cologne smelled so familiar, but honestly, I hate it. Come here." She motioned him closer. Danny bent down and she whispered, "I'm scared, and I'm so alone."

"I know, I know, but I'm here, and never forget, you are never alone."

"Will you tell me something?" She looked up at him. "How old am I?"

Danny took in a breath that pushed tears onto his cheeks that fell onto hers. "MaryAnne with an e, you're fifty-nine."

She's going to cry. Who wouldn't? What a shock. It's like she went to sleep at fifty-nine and woke up at age fifteen. She's Rip Van Winkle in reverse. Who can survive such a thing?

"Fifty-nine, you say? I'm still younger than you." Her eyes squinted as a smile crossed her face. "Well, I didn't expect you back until I was a hundred. I'd say you're early."

Danny laughed and squeezed her hand lightly. "That's my MaryAnne, always looking at the bright side. Do you want me to leave and come back in forty-one years?"

"No, no, please, that's not funny. You can't leave, you can't." MaryAnne reached for him.

Danny bent down and hugged her back as best he could. When he looked up, he saw half the nurses at the nurses' station looking back. He pulled up a chair with his back to them and held MaryAnne's hand out of their line of sight.

"I'm not going anywhere. But I do have a home now, and I'll have to go home sometimes. But I'm here, and my job is to help you get better."

"I'd like to see myself."

"What?"

"I want a mirror. I want to see what I look like."

Sully frowned. "I'm not sure that's such a good idea."

"Please get me a mirror."

Danny looked around the room. He rummaged through a couple of drawers and found a small mirror hanging on the back of the bathroom door. He sat back down with it in his hands.

"Look at me," he said.

Their eyes met.

"You still have the most beautiful brown eyes, I promise. And you will get your beautiful skin back—promise again. And this whole time, people have been saying that you look like an angel. Just remember that, okay?"

She nodded, and he slowly turned the mirror around.

She gasped, winced, and shut her eyes. He started to pull the mirror away, but she opened her eyes and clutched his hand tighter in hers, bringing the mirror closer. MaryAnne transferred the mirror to her broken arm and with her right hand began to outline the wrinkles beside her eyes. She pushed back her hair not captured by the head dressing.

"Danny?"

"MaryAnne, you are beautiful. You don't just look like an angel. You are an angel—my angel."

He took the mirror from her and hung it back up in the bathroom. When he sat down again, neither of them talked. He held her hand long after she fell asleep.

Finally, when he could stay no more, he tucked her hand beneath her sheet and walked out of the room. Out of the corner of his eye, he saw both doctors and nurses stopping their normal routines to watch him. Some, he thought,

Always

wiped tears. He kept his head lowered and headed for the elevator.

Downstairs, he walked toward the exit when he heard his name being called.

"Sully, Sully ... oh Sully?"

He turned. "Yes, mum."

His supervisor's hands were on her hips. "I hear you're headed to nursing services."

"Yes, mum, but I'll be in tonight."

"What, so you can fall asleep on your first shift tomorrow? And who do you think they'll blame? Report to PT tomorrow at seven and ... do us proud, ya hear?"

"Yes, mum." Sully smiled.

July 1974

Danny squinted through the raindrops and pushed harder, but he rode no faster. His thighs felt like cinderblocks and his palms felt like bone mashed against the wet handlebars. Every divot, rock, and drop in the road jarred his body. Every deviation drove him farther into despair. He saw his MaryAnne staring out the window of their station wagon as rain rolled down the outside of the window but the inside was smeared with her tears.

Her mother must have reached back for her.

Maybe they tried to convince her he was like any other boy. He could hear her mother saying, "You'll meet plenty of other boys, honey." And MaryAnne saying, "No, I won't."

But her protests wouldn't do any good. They would still be driving farther and farther down the road, farther away from Danny. And the farther they went, the deeper into his imagination and sadness Danny ventured. By the time he made it home, the rain had stopped, his tears were dry, and his hands no longer trembled but were bleached white from the strain.

"Danny, Mr. Bill called. Honey, I am so sorry," Aunt Clare said, standing on the porch. "He asked if you would call him when you get home."

Danny didn't look at her, just grabbed his fishing rod leaning in the corner.

"You call him. I'm going fishing."

He snatched the rest of a loaf of Stroehmann's bread on the counter, took a birch beer out of the fridge, and headed out the back door. He imagined his aunt wanting to come after him, wanting to hold him and dry the tears that had long ceased along with the rain. He pictured his uncle saying something like, "Let the boy go, Clare, nothing we can do for him."

And his uncle would be right. His tears would not return. But it sure would have felt good to be held by Aunt Clare.

Oh man, this hurts. I'd rather have hypothermia and die. Least with hypothermia, you get delusional and think you're warm and all right. And death wouldn't hurt, not like this.

He walked through the weeds still wet from the rain and found his spot on the little dock. He wet the bread and kneaded it as he had done countless times before, pasted it around a number 6/0 hook, and squeezed two split shots on the end of the line with his teeth. And like he had done a million times before, he cast his line from the old Zebco 33 out to the middle of the little pond.

He felt his shoulders relax slightly at the familiar plop as the line hit the water. The bobber resurfaced and took him to a time when the only thing that counted was what was on the end of his line. He was always so sure he would catch the big catfish, "Ol' Masa." Uncle Vern had bragged about how the big catfish owned the pond for years. Danny could imagine the old fish scouring the bottom when the dough bait dropped in front of him just high enough to keep from getting snagged on a fallen branch.

He envisioned Ol' Masa smelling his bread and chomping down on the bait. Immediately, he'd reach back and snag his

Always

little hook. Danny could see the fish give fight, first coming up near the surface, then diving down to break his line. He pictured his rod bending and heard the drag on his Zebco screaming out the joyous sound of what could only be the biggest fish in the Poconos testing his twenty-pound line.

The sound of the drag woke him from his imagination. He saw his rod bending as a fish took his line toward the opposite shore. Danny snapped back on the line, setting the hook and maybe the fish's fate.

Got one, got one. Let him take some line, but don't let him go deep under a log or something.

Danny obeyed his uncle's voice in his head like he was six. He reeled in the line when the fish started swimming toward him, but he let him run when the fish turned away.

He's the big one, Uncle Vern. He's smart, I'll give him that.

Danny zigged when his fish zagged, reeled when his catch slacked, and waited when the old boy ran. His muscles ached after a time. Ol' Masa was the only thing that mattered now. Two minutes or ten might have passed when Danny saw the fish come to the surface to make one splendid leap. It was as if he was saying "You don't have me, yet."

Bring it, Masa. Bring it, old fish.

Danny reeled hard but didn't have to reel much before scooping the big fish up with his net.

"Ol' Masa, everyone says you're ugly but you're beautiful to me." Danny reached into his net and lifted him out with both hands. "I believe I caught the Ol' Masa ... or at least his heir. You're what Uncle Vern would call a 'big-un.' Shoot, if you're eight pounds, you're ten."

He extracted the clean hook from the old fish. Danny was about to feed the stringer through his lip when he caught a good look at the fish's big black eyes.

"You're more than those long whiskers and muddy tail, aren't you, fella? You look so scared. Dang, you're all alone, aren't ya, fella?"

Danny held him up and kissed him. The fish slipped from his fingers and flopped once on the dock, rolled over, and splashed home.

"Go on now. Supper's waiting for you. Now you got something tell the boys and maybe that girl that's waiting for you, Masa."

Danny would tell Uncle Vern about the one that got away. How the old fish would have been enough to feed them all for dinner. How he was the next generation of Ol' Masa and how he'd inexplicably ended up back in his watery home.

Danny tucked his hands into his back pockets and surveyed the pond, satisfying himself with thoughts of his catch. But he felt the letter still in his pocket. He cautiously opened the envelope and pulled out the lined paper folded by its length and width to fit into the bulging envelope. He unfolded the papers like they were the Dead Sea Scrolls and sat down on the deck with his feet dangling over the edge.

> Hey Fred,
>
> As soon as we got to Uncle Bill's, I could tell Dad wanted to leave before you got here, so I'm writing this letter, and I'll leave it on my bed. I'm hoping Uncle Bill will do the right thing. I know he will. I have so many feelings, I don't know where to begin. First, I am so sorry if I don't get to see you. Just leaving is breaking my heart. Last night was special. As long as I live, I know there will never be another night to compare. Never. You saved me. You are a gentle man. Get it? You are so gentle, and last night, you were my man. And that's simply how you will always be to me. I don't know if I will ever be back, if I will ever see you again, hear your voice, see

Always

your paintings, or share your pain. But I know this, right now we're sharing a pain so deep and so real. So please know this, Danny, you are not alone. I am with you. God is in my heart, and you are there too. I feel you more than I feel this stupid Bic pen between my fingers. Last night, I felt you through every part of my being. It still takes my breath away. I have no one to share this with but you. For that alone, we will always be together, never alone. Please believe that, please. And please do this for yourself and if not for yourself, then for me. Be happy! Every day, just like your painting. Today, even, be happy! I'm happy. Okay, maybe not totally happy, but I'm happy I have you. Present tense, not just "had." I have memories so sweet, so beautiful, if I live to a hundred, I will remember us. And that has made all the difference. You know, like "two paths diverge in the woods, I chose one ... and it's made all the difference." Sorry, but I'm kind of a poet, at least the reading part. So be happy! Pick up your fishing rod, walk down to the dock, and catch the big one for me, kiss him on the lips, and let him go! K?

My address is on the backside of this page. If you want, you can write me. I think that will be okay. I didn't ask ... well, now is not the best time, but who knows? And then I'll do the same and even if our letters don't get to each other, we'll have something to share when we are a hundred and you find me. Because a promise is a promise, and you've saved me at least twice so far. Gotta go. They're all downstairs, and Dad's calling ...

Wilma

Back at the farmhouse, Danny told his grandparents about the big one.

"Home, Danny, the fish is home?" Uncle Vern said.

"Pond. I mean pond."

"Slipped, did he?"

"I guess."

Danny put his gear in the corner and headed back upstairs.

Aunt Clare wiped her hands on her apron. "Make sure you wash the pond off before dinner."

His steps grew heavy the closer he got to his room. He didn't want to open his door, but he couldn't just stand there in the hallway. Not all night, anyway. He pushed on the old cross-and-Bible wooden door, feeling the slippery porcelain knob that fed into a cast metal box. The skeleton key was more show than security.

He pulled his letter out of his back pocket, flopped on his bed, and kicked off his shoes so they made a *thud* on the floor. Lying on his back, he read her words again, and again. *Be happy! Be happy!*

Geeze, did she have to use all those exclamation points? How am I going to do that, anyway? I wasn't that happy before I met her and now that she's gone ...

He read the letter again, most of it, anyway, before drifting to sleep.

It was dark when he awoke. He stumbled to the door and flipped the light switch. A plate of meatloaf, green beans, and mashed potatoes covered with waxed paper sat on his bureau. A glass of lemonade and lemon meringue pie sat next to the plate.

Aunt Clare must have left this.

Danny's hands still smelled fishy, so he walked down to the bathroom. He could see the light was on, but it was too late to turn around. The door opened as he drew near, and Uncle Vern walked out.

Always

"I go more times than I can count these days. It's the cost of getting old. Someday you'll understand. Did you see the food?"

"Yessir. I just wanted to wash up some before I eat it."

"Gotta be your aunt Clare's best pie yet."

"Lemon meringue is my favorite."

"Is that right? I will have to tell her."

"Uncle Vern, I know you know she knows."

"Well, I don't know what you just said, but boy, know this—we love you, son, and we're hurting for you. After last night, I realize you are a man. I have never been so proud of anyone in all my life."

Vern put his hand on Danny's shoulder. Danny reached forward and pulled his uncle into a hug.

"Aw, now, what's all this?" Uncle Vern said as he hugged harder. "Now I'm gonna smell like fish."

Danny shook his head, let go, and went into the bathroom. Back at his room a few minutes later, he cleaned his plate with a piece of buttered bread, then licked the last of the meringue from the pie plate. He climbed into bed, feeling full and weary, and shut his eyes as he felt MaryAnne against him. *She was right, she's still here.*

Crack! The sun peered through the trees.

Nothing beats the sound of wood splitting. Good for the arms too.

Danny bent over and righted two halves of cut oak onto the larger base wood then rubbed his gloved hands over the rusty handle of the monster maul. The six-pound wedge was a veritable wrecking wedge. Just a few yards from the back door, Danny was working up quite a sweat. It took both hands to raise it over his head but just a little effort to get the massive tool started before inertia and gravity had its way with the broad oak billet. The tree had taken decades to grow but now lay in pieces on the ground in a matter of minutes.

Danny picked up the broken quarters, loaded them onto the already top-heavy wheelbarrow, and rolled the mass of potential heat to a four-foot-high row of firewood. He crisscrossed the wood on the end before filling in the middle. After loading the last piece, he turned around and headed back to the unsplit pile.

"How long you been out here?"

Danny jumped at the sound. "Uncle Vern, you scared me. I dunno. A while. This is my third load."

"You hungry?"

"A little. Let me make one more pass, okay?"

"Okay, but be careful, if that wedge hits your foot, it'll be your last pass, and we won't have wood this winter."

Danny's T-shirt was drenched from his exertions. Even his jeans were wet from his waist to his thighs, and both were covered with bits of wood. Snot ran from his nose, and despite the gloves, his hands had been rubbed raw. His wet hair flapped with each swing, slapping across his face and the back of his neck. His triceps and biceps were engorged with blood, but his mind was empty.

After he split another log, he looked up and saw Aunt Clare looking through the kitchen windowpanes.

She is beauty—real beauty.

Danny paused and waved.

There is more than one angel in the world. Two at least.

He couldn't give up MaryAnne's memory, but he could work. And when he worked hard enough, his sadness no longer lingered. Smelling the cool air in his nostrils and filling his skinny chest brought a sense of security with each

Always

blow. He simply did not want to quit. The maul bounced off the corner of a knotty piece and ended up digging a hole next to his sneaker.

I see what he means. Probably should have boots.

He could smell breakfast coming through the kitchen vent.

Smells like scrapple.

Finally, Danny got out the grain shovel and broom. He made a neat pile and scooped it up in one swift motion before tossing it into the compost pile.

Everything here's got a purpose, even the waste. A guy really wouldn't want for anything if he worked it right. He shook his head. *I'll never be that guy. Not anymore.*

"Don't take another step. Drop your clothes right there at the door," his aunt commanded as he came to the door.

"But, Aunt Clare."

"You have underwear on, don't you? Whitey tighties? Who do you think washes that underwear?"

Danny did as he was told. He ran upstairs next and put on a pair of new overalls before hustling downstairs again.

"Now, don't you look like you're ready for the day?" his uncle said over his pile of eggs. "I didn't think you liked overalls."

"I was just waiting for the right time. They fit me pretty good."

"Yeah, they do. You look like a real farmer. What's gotten into you?"

"Let him be, Vern. Here, Danny, take this scrapple. Your dippy eggs are cooking."

Danny watched his uncle pour the right amount of maple syrup on his scrapple before cutting the mushy rectangle with the side of his fork and scooping up his first bite. Danny did likewise.

"Pretty good," he said.

"Pretty good? That's our pork you're eating, boy."

Danny shrugged. "I have to confess ... I've never had scrapple before."

"We just ruined you, because you'll never have it that good again anywhere else—not ever."

"Yeah, well, that's been happening a lot to me lately." Danny's eyes welled up.

"So, Vern, what's your plan for today?" asked Aunt Clare, obviously hoping to divert the conversation.

"TSC. I need to go to Tractor Supply for parts and while we're there, we can pick up some Huskies for Danny."

"Dogs?"

Vern laughed. "No, some work boots for *your* dogs. People will pick you out as a poser a mile away if you come in wearing overalls and Adidas. Especially if you're missing a toe or two."

"You saw that?"

"I did. Don't worry, all good woodsmen are missing at least one digit."

The pair took their plates to the sink when they were done eating, rinsed them off, and turned to the door. Outside, Danny climbed up in his uncle's old Ford like he had done for years. But this time when he slammed his door twice, like always, he had a new thought. He looked over at his mentor.

Things don't always stay the same. People grow up, they go away, and sometimes they die. Please God, let me never forget this moment.

They drove down the road with the windows open. Danny waved his hand in the wind that went up his short sleeve. The wind blew his hair back.

As they walked into TSC, a man called out from the middle of the store, "Oh no, here comes trouble."

Always

"Melvin, you rascal. This is my nephew, Danny, so watch what you say. He still thinks I'm pretty special." Uncle Vern slapped him on the shoulder. "Fix him up with some work boots, will ya? And while you're at it, find him a mesh cap to cover that mop of his."

He turned to Danny who was backing away under a rack of western wear. "Well, if you're not going to cut it, you can at least cap it!"

Danny walked behind Melvin who showed him the boots and got him the right size. After trying on a couple of pairs, he picked out some dark brown, eight-inch Justins.

"These fit good. Uncle Vern said don't get anything with heavy lugs because the manure will get stuck in them, and Aunt Clare will give me the dickens."

"Yeah, that sounds like your uncle. You know we go back a ways, we do. High school and even the war."

"World War II? I saw a picture of him in his uniform, but he never says anything."

"Well, let me tell you, when you look at your uncle, you're looking at a dad-gum war hero. And if you don't believe me, have him bring you down to the Legion some night, you know, for a root beer." Melvin elbowed Danny.

What's with old men and their elbows?

Vern walked up behind him. "Got what you came for, Danny?"

"Yessir."

"Justin boots? Whoopee!"

"I don't want to look like a poser." He winked at his uncle. "Melvin was just telling me he knew you in WWII."

"Shoot, Melvin, quit filling this boy with stories. Did Danny tell you he saved his little girlfriend's life?"

"She's not my girlfriend, and truth be known, she saved me."

Melvin took the shoe box from Danny. "Sounds like the acorn doesn't fall far from the mighty oak."

"Yeah, well, this skinny kid split a half a cord of oak just this morning while you were still in bed."

"You too, Uncle Vern."

"Watch it!" Vern crushed a new red CASE hat on Danny's head.

"I thought you were an International man?" Melvin asked.

"Same thing."

Melvin rang up the sale. "Let's see, belts, bolts, filters, and oil, and boots ..."

"And the hat, sir."

"Hat's complimentary. Can't have your uncle start buying caps at his age. It'd kill him."

Vern raised his fists. "I could still give you your comeuppance, junior."

Danny bent the brim of his new hat. "All right, you two, I can't take this. I'm heading for the truck. Coming?"

Vern reached for the cap, tightened the back, and put it on Danny's head so its band rested on his head and the brim came to eye level. "There, now you look like a Marine."

Danny gathered the packages while Vern carried the oil. Together they left, together they got in the truck, and together they headed back to the farm.

"Uncle Vern, think you could take me to the Legion sometime?"

Vern gave his nephew a puzzled look. "Sure, Danny, sure. Guess you're old enough." His uncle edged his truck into the farm lane. "I think that'll be just fine," he said as he warmly squeezed the back of Danny's neck.

Our farm, back where I'll always want to be.

April 2021

After Sly from the physical therapy department had handed Sully a form to complete and some scrubs, Sully went to his locker and changed from the crisp tan slacks and white button-down dress shirt he'd put on this morning. The dirty boots he'd put on—having nothing else to wear—glared beneath the clean raspberry-colored scrubs.

These pajamas and boots make me look like I'm planning to break out of the asylum.

Sully returned to the physical therapy department and asked Sly, "Where do I punch in?"

"We don't do that in PT. You'll need to get a time sheet from human resources and turn it in at the end of the week. Let's head over to Dr. Chavez, the head therapist. She can be brisk, but she's eager to meet you."

As Sully followed the therapist, he checked out his coworker. Sly seemed to be half Sully's age but towered over him and was in incredible shape. Sully could tell he took pride in working out as evidenced by his rolled-up sleeves that accentuated his biceps. His scrubs looked tailored, pressed, and his name was even monogramed on his shirt.

The doctor's office door was open when they reached the end of the hall.

"Hey, doc," Sly greeted the middle-aged doctor. "This is Sull—uh, Mr. Sullivan."

"Good morning, Mr. Sullivan," she greeted, looking at Sully over the top of her glasses. A chain hung from the sides of her glasses and around her neck. Her coal black hair with graying roots was pulled back into a bun so tight it looked like it hurt.

"Mum."

"So, you're Sully. You've created quite a buzz around here." In one motion, she told him where to sit and for Sly to leave the room. "I heard about your conversations with our coma patient. I've also heard about your ability to calm tense situations. You have a way about you, and it has won over some rather influential people." She waited a beat for him to respond. When he didn't, she continued, "Mr. Sullivan, down here it's good to have bedside manners, but I also expect professionalism in your interactions with other professionals and in your progress notes. You now represent me, us really. To be frank, you will be on a short leash, which is something I'm sure you will find disagreeable. If that idea is too difficult for you, please tell me now. We can work on your transfer back to housekeeping." Dr. Chavez folded her arms and sat motionless.

"I see, mum, I'll watch my P's and Q's."

"I've gathered some books from my personal library for your perusal ... no, for your *crash education* into physical therapy. And Mr. Sullivan, 'Above all, do no harm.' This phrase comes from—"

"The Hippocratic Oath, mum. I am required to swear by Apollo Healer, by Asclepius, by Hygieia, by Panacea, and by all the gods and goddesses, making them witnesses that I will carry out, according to my ability and judgment, this oath and this indenture." Sully smiled. "I had to memorize that bit as a navy corpsman."

"I hope that's a good thing." Dr. Chavez pointed at a stack of books on the corner of her immense desk that overpowered the room. "Here's *Braddom's Physical Medicine and Rehabilitation* by Cifu, *Recovering from Your Car Accident* by Zender, and *Physical Therapy for Traumatic Brain Injury*, a personal favorite, by J. Montgomery."

"Thank you. I just picked up *Retrograde* by Kat Hausler."

Dr. Chavez frowned. "Not familiar."

"Well, it's a novel about a woman who lost years of memory after a traumatic car accident."

"Mr. Sullivan, although I'm providing you with some education, your job here is not to diagnose. Your job is to carry out the doctor's orders and to be a conduit for observing, recording, and communicating progress. Nothing more, but a little theory won't hurt, either. Understood?"

"Yes, mum." Sully knew it was his time to leave.

"And get something clean on your feet. You can't wear those dirty, old boots in here."

She dismissed him with little more than a hand gesture and a grunt.

Sly waited outside her office. "How'd it go?"

"Not so sure everybody likes the idea of having me here."

Sly patted him on the back. "Don't worry about Dr. C. She's old school. Do the right thing, and she'll back you all the way to the quarterdeck."

"Quarterdeck? Are you navy?"

Sly nodded. "I did my four as a PT Tech."

"Well, shipmate, nice to be aboard." Sully beamed.

Sly scratched at the black chest hair creeping over his V-neck. "Yeah, well, anyway, we've already missed the morning meeting. This here's the whiteboard, like your board in housekeeping only this one can change at any moment. Check it regularly and after each patient. Got it?"

Sly didn't wait for a response.

"Let's talk while we walk up to the fourth floor, no elevators for us."

Sully winced.

He was a flight of stairs behind but caught up to Sly at the top of the stairs.

"I'm sure you know, we're assigned to Ms. Mills this morning. You've been assigned her even though she's a complicated case, so the probability of screwing up is pretty good. The good news is right now she's your only patient, so you have time to study and learn specific PT and OT techniques as well as how to teach simple ADL skills."

Sully wrote down the acronyms and other words into a palm-sized spiral notebook.

"You know, you can use your phone to record this, if you want."

"I don't want."

"Okay, man, just sayin'. Let's keep moving."

They stopped at the nurses' station where Sly sat down in front of a computer. "This is where you type in your username, password, and PT code. Then your patient's name."

Mary Mills's file appeared on the screen.

"You're allowed to read her chart?" Sully asked.

"Yeah, man, you too. But only the records you're assigned. You only have the keys for PT. Got it? So anyway, here's my system." Sly pecked away at the keyboard using two fingers. "First, scroll down to orders, look for anything that says PT Tech. Here." He pointed to some verbiage on the screen. "So, the PT—the new ones are doctors too—takes

Always

the order, does a patient assessment, consults with the doc, then writes a treatment plan that dovetails the main plan. Now let's look under Treatment Plan—PT." Sly scratched his chest with one hand and pressed on the keyboard with the other. "Here, looks like they want us to simply work on getting Ms. Mills out of bed. She doesn't even have to go to our treatment room. They just want to acclimate her slowly to the hospital and therapy." Now, Sly rubbed the back of his neck. "They also want us to do some therapeutic games to help stimulate memory."

"Like a current events quiz?"

Sly frowned. "Absolutely not. That would only scare her. I'm talking crosswords, hangman ... we have a bunch of games downstairs. Remember the stuff we played as kids? Okay, you played different games, but that's how we learned. Thing is, you don't want to belittle her, but you don't want to frustrate her either." Sly rolled his eyes. "*Wheel of Fortune*, not *Jeopardy*. Not yet, anyway. She knows she's fifty-nine and can process some things like she's fifty-nine but can only remember as if she is sixteen. Man, that's really gotta mess with her mind, ya know?"

Now Sully rubbed the back of his neck as the Hippocratic Oath loomed in front of him. *I could really mess her up.*

"You'll be fine," Sly reassured him. "Ask open-ended questions. Don't remind her of things she may not remember, otherwise you can create false memories. She needs to own them, and that could create doubt. I'm sure she already has plenty of that."

Sully started to shift back and forth in his boots.

"Just go with what she gives you and ask, 'What else do you remember,' or 'How did it sound?' 'What did you see?' 'How did it smell?' Smell is a good one. Your olfactory sense is hardwired to a part of your brain that triggers long-term memory. That's like when you smell perfume and think of your aunt. It can take you back like no other sense."

"You mean like the smell of something burning?" Sully thought about the Humvee in Iraq, upside down and on fire.

"Exactly. Then in this section"—Sly pointed—"progress notes, is where you will write your SOAP note. I'll go over that later today. Just don't write anything until I've approved it. I mean not one thing." Sly stood and looked down at Sully. His dark features gave him a menacing look when he was serious. "Ready to meet your patient? Let's go."

Sly walked into room 9 followed by his protégé. Sully noticed immediately the orchids were gone. *Wonder if he flew them back to China?* But in their place were scads of tulips in all different shades, vases, arrangements, and simple bouquets. There was even a dog made out of tulips. The flowers stretched across the window and onto the stand next to the bed. He noticed the tulips he'd brought sat next to the bed in the corner but were overshadowed by some other exotic genus type.

"Hello, ma'am, I'm Sly from physical therapy and this is my coworker, Danny Sullivan."

"Hello, Mr. Sullivan." MaryAnne shot forward her right hand as if she were still in the Poconos, her eyes sparkling. Her smile couldn't be ignored. Sully instantly recalled the first time they met.

Sully looked at Sly, who nodded. "You still have a firm handshake, MaryAnne," Sully remarked.

Sly gave him a quizzical look.

"That's Ms. Mills to you," Sly mumbled. "And how do you know about her handshake?"

"Oh, um, from when she woke up. I doubt if that would have made it to the progress notes."

As Sly moved to the left side of the bed, Sully held up his index finger against his lip and winked at her.

"So anyway," Sly continued, "this morning, we are working on getting you out of bed. The sooner you get out of bed, the sooner you can use the bathroom, and the sooner you can say goodbye to your catheter. Unless you want to keep it."

Sly smiled, but MaryAnne was not amused.

"Funny."

Sly slid a chair parallel to the bed and lowered the bed to the same height as the chair.

"After this, we'll try a wheelchair." He looked at Sully. "See how the bed is the same level as the chair, angled in the same direction, and low enough for her feet to touch the floor?"

When Sully nodded, he turned back to his patient.

"Ms. Mills, can you lie on your left side, facing us?"

MaryAnne looked at Sully who nodded. Slowly, she groaned her way to her left side.

"If you are in any pain, please tell us. We will not do anything to hurt you, I promise." He turned back to Sully. "Be mindful her right side is very sensitive due to the burns and grafts. We can't use a gait belt or a slide board because of it."

Sly turned back to MaryAnne and lowered the bed rails. "I'm going to raise the head of bed to help you sit up. Just go with the flow, allow the momentum to bring you upright."

Sly raised the head of the bed, and MaryAnne's eyes grew wide as she teetered onto her bottom like a blow-up punching bag.

Sly held out his arm for her to cling to. "You are doing so well."

Sully realized how tense he had become. The simple act of sitting up, something he did every day was now more than work for her—it was therapy. MaryAnne was at base zero, and the simplest of acts needed to be planned and executed intentionally.

"Now place your hand on my shoulder, ma'am."

Sly slid his hand around her back and took her hand.

"Fortunately, she was not burned under her arm," he said to Sully. "Okay, hun, let's lift together."

MaryAnne instantly began to panic. "Oh, no, no, I can't."

Sully didn't know what to do. His arms froze, his feet planted in cement, his voice mute.

"Okay, okay." Sly's voice never wavered, his movements just as smooth. "Just breathe. Take your time. Let me know when you're ready."

MaryAnne looked over at Sully who had regained his voice. "You can do this, MaryAnne."

Sly gave him a stern look. "Ms. Mills, Sully." Then he turned back to her. "Okay, let's do this together."

MaryAnne shifted her legs, so her feet reached the floor, straightened up, and stood for the first time in weeks.

Sly held her securely. "Now would you like to sit on this wonderful plastic chair, or would you like to lie back down?"

"Lie down. I want to lie down."

Sly lowered her back down to the bed with ease. Sully noticed her breathing had grown heavy.

"You must think I'm such a baby."

"Not at all, look what you just did. That's something you haven't done in a long time. Something the doctors didn't even think about just a week ago. And you did it." Sly smiled.

"I guess."

"Let's do it again." Sly didn't ask this time. "But now we'll have Mr. Sullivan assist."

Always

"Me?"

"Yeah, you." Sly stood and pushed Sully to where he'd been stationed a moment earlier. "If Ms. Mills can do it, so can you."

Refusal was not an option as MaryAnne looked deeply into his eyes. Just as he had observed, Sully put his right hand under her arm, and his left hand took her hand.

"Ready, Wilma?" he whispered.

"Ready, Fred."

Together they rose. This time, she didn't groan. She may have giggled. Their eyes met, and he felt like he was falling into the back of her brown eyes as he'd done so many years before.

In the distance he heard Sly say, "Okay, do you want to lie down or sit in the chair, Ms. Mills?"

But MaryAnne just kept looking at Sully—her Danny—and not replying.

"Ms. Mills? Do you want to sit in the chair or lie back down? Mary?"

She snapped out of their trance and turned her head toward Sly. "Oh, um, sit in the chair, and it's MaryAnne."

Together, the two pivoted like kids slow dancing at the sock hop.

"Just bend your knees, Sully."

He lowered his partner to her awaiting chair where she closed her eyes for the longest time. Long enough for both Sully and Sly to look at each other with raised eyebrows.

As if sensing their worry, she said, "It just feels good to be upright, like I'm normal again."

"You're better than normal, MaryAnne, you're a survivor."

"*Sully*, it's Ms. Mills." Sly stood with his arms crossed.

Sully nodded.

Sly looked at his watch. "Only took a half-hour, but hey, you're up. I'm going to leave you two. I have a patient waiting for me downstairs. You can move back to the bed when you're ready. And you can try the transfer again or try getting in the wheelchair." He turned to Sully. "It's really just the same as long as you remember to lock the wheels—both wheels—and put the footrests off to the side before lifting her. Got it?"

"Yessir."

"And remember, it's Ms. Mills."

Sully gave a half-salute before Sly wrote down his number on a sticky pad he kept in his pocket.

He slapped the note on Sully's chest. "Call me if you need me."

Sully nodded as the tech left the room. He turned back to MaryAnne.

"What's your pleasure, *Ms. Mills*?"

"Danny, I really don't know who that woman is. I just want to sit here and look out this warm window." She gazed out onto the scene below. "Oh look, there's a pond. Wanna go swimming?"

"Sure, except I forgot my cutoffs. Maybe some other time. 'K?"

She smiled. "'K."

The pond was surrounded by a carpet of green that rolled over a hill until it met the stark blue sky. Two white swans swam together surrounded by green reeds that bowed to the water. Leaves left on the trees blew gently, clinging to what was once their lifeline. Now they hung on because it was all they knew. The sun shone sharply, creating long shadows and deep contrast.

"I can almost feel the sun." She tilted her face up to the sky.

"They mate for life."

"Who?"

"The swans." Danny pointed. "They mate for life. Oh, I'm supposed to ask you open-ended questions."

She opened her eyes and looked at him. "What's that?"

"Open-ended? Just not yes/no questions. Like, 'What do you remember' and not, 'Do you remember when Max tried to take my head off?'"

"I do remember Max our German shepherd, but I don't remember him taking your head off."

He forgot that even though MaryAnne was an adult now, some of her thinking would not be fully developed. She wouldn't understand sarcasm and could be very concrete and literal.

"Is he still ..." she began, then stopped. "No, no, of course not. I've lost so much."

Tears began to form, and Sully reached for the tissues. He realized he had already pushed too hard with such an innocent remark. Now he grasped the gravity of her situation and feared even more of doing the wrong thing. *You were sixteen then, but you're fifty-nine now. You can do this.*

"Hey, I pushed you too hard. Take your time. It will come back, it will."

She put her head in her hands. "But what if it doesn't?"

"Look at it this way, you are sitting up, looking out at a nice little pond. That's enough for today. Go with that."

"You're right. I'm grateful. For the swans, for the pond, even for this plastic chair. Where's that wheelchair?"

Sully didn't hesitate to push the wheelchair in front of her at a slight angle. Helping her into it was easier than the chair. He hated letting go as she sat down, but his smile revealed his pride in her as the two wheeled down the hall together.

MaryAnne received numerous "Hellos" at which she politely smiled and shyly waved back. They rolled past the visitors' room where they saw a family of five playing a boardgame. The sun shone down the hall from the end windows that reached from floor to ceiling.

"This is perfect, let's stop here." MaryAnne folded her hands.

"We have to—there's nowhere else to go."

MaryAnne let her arms go limp, shut her eyes, and leaned her head back as Sully sat down on a small chair. She reached over and took his hand. He wanted to look around to see if anyone noticed, but instead, he shut his eyes and basked in the warmth.

"Danny?"

"Yes?"

"What happened to ... to us?"

"Oh, I hate to think about it."

He wasn't sure if the truth would hurt or help her, but he took a chance.

"I got your letter from Mr. Bill and read it a bazillion times before I wrote you back."

"Did I write to you again?"

"I don't know. I never got it if you did. But I kept writing anyway—all through my senior year. Then college came up, I met Martha, got married, and worked to help support our family. Then, the war got in the way, and well, things really changed then."

MaryAnne gazed out the warm window. "I can't believe I didn't write. I don't remember getting anything from you. I think I would remember if I did."

Sully turned his head toward hers. "I figured, so if you weren't writing, what chance did I have?"

"I'm sorry." She squeezed his hand.

"Don't be. It's not you, it's me. Isn't that what they say? Anyway, things worked out."

When she tensed, he wondered if he had said too much and looked to her for confirmation.

"It's okay." She shook her head slightly. "Who was the man with the orchids? Is he the florist?"

Sully laughed. "Well, that's funny."

"No, it's not." She frowned. "You're laughing at a disabled person."

"You are not disabled, MaryAnne. You have me, and you have ... the florist, and you will leave that wheelchair behind when you leave here. But that man, he's your uh, your fiancé, I think, and he's some kind of high-powered lawyer."

MaryAnne turned. "Oh ... does he seem like someone I would ... be involved with?"

Sully let go of her hand and turned to face her. "I live in a trailer. My only friends are Kat and Sierra, my cat and my truck. I work nights. I don't have a real friend because people think I'm a grumpy old man, and I sleep most of the day. Does that sound like me?"

Again, she frowned. "Not at all. What happened?"

"Life, I guess. No ... death. First, it was Stephen, and then Jimmy in the war. When my wife Martha died, I was done. Her death left a sucking wound that won't heal, like a bullet through my chest. Even breathing became a struggle." He looked at her with a cold expression. "Well, listen to me rattle on. I'm supposed to be here for you."

"You are ... you are." She squeezed his hand again. "Maybe it's time to take me back."

Sully turned her wheelchair around and headed back to her room. Each person they passed smiled as if they were looking at an older couple who had weathered life together in sickness and in health. They didn't know how young and alone Sully and MaryAnne felt.

"Here we are, track number nine," he said.

MaryAnne looked puzzled.

"I mean, room number nine."

A nurse's aide brought in a tray as Sully locked the wheelchair in place.

"Good afternoon, Ms. Mills. I have your lunch."

"Please, call me MaryAnne." She looked over the meal. "Yum, tomato soup, grilled cheese, crackers, applesauce in a cup, and fruit, also in a cup." She picked up a third cup and frowned. "I didn't know Jell-O came in a cup."

Sully started to ask if she remembered Aunt Clare's homemade applesauce but stopped himself. Instead, he sat there in wonderment, watching his first love dig the last piece of fruit out of the little plastic cup, then raising her eyebrows and a mini carton of chocolate milk at the same time before taking a swig and leaving a chocolate mustache behind.

When she'd finished most of the meal, she said, "Maybe I should lie down."

Sully helped her to her feet, and they pivoted toward the bed. She sat on the bed as Sully helped her lie on her side, then rolled onto her back.

The last time we did this we were wearing the same sweater.

"You're a chocolate mess."

He handed her a napkin, but she grabbed his hand and held on until he exhaled and let go.

I'm more confused than she is. I don't know who I am either. I mean, am I a PT tech, an old boyfriend, or just a figment of an organically impaired TBI patient's memory trapped in time? When will this house of cards fall?

Sully heard a noise and turned toward the door where Jonesy stood with a small bunch of tulips in his hand.

August 1974

Danny continued his ritual of splitting firewood before breakfast. By the time the scrapple sizzled, he had worked up quite a sweat and appetite. Neither Aunt Clare nor Uncle Vern complained about the sweaty sixteen-year-old in need of a haircut who took the last of the pancakes, last of the orange juice, and last of just about everything. Little was said about the Beckers or even Mr. Bill until one evening after dinner.

His uncle had come down the steps clean shaven, wearing a clean shirt and a blue ball cap with gold lettering, *FMF Corpsman*.

He looked at Danny. "Well, you comin' or not?"

Startled, Danny didn't say a word, simply grabbed his denim jacket with a peace sign drawn in magic marker on one shoulder, a dove and olive branch patch sewn on the other, and an upside-down American flag sewed on the back. Vern didn't say a word, but the look he gave Danny said it all. He hung up his jacket and picked up a flannel shirt he'd left on the chair instead.

"Ready."

Danny knew Wednesdays meant they were headed for the American Legion.

"Will Melvin from the store be there?" Danny asked as they got into the truck.

"I s'pose. Mr. Bill, too."

"Oh." Danny stared out the split windshield of the old Ford.

"Guess you haven't seen him for a while."

Danny didn't say a word.

"It'll be all right. Mr. Bill likes you. He called to see how you were doing."

"Oh."

"Oh," his uncle mimicked. "Well, you don't have to talk to him. But you better talk to Melvin. He keeps bugging me about you and asks about your boots. I don't know why he likes you so much, but he does."

Danny smiled and put his hands on the warm dashboard vents on this chilly evening in the mountains.

They drove in silence until Uncle Vern parked the green Ford in front of a building with a gray World War II cannon on massive metal wheels standing guard at the edge of the lot. There were no windows at the front of the building.

The parking lot was quiet with only a couple of expected creaks coming from the Ford's suspension. But the place exploded with sound when his uncle opened the front door to the building.

"Stand by Your Man," blared on the jukebox, and pool balls clacked together in the background. "Love me some more Tammy Wynette!" someone bellowed. One old couple slow danced in the middle of the room and didn't seem bothered by the shouting, laughing, and spilling of beer happening all around them.

Neon signs spelled out Schlitz, Yuengling, and Ballentine Beer along with pictures, plaques, and patches from the wars and all branches of the service covering the

Always

paneled walls. Cigarette smoke filled the air and clung to the dusty, white, drop ceiling. A pinball machine banged and clanged with irregularity as Danny's eyes darted from patron to patriot, barfly to waitress, and back to his uncle.

Uncle Vern gently grabbed the back of Danny's neck. "Keep your head on a swivel, boy. Any one of these men would die for you, but no telling what they'll do tonight."

"Doc!" old men shouted as they slapped his uncle on the back.

"Danny," Melvin shouted, "Let me be the first to buy you a beer. What'll be? Birch or Root."

"Birch, sir."

"My man. Raised him right, Doc, raised him right."

The three jostled to the bar and squeezed between two men arguing about whether some fighter jet was first made in 1952 or 1953. A skinny man with slicked back hair nursing a near empty glass of beer and a long ash on a shortened cigarette sat at the other end of the bar.

A barmaid made her way to the group. "Well hey, sweetheart, what'll be, good-looking?"

"Careful, Marge, this is my nephew. Better not say that in front of him."

"I figured who he was. Anyway, who did you think I was talking to, old man?"

"Don't let her fool you, Danny. Marge here was a WAC, Woman's Army Corps, and flew on B17s," Uncle Vern told him. "He'll have a birch beer. Give me the usual."

"Guess I can expect the usual tip then." Marge turned to grab their drinks with a wink.

"She's in rare form tonight, how about it, Mel?"

"Sure is, old man."

"Danny, see the skinny guy next to Melvin?" his uncle whispered. "Doesn't look like much does he? Silver Star and two Purple Hearts at Guadalcanal."

"What about you, Doc?" Melvin started. "Your uncle pulled his CO from an overturned jeep, all under enemy fire. And that's just the one he got his medal for. Back then, corpsmen wore a big red cross painted in a white circle on their helmet. It was a bullseye, I tell you. The enemy knew if they killed a corpsman, it was like killing seven Marines. And I was one of the Marines he saved."

Vern waved his hand at his friend. "Oh, quit exaggerating, now."

Melvin leaned into Danny. "See, that's what he does, but me and the machine gunner were pinned down after our Browning M1917 overheated and wouldn't fire. A grenade got tossed in our fighting hole. We both looked at it before this knucklehead jumps on it out of nowhere."

Danny squinted at his uncle.

"It didn't go off," he said, then sipped his beer.

"Now, that's not the point, not the point a' tall," Melvin said. "It sure could have gone off. It should have gone off. And you didn't know it was a dud."

"It didn't go off." His uncle took another sip. "Besides how do you know what I knew? Maybe they didn't bother to teach the Marines what a real grenade looks like."

"So that's why you saved me? Just to insult me and the corps for the next thirty years?"

"How come you never told me about that, Uncle Vern?" Danny asked as he accepted his birch beer from the bartender.

"It's like this. Down in DC, they're building a war memorial for the men and women we lost in Vietnam, and they should—war is horrible. But did you ever wonder why there's no WWII memorial? Because we don't ask for one. Maybe someday, but all of us were lucky enough to come home, and a lot of it was luck or the good Lord. We got

Always

jobs, got married, bought a place, and put that stuff in a suitcase somewhere, because we leave it in the past, and that's where it should stay."

"Now, just wait a minute." Melvin leaned in, crushing Danny between him and his uncle.

"Don't go filling this boy's head with glory and honor because it wasn't all glory," countered Vern.

"I just think the boy ought to know the truth. Ain't that why you brought him here?"

"I guess." Vern took another swig.

Danny looked in the mirror and saw Mr. Bill walking toward them.

"Hey fellas, what'cha talking about? Let me guess, Iwo Jima?" Mr. Bill slapped Danny on the back, but Danny didn't turn around

"You were at Iwo, Uncle Vern?"

"Next round's on me," shouted Mr. Bill.

"Now that guy's got my back." Melvin laughed.

"Did you serve too, Mr. Bill?" Danny asked as Mr. Bill took a seat next to him

"Korea, the forgotten war. But here's the thing, Congress never declared it a war, and we never signed a peace treaty. They signed 'an armistice agreement.' What is that, anyway? Far as I'm concerned, that war never ended. These fellas here came home heroes. We just came home. But it was even worse for the boys in Vietnam. They came home baby killers."

"Important thing to remember is"—his uncle raised his beer—"a lot of boys didn't come home at all."

Melvin and Mr. Bill raised their glasses in a salute and together they declared "Never forget." They drank to the empty chair sitting next to a white-clothed table in the corner of the room—a tribute to all those who still had not come home. On top of the table was a flower, a candle, a plate with a lemon slice, and some sugar for the bittersweet truth.

The men grew quiet. Marge was still pouring, the jukebox was still blaring, and another old couple was dancing. All around them men and women laughed, threw darts, and shot pool while these four men looked down at their empty glasses.

"Fellow veterans and guests, it's a quarter to ten and time for one last round," Marge shouted out a little while later. The jukebox went silent. "We have our tradition, so if you'll turn with me to the flag and say the pledge."

Danny gazed around the room to see old men, some with ponytails, some bearded, take off their dirty caps and cover their hearts. Others stood in perfect salute or put their hands to their heart. He choked up to see some fellas' fingers were crooked from age, but they did their best to honor their country. Some guys gave shoulder hugs after they'd recited the pledge. Most headed to the bar to buy a last round or settle up.

"One more?" Marge asked his group.

"No, we're heading out." His uncle pulled out a ten from his wallet.

"I got this, old man," said Melvin, pushing his money back at him.

"You said it was my turn this week," added Mr. Bill.

"Now look, he's my nephew and I'm paying, and quit calling me 'old man.'"

"Knock it off, the three of you," said Marge as she wiped the bar with a dirty white dish rag. "Joe already picked up all your tabs."

The skinny man at the end of the bar put out his cigarette and tipped his empty glass to Danny.

Always

Outside Vern and Danny were quiet again. They got in the old Ford 100 and drove past the single light on the Legion sign and the rusty cannon still standing at the watch.

"That was something," his uncle started, "Old Joe's never done that before."

"Why did that old man pay for our beers?"

"Leadership."

"I don't get it."

His uncle laughed. "Most people don't. They think leadership is telling people what to do. It ain't. Real leadership starts with taking care of your people. Most important thing. Without that, no one would follow you in battle. You do it for the guy next to you, not for Old Glory, or even the girl back home. Old Joe can't rub two nickels together, but I suspect he saw you, and something inside him stirred."

"Me? Why me?"

"Danny, you gotta understand, there's two things that motivate a man to stay true to the mission—the young PFC standing guard and the old farts showing up with their scraggly beards and raggedy Legion caps. And when you get to be Joe and me, you look around and most all the old farts are gone. Joe sees you, and he sees hope. You motivated him."

Danny thought about this truth as they trundled down the road back to the farm. Soon, he felt himself nodding off. He had been up early and had worked all day. The only time he had sat down was at dinner and at the Legion.

The next thing he knew, Uncle Vern was nudging him awake. He went inside where Aunt Clare sat in her chair next to the woodstove working on some patches for Danny's blue jeans.

"Glad to see my boys are safe," she said.

Danny watched her a moment before asking, "Aunt Clare, do you have something to rip out threads and stuff?"

"My seam ripper is in here somewhere." She fumbled around in her sewing kit for a moment before coming up with the tool. "Here it is. You doing some sewing?"

"Sort of." He took the ripper from her gnarled hands. "I have to fix this flag on the back of my jacket. I got it upside down." Danny hugged his uncle and whispered, "Thanks, Doc, you motivate me." Then he headed up the stairs.

He threw his jacket and himself on his bed and rolled over. Remembering the letter on his desk next to a blank pad of lined paper, he got up, sat down at the desk, flipped on his little desk lamp, and picked up a pen.

> Hey, Wilma,
>
> Your letter means everything to me—everything. I read it every day. Sometimes, I wake up in the morning and it's lying next to me. It's all I have of you, but for now, it'll do, I guess. Even though it seems like years since you left, not much is happening around here. I'm trying to do what you want. I'm trying to be happy. I guess you could say I'm doing happy. I get up early before breakfast and split wood like honest Abe. So far, I split about a cord, which doesn't sound like much, but it's a four-by-eight-foot pile stacked four-feet high. Then we have breakfast together. I'm starting to like scrapple, but I still like my dippy eggs best. Aunt Clare says I'm filling out. I don't know, but I am getting stronger, and the blisters on my hands are now callused. Aunt Clare got me overalls, and Uncle Vern got me work boots. And I got me a farmer's tan.
>
> I go down to the pond, but it makes me sad. There's no reason to row the boat, and there's nobody to splash with my cannonball. (My splash is still bigger than yours.) But

Always

guess what? I caught the big one! No kidding, he was a monster catfish. Second or third, who knows, generation to Ol' Masa. Vern says he's reincarnated, but Aunt Clare says we're Presbyterian, and we don't believe in that stuff. Anyway, I caught him before I read your letter, and you won't believe it, I kissed him on the lips, and he slipped through my fingers and fell back into the water. You predicted it, and it came true. You're Rasputin! Do you have any other supernatural powers? If you do, I hope you are clairvoyant, because then, you would know what I'm thinking right now.

Tonight, Uncle Vern took me to the American Legion for a beer. Okay, okay, it was birch beer. Your uncle Bill was there and a guy named Melvin. They told war stories and everything. I used to be for peace and all and I still am, just now I got a lot a respect for what they did just because they were told to do it. But there's a real closeness there, a brotherhood like no other. Not scouts, not even church, I think anyway. I know Uncle Vern wouldn't want me to join, says he'd worry too much, but it really made me think.

Anyway, I'm sort of happy. I'm thinking maybe I'll go out for lacrosse this year. I know it's kinda late to start a new sport, but I'm a good runner, and you don't have to be tall. You even get to run into people, as long as you go for the ball. Working up here is getting me in shape, so why not?

I sure hope I get to see you again and soon. Sometimes my stomach hurts I miss you so much. Oh, but I'm happy, right? I really hope you get this. It just feels good writing so I will keep doing it.

Hoping your prediction about seeing you when we're a hundred comes true too.

Till we meet again,

Fred from Bedrock

Danny folded up his letter and put it in a business-sized envelope, the only one he had. *This looks dumb. It looks like a bill—not a letter to a girl.* But he sealed it up and hoped to get a stamp from Aunt Clare. He got undressed, then turned out the light and burrowed into his bed. After a minute, he turned the light back on. He got up, picked up Aunt Clare's seam ripper, and freed the upside-down flag from the back of his jacket. He made sure all the errant threads landed in the wastebasket.

There. Tomorrow, I'll sew it on right.

And he went back to bed.

April 2021

Sully didn't know what to say as he and Jonesy looked each other over like waring Samari in the doorway of MaryAnne's room.

"Sully." Jonesy nodded coldly to the new physical therapy tech.

"Sir, ah, we ah, we just had MaryAnne for a stroll. To ... to the end of the hall and back in her wheelchair." Sully nodded, affirming his words.

"Is that what you were doing?" Jonesy's tone sounded sarcastic.

Sully knew sarcasm, and it took everything he had not to fire back. Instead, he bit his lip.

Finally, Jonesy turned to MaryAnne. "Mary, have you remembered me yet?"

"You're Mr. Jones. They tell me I know you."

"Honey, you do know me. You call me Jonesy."

She frowned. "I see. And you call me Mary. Why don't you call me MaryAnne?"

"I dunno." Jonesy shrugged as he walked closer. "'Cause I like Mary better, I guess."

Sully backed up and watched the two feel each other out like boxers circling in the ring but never getting too close and never connecting.

"I brought you these flowers. I understand you like tulips." Jonesy looked for somewhere to put them. Sully took them from him and squeezed them in a vase after taking out the older, limp ones. "In fact, I got you all of these." Jonesy waved his arms about the room.

"Danny brought these." She pointed to the one small vase near her bed. Sully was startled to realize she had even noticed.

"We expect to get Ms. Mills downstairs to PT tomorrow or the next day after potty training." Sully looked coyly at his patient who busted out laughing.

MaryAnne shook her head. "You always were so funny."

Jonesy pointed his finger inches from Sully's chest. "My gal does not need to be potty trained."

"No, sir. I just meant learning how to get up and sit down on the head, er, toilet."

"And Mary, what do you mean," he said, turning back to her. "You *always* were so funny?"

MaryAnne changed the subject. "Mr. Jones, is it? I really don't like your tone. My name is MaryAnne with an e. Do you talk to everyone that way or just *your gal*?"

Sully dropped his chin to his chest. *Pretty sure he doesn't like feedback—not from MaryAnne, anyway.*

"Now look! You"—he pointed down at MaryAnne—"are my girl."

The charge nurse was in the doorway in an instant. "Mr. Jones, please come here."

Jonesy scowled at her as if to say "Who are you to command me?"

She simply crossed her arms over her chest. "Mr. Jones. Now, please."

He looked back at MaryAnne who had turned to look at the wall and Danny's flowers.

Always

"I see what's going on here. I've underestimated you, old man."

Sully thought of the Great Gatsby who had cheated with a neighbor's wife. Jonesy stormed out of the room and began having an animated conversation with the charge nurse standing near the nurses' station. Other nurses and interns distanced themselves. Sully turned back to his patient.

"I'm so sorry, MaryAnne."

"That petulant little boy," she quipped.

Sully turned back to her. "This has been hard on everyone. He was in the accident too. He was driving, and I'm sure he feels guilty."

"He's got a weird way of showing it. He could take a line from you."

"Huh?"

"Well, you've said I'm sorry several times already, even when it wasn't your fault. You've been so thoughtful."

Sully flashed back to something his uncle had said years ago about leadership. *Leadership is taking care of your people.*

"I need a hand, not a florist."

Sully smiled at MaryAnne's renewed spunk. "You're tough."

She looked confused, then said, "Oh, I'm sorry."

"No, don't apologize for being tough. Tough is good. Tough kept you alive when others would have given up. I know I'm not one to talk, but MaryAnne, it's going to be grace that gets you through. Your brain's been shaken ... like shaken baby syndrome ... and it's going to take a while for it to settle down. But there's something I want you to remember. You were always full of grace. It's your best quality."

"Thank you for finding me." She raised her hand toward him, and he took it, then backed away with his head down as if to bow.

Sully moved MaryAnne back into bed, then left with a promise to return. When he passed the nurses' station, he felt eyes upon him but didn't look up.

But he noticed the charge nurse standing in front of Jonesy, who turned to walk away from her scolding. "Mr. Jones? Please sir, I'm still talking to you," she said as Sully quickly exited to the elevators.

Downstairs, he walked through the double doors leading to the PT clinic. To the left were six tables where techs were helping patients stretch, flex, turn, and twist their way back to life. The large room to the right contained weights, bands, bars, and other props, where patients were regaining their balance, gait, and posture. Various shapes and ages were spinning the reclining and upright stationary bikes.

He turned into the staff room to retrieve his tuna fish sandwich and napkin, pouring himself a coffee before sitting down. Sly sat down next to him with a lined form and a box outlined at the bottom to write the patient's name, birthdate, and other identifying information.

"How's it going, Sully?"

"I'm thinking today might be my last. Mr. Jones wasn't very happy with me."

"Mr. Jones isn't your boss."

Sully eyed his sandwich, suddenly not hungry. "Tell Mr. Jones that. He got mad that MaryAnne seemed to know me better than him, so he ended up yelling at her, and the charge nurse took him aside."

Sly shook his head. "Just do your job. The patients are easy, but the patients' families are tough. He's putting too much pressure on Ms. Mills." He moved the lined paper

Always

closer to Sully. "I dug up some old progress notes to teach you how to write a SOAP note. Because you are new and don't have access to our computer system, I think for now, until you take the class, you can write your notes on these forms, and I will put them into the system. Just keep the notes in the clinic so we don't violate HIPAA and go to jail."

Sully nodded and acted like he knew what HIPAA was.

"Anyway, S is subjective, O is objective, A is assessment, and P is plan. How did Ms. Mills look today?"

Sully shrugged. "Good."

"Give me some specifics, draw me a picture."

"She was lying in bed, soft cast on one arm, hard cast on her leg. She talked to me about the past."

"Okay, good, that's S." He jotted down the notes in the S column. "Now, what did you two do?"

"I helped her get out of bed and into her chair. Next, I helped her get into the wheelchair. I wheeled her down to the end of the hallway, and we talked. I helped her back to bed, and she ate her lunch. Then, Mr. Jones showed up, and things went to hell in a handbasket."

"Okay, that's Observation. Let's leave him out of it, though, it's not his note. So, how is she?"

"Good." Sully took a bite of his sandwich.

"Specifics, behavior, man, behavior."

"She is capable of sitting up, standing up, sitting down with minimal assistance. She's angry. I think she's sad. I think she misses her life, even though she doesn't know what it was."

"Great, A for Assessment. Now what's the plan for tomorrow?"

Sully held his tuna fish sandwich with one hand. "I'd like her to get to the toilet. I'd like to see her do it without my help."

"Perfect, P is for Plan. Here's your note."

Sully looked over the sheet. In the corner was MaryAnne's identifying information. On the left, the date and time. Then SOAP was written down the side and filled in with what he had told Sly.

"I get it."

"Think you can do that tomorrow?"

"I can do it today. I'm going back up." Sully sipped his coffee.

"Slow down, cowpoke," Sly said. "She got several hours in today. Her brain needs to process. She will take in all this new data, chunk it into meaningful categories, and file it away. Believe it or not, she needs sleep to do this. Best not to rush her. Besides, she has to follow up with the burn unit. And ortho needs to see her about her breaks which means x-ray, maybe another CAT scan for neurology. Who knows? They may schedule the social worker to talk to her and her fiancé after what you just told me. You were lucky to get this much time."

Sully finished his tuna fish and held his napkin around his hot coffee. "So, what do I do?"

"Grab one of your books and dig in."

Sully went to his locker and reached into the pocket sewed on the front of his scrubs to pull out a ripped paper with his new combination. He pulled out a crumpled tulip. *MaryAnne. She must have put this in my pocket when I was helping her get into her bed.* He smelled the flower and lay it on his top shelf. He pulled out one of the large textbooks and his novel.

I can't believe they are paying me to read. He returned to the staff room with *Braddom's Physical Medicine* and *Retrograde* and found a soft chair where he began reading. He leafed through to the pictures and the captions.

Always

Reminds me of those plastic overlays of the human body in Biology class. Hmm, okay, Braddom, what can you teach me? He turned to the table of contents and ran his finger down the columns. *Evaluation: Physiatric History and Physical Examination. Physiatric? Is that even a word? I'll definitely read this section first ... Oh, here's a section on burns. I'll save that for later.* He turned the page to the last section. *Traumatic Brain Injury.*

He read about the "Chief Complaint" and "History of Present Illness." *Oh, yeah, I remember this from corps school.* He continued through "Functional Status and Activities of Daily Living (ADL)." *Hmm, this is new.* He continued until he got to "MSE, Mental Status Exam." He knew this well from seeing so many of his Marines after an IED, but now there was so much more to consider. He knew the docs were doing this too, but he wanted to know what they knew and maybe he'd find something they didn't know.

His distrust of doctors wasn't because of Stephen or even Jimmy. He simply distrusted anyone with more control than him. He did his best to digest "Cranial Nerves," the section on Sensory Examination, but by the time he got to "Musculoskeletal Assessment," his head started to droop.

Doctors and their big words.

"Hey, Sunshine, they're paying you to read, not sleep."

He lifted his head off his book and saw Sly standing behind him.

"Oh, there's so much here. A lot reminds me of my C-school in the navy, but I was younger then."

"It's good that you're interested. Take some notes, hit the wave tops, and when you're with your patient something will remind you of what you've read, and you can go back to the text."

"Smart. I'll do that. Maybe now, I'll go for another coffee."

"Done."

Sly handed him one of the two cups he had just poured. But Sully got up anyway and walked through the clinic to wake up his body.

An obese senior citizen sat at the reclining stationary bicycle and turned the hand cranks. Next to her, a thirty-something man turned his cranks at the same speed with about the same enthusiasm. He wore tan canvas shorts and a T-shirt. His shoulder was inked with a familiar trident emblem.

"You a navy SEAL?" Sully asked him.

"Was, 'til I blew out my shoulder."

"HM2 Sullivan." Sully reached out his hand. The patient stuck out what was left of three fingers. *His shoulder isn't the only thing blown.* "You SEALS are the big men on campus."

"Well, like I said ... was."

"Nonsense. That ink runs deep."

The man stopped his cranks and squinted at Sully. "Were you downrange, Doc?"

"The Gulf, 2nd Mar Div."

"Right on, dude, that highway of death was real." He began cranking on the machine again.

"Yeah, well, like you said, shipmate ... was."

"Now it's my turn to call nonsense. Like *you* said, man, that stuff still runs deep."

"I'll check on you later, SEAL. We should talk." Sully walked back toward the staff room, passing Dr. Chavez on the way.

"Mum." He nodded to her.

"Sully, what did you say to that patient?"

He stopped and frowned. "Nothing much, just navy stuff. Is there a problem?"

"Turn around."

Always

Sully turned and saw the SEAL now cranking his bike at twice the velocity.

"We've tried to motivate him for days and nothing seemed to work."

"Sometimes seeing an old sailor will do that." Sully thought about old Joe from his past.

"Nice, Mr. Sullivan, very nice."

Sully returned to the staff room and sat down to his books and coffee.

Let's try Retrograde, *even though it's a novel.* He read the back cover. *"On a warm summer day in Berlin, Helena is hit by a truck while crossing the street. She awakens to the loving face of her husband Joachim. In addition to a few broken bones, she realizes she can't remember anything about the accident or even the last few years leading up to it. Retrograde amnesia, the doctors call it, and assure her that with time, she should regain her memory."*

Man, this sounds too real. I wonder how soon this character regains her memory.

Sully started reading and didn't look up until he heard his name.

"Sully? PT doesn't work nights."

He smiled up at his one friend. "John, my man, how did you find me?"

John turned the chair next to him around and sat down, facing backwards in the chair. "I came in early, so I thought I'd see if you were still around or if you got fired yet."

"Not yet, but Mr. Jones isn't real happy with me."

"If it means anything to you, I saw Dr. Chavez and she's really happy with you."

"Oh, yeah. I say one thing to one patient, and now, I'm the heir apparent of PT." Sully stood. "It's late. I'm not used to these hours. Kat will be wondering where I'm at."

"Cat people." John shook his head. "So, how'd it go today?"

"Good or is it *well*? I helped Ms. Mills get out of bed and into a wheelchair. It was going good until Mr. Jones showed up and got jealous."

"Jealous?" John walked with Sully to his locker.

"Something MaryAnne said."

"MaryAnne?"

"Ms. Mills. She said I was always so funny, and he blew a gasket."

John leaned against the bank of lockers while Sully gathered his things. "I've been meaning to ask you. Did you know Ms. Mills before?"

Sully zipped up his jacket and decided to take his novel with him. He shrugged and tried to pass John, but the PA put a hand on his chest.

"You knew her. How?"

"It was just for a short time, way back in high school. We weren't boyfriend and girlfriend but … let's just say we had feelings."

John frowned. "Feelings?"

"Would you quit repeating everything I say?"

"You were a corpsman, Sully. You *do* know about conflict of interest, don't you?"

"Conflict of interest? I worked, played, ate, and slept next to my patients who, by the way, were my best friends. And I do mean were."

"You're not in Iraq, Doc. You have to tell someone, or this could blow up in your face. You've seen Jonesy in action. He'll have your hide."

"I never left Iraq, but that's another story. It's fine, don't worry. He asked me to look after her, remember? I got it under control."

Always

"Under control?"

"Knock that off!" Sully pushed John's hand away and began walking.

"Have you seen a professional yet? You know, for your PTSD?"

Sully took a deep breath and let it out slowly, wanting to punch his best friend in the face. He relished feeling the pain of broken flesh and bone. A throbbing, excruciating fist, anything, was better than the tension that now wrapped around his head like a hot metal band. PTSD had never been mentioned before—not directly, anyway. In the past, he could skirt the issue. Now it was out, and he wasn't getting it back.

"I gotta go." Sully walked down the hall and past the small metal sign above a door advertising Mental Health Services. A bulletin board had the usual flyers about wellness, a suicide hotline, and seasonal updates. One flyer caught Sully's eye, but he barely slowed down to read it. *Employee Assistance Program. Just drop in. Yeah, right.*

He walked out to Sierra, then drove away into the darkness.

August 1974

Dear MaryAnne,

It's been months since we were together, but it seems like years. In some ways, that time feels like a dream or even a fairytale. It was so great, but unreal. But I guess that's why so many songs, poems, books, and movies are out there about love stories. Yet none of them come close to our story.

I sure wish I would hear from you. I'm certain you've tried. I'm now certain my letters are not getting to you. That makes it all the harder, and me all the more determined. But I have to admit, it hurts. Earlier, Aunt Clare came into my room because she heard me crying. I couldn't lie, and I told her how lonely I feel, not hearing from you. No one really gets it because they think we're young and weren't together long.

But she told me how she and Uncle Vern met—at a Friday night sock hop at their school. That's when all the kids take off their shoes, so they don't scuff the gym floor. I asked why they just didn't wear sneakers, and she told me a lot of kids didn't have them then, and besides, sneakers are hard to dance in. Sneakers are all I wear at home, to school, and even church if I don't get caught.

Anyway, she knew Uncle Vern was the one before their first dance was over. She had told a friend she thought he was good-looking, and the friend told his friend, and then, those two friends brought them together. The music started, and Uncle Vern didn't know what to do so Aunt Clare just picked up his hands, put them in the right places, and started to move (like you did with my hands). She said he was so scared he didn't move his feet until about halfway into the song. Benny Goodman, she says. Anyway, after they danced, she said she was thirsty, but she still had to tell him to get her some punch. Then he spilled it on her!

But guess what? It all worked out because he lent her his letter sweater and walked her home. Her dad was pretty mad about the red punch, but her mother invited him in for apple pie, and he ate three pieces. Later, he told her he really wasn't hungry, but he didn't know what else to do to keep from leaving. He had a stomachache all the next day. Aunt Clare said he still doesn't admit whether it was love or just a stomachache.

So, what am I supposed to do with that? I mean, if they didn't have it together, how do they expect me to act any better? Except I feel like I do know better. I mean, I know what I want, but it's making me sick, and I didn't eat three pieces of apple pie.

I just don't know what to do. I'm still doing my chores. I go to the Legion. I even ride ole Betsy when I get the chance. I go fishing some, but I don't jump in the pond anymore. I fixed more holes in the barn floor. I toss around my lacrosse ball and shoot my bow and arrows, but it's just not enough—not anymore.

So, every day I write a little something to you. By the end of the week, I have a letter that I mail. I know it gets mailed because I hand it to the mailman, and I think it's a law or something that tampering with the mail is a federal offense.

I guess this is four or five letters now. I should start numbering them. It's really tough, you know? It's worse than praying. When I pray, at least I think God hears me. But this feels like I'm writing into a black hole or something. We learned about those in Science, but to be honest, I didn't do that good on the test. Or is it "well"?

I painted another picture, this one of Betsy. It's little, so I could mail it to you. Hope you like it.
Danny.

Danny reread his letter several times before putting it in its envelope. Reading it over and over made him feel like he was really talking to MaryAnne, but when he sealed the paper in the envelope, it was like he was sealing something special in a vault or a tomb or something. Normally when a letter is written, it's sealed with hope. Making sure the flap sticks to the envelope feels good, and when someone jiggles the mailbox lid, they do it to make sure it'll get sent. But the more letters Danny sealed, the gloomier he became. And more cynical.

All the sweet corn had been picked a while back, and the last of the hay had been brought in. In the vegetable garden, all but the last of the kale and pumpkins were ready to be turned over. The deer were getting restless, rubbing their antlers on saplings, and were coming down from the mountain looking for field corn, acorns, and anything else within reach. It wouldn't be long before the rut would be on, and they'd need as much extra energy they could find before food got scarce.

Danny grew restless, as well. In past years, he had looked forward to going home. He looked forward to something different, seeing his few friends, and being back in his house. But the end of this summer drew angst and discontent. He pulled his duffle bag out from under his bed and slowly loaded it with T-shirts, jeans, and sneakers. Whitie tighties, long white socks with blue and yellow stripes around the tops, magazines, books, a deer skull he'd found, and an antler shed. He left his overalls and boots out just in case Uncle Vern needed him for a last-minute run to the field to dig out the tractor or shoot a groundhog.

He looked out his window when he heard a car driving up the stone road. The rust-brown Malibu with the black vinyl top was easy to identify. He watched from above as three people got out of the two-door vehicle—first his mother, then his father from behind the steering wheel, then his sister from the back seat. He could see Karen's new haircut, still long but now layered and parted down the middle with just a little puff on top. *She looks older. She never was one for the farm.* But his mother and father looked the same—Mom in a predictable comfortable dress and blue sneakers, Dad in a collared shirt and thin, gray pants. *Looks like he let his sideburns grow—trendy.* But his hair was still short, still slicked back, and his glasses still black. *He may have lost some weight, but did it really matter?* And his mom, she was who she was—naïve to the new world of rock and roll, long hair, and really anything cool. But she did sew a wide ribbon around the bottom of his bellbottoms when they got too short, and she let him wear T-shirts that advertised Budweiser and Boone's Farm Apple Wine—just not to church youth group.

"Danny boy, get down here, your parents are here."
Surprised Uncle Vern doesn't ring the dinner bell.
CLANG, CLANG.
Figures, he had to do it. "I'm coming. I'm coming."

Danny clunked down the stairs in his Justin boots and overalls.

"Oh my gosh, look at you!" cried his sister Karen. "You even have a farmer tan."

"Yeah, he does," said Uncle Vern who crushed Danny's Case hat on top of his head. Danny tried to duck. He had just fixed his hair, but he was too late.

"Would you look at that hair," his mother said.

"I'd rather not," replied his father.

"How do you like *my* haircut—it's a shag," said his sister.

"Good, I guess." Danny looked at his *boots*. "You always were a city girl."

Aunt Clare, who had stood in the background, wiped her hands on her apron and changed the subject. "All right everyone, come on in the kitchen for some shepherd's pie."

"What else," said his father. "Did you use your own sheep?"

"Dear, shepherd's pie is not made from sheep," said Danny's mother.

"Oh, I knew that."

Danny rolled his eyes. His father had always longed for the suburbs while his father's older brother inherited the farm. He didn't know when his father was joking because basically nothing he said was funny. People would laugh, but Danny assumed it was out of politeness or because they were uncomfortable. When his father sat directly across from him, Danny grew increasingly uncomfortable with each look his father gave him.

He knew a trip to the barber was imminent. Danny hated barbers. Not because they cut his hair too short but simply because the barber was a stranger in his personal space with his hands in Danny's hair and on his person. Way too close. Way too uncomfortable. Way too long for him to hold his breath. He had to endure breathing the same air, smelling the same cologne, and wishing to be done or dead, whichever came first.

After bowls were passed, plates filled, and glasses emptied, Danny's father asked, "So, Vern, what's new on the farm?"

Guess Dad doesn't want to talk to me anymore than I want to talk to him.

"I want to hear from Danny," his mother said. "What did you do this summer?"

Danny shrugged. "Nothing."

"Oh, come on, you must have done something," his father said.

Danny looked down at his plate of food.

"Danny learned to water ski," his uncle offered.

"You did?" his sister asked, eyes wide.

"Yeah."

"And he split all that wood you see out there," Vern said.

"Not all of it," said Danny, "but I got up and split it every morning, almost."

Why'd I tell them that? Now they're going to expect that at home.

"Well, maybe now he won't be late for school," his mother said.

"He learned how to sail too," Uncle Vern said.

"Did you now?" His mother held a piece of bread in one hand, a fork in the other.

"Yeah." *I know what he's doing. If I tell them, I'm going have to tell them about MaryAnne.*

"And he rode a horse."

"You did?" His mom had a mouthful of shepherd's pie.

"No. It was a mule."

Uncle Vern scooped up a bite onto his fork. "Did he tell you he saved a girl's life? Twice?"

"C'mon, you didn't," Karen said.

Always

"Did too." His fork clattered to his plate. "First, I had to pull her out of a hole in the barn floor, then I had to keep her from getting hypothermia in the woods."

Everyone stopped eating now, even his father.

"How on earth did you do that?" his mother asked.

Nuts. He picked up his fork and moved bits of mashed potato around his plate. "I ... we just built a fire and blocked the wind with a tarp at night."

"At night? *All* night?" his father asked.

"You were with a girl all night?" his sister repeated, staring at him with what might be a bit of awe.

Danny didn't look up at their inquiries. He'd rather sit in the barber's chair for three days than take any more of this interrogation.

"So, what's her name?" his mother asked, a smile pulling at her lips.

After an awkward silence, Aunt Clare answered. "MaryAnne. Her name is MaryAnne, and she's a lovely girl, and Danny was a true gentleman. She called him Sir Lancelot."

Danny could feel the heat reach his forehead. He tried to drink some milk but spilled it on his shirt.

"Danny's got a girlfriend, Danny's got a girlfriend," his sister taunted.

He slammed his glass back down to the table. "Shut up. I do not."

All this was too much. Girls had never been a subject at home. Being close to someone, love, any relationship other than sports, were not discussed. Even hugging or kissing were rare occurrences back home. All of this was too close, too personal ... too real.

"Oh now, that's okay, Danny," his mother offered, reaching out to pat his hand.

"That's okay, Danny," his father mimicked.

"Just shut up." Danny looked up with wild eyes, knowing he'd said the wrong thing. Words like "shut up" were good cause for a swift smack from his father.

Before his father had a chance, Danny jumped up and stormed out the back door, heading down to the pond. He didn't stop until he got to the dock where he sat down at the spot he did his best thinking. He threw a couple of rocks that simply *plopped* into the water. He was never good at skimming.

Nuts. Can't even skim rocks. How could my family act like that? They're so immature. They're so stuck. They can't talk about anything without making fun. They don't know anything, that's for sure. I can't go home. I can't get in that car and sit there for all that time. It'll kill me, I tell you. It'll kill me.

You'll be okay.

No, I won't. I can't do it. I'm not like you.

Danny realized he was no longer talking to himself.

I'm so mixed up. Whoever told me sixteen is a great year is a big liar, a poser. This is the worst year of my life. Fifteen was tough but sixteen, sixteen sucks. I tell you, it sucks.

I wish we were eighteen.

I wish you were here. Then I could just show them and wouldn't have to say anything. I don't even like eating with them. It's so boring at our house now without Stephen. I eat, and I go to my room. But here I can't. Here my two worlds collide. My life with Uncle Vern and my life with Dad.

What about me?

And you, MaryAnne, you make three worlds. I couldn't balance two. I'm no juggler. I mean I used to be such a clown, but I was never a juggler. I can't do it, I tell you. It's not that

Always

I don't want to. I do. I just don't know how. I don't know how to talk to them. I don't even know how to say hi without my voice going all weird. I can't shake hands without fumbling. Without you, I'm just a clumsy mess, I tell you.

You're not. You're not a mess. You're mine, always.

Danny stopped right there. He had always thought too much. But what could he say to that? What was there to say? He breathed in, "You're mine." He let out, "*always.*" He repeated the words and breath again, again, and again. *You're mine ... always.*

His muscles relaxed. His body went limp. His mind barely stirred. Danny shut his eyes, and when he opened them again the day had grown dark. He could see the light from the house and looked up at the early stars on a clear night in the mountains. A star shot across the sky. *Always.*

Danny got up and moped back to his family.

No one said a word, they didn't look up as he came through the door. Mom and Aunt Clare were doing dishes, his uncle and his father were watching baseball on TV, and Karen was reading a book.

"Whatcha reading?" Danny asked.

"A book," she answered without looking up from the pages.

"Funny." He knew he deserved her snark. "Wanna play a game?"

"Which one?" Karen asked, finally looking up at him.

He shrugged. "I don't know."

"How about Parcheesi?"

"Sure."

Danny pulled the broken box from beneath the Scrabble, Sorry, and Monopoly boxes. As they set up the game at the kitchen table, Aunt Clare and Mom sat beside them. Danny used to always take green, but now he had blue, and Karen had to have red. He knew he wouldn't win. It would be okay if Mom or Aunt Clare won, just not his sister.

But she did.

After the game, Danny worked to put the game away, hoping someone would notice he really wasn't a big baby after all, but no one did. Aunt Clare pulled out her famous lemon meringue pie. Danny smiled. He would rather have pie than cake even on his birthday. Dad and Uncle Vern joined them at the table. He wanted so much to lick his plate, but he knew Karen would make fun, so he decided to just help clear the table. He even rinsed the plates.

"I'm really going to miss you, Danny." Aunt Clare pulled him into her soft body.

"Yup, the boys at the Legion are going to miss you too." Uncle Vern held out his hand and then pulled him in for a rough hug.

"Well, I'm not leaving until tomorrow, so I'll say goodbye then."

More than saying hello, Danny dreaded saying goodbye. He didn't mind goodbyes, he just hated saying goodbye because if the words came out wrong, there would be no way to get them back. Goodbyes always sounded better in his head. After messing up, he'd find some way to make a joke out of it and everyone would laugh, but he'd go away feeling like a clown.

He went to his room and sat at his little desk.

> Dear MaryAnne with an e,
> Thank you. Thank you for getting in my head and in my heart. Thank you for never letting go. And for always being there. Always. Talk to you tomorrow.

He brushed his teeth, climbed into bed, and turned off the light.

Always

The next morning, Danny was the second one up and followed Aunt Clare into the kitchen where he helped with the bacon and scrapple. He knew how much his dad loved scrapple and how he would get all goofy, his eyes all big, he'd pour on the syrup and dig right in.

After breakfast, Aunt Clare wouldn't let anyone help clean up the plates, so they all filed out the front door and moved toward the car. His sister sat in the back seat as his father started up the car. His mother waited on the other side of the car with the door wide open.

Danny grabbed his aunt around the waist. He hadn't realized how little she was until this moment. His chest heaved trying to pull back his tears. The effort was useless as tears flooded his face.

"Now, now," she said as she patted his back. "Now, now."

"Best summer ever, Auntie, best ever" was all he could say.

He grabbed Uncle Vern next and held him tight. He knew he'd get some ribbing, but he didn't care. "Tell the boys at the Legion to have one on me. And tell Old Joe I said hey."

His uncle smiled, looked into his eyes, and said, "Of course I will."

As they drove away, Danny imagined his aunt and uncle going into his room and finding the watercolor he'd left behind. He could see them picking up the frame and looking at the painting of the backs of two people, husband and wife, sitting on their swing at sundown. Another happy picture—his best work yet.

No one said anything about his sniffling as they traveled down the road. His mother gave him a little packet of Kleenex, but he stared motionless out the window until they came near Mr. Bill's. He turned to look out the back window as they drove past the house.

"Know someone there, Danny?" his father asked.

"Always," he said, "Always."

April 2021

After the confrontation with Jonesy, Sully had expected the axe to fall the next day, but it didn't. The axe didn't fall the day after, either, or the day after that. He kept his head down and did the only thing he knew to how do—he worked. *It worked for Dad, it worked for Uncle Vern, and it will work for me. Always has.*

When MaryAnne woke up, she had awakened something long lost inside him that he couldn't shake, and this feeling followed him to work each morning. Hope was there when he smelled her hair—as much as he tried not to—and hope was there when he opened a can of food at night for Kat.

With hope came a light that hadn't shined in his life for a long time. Now he prayed with hope. He just couldn't shake hope.

On his days off, he cleaned his old trailer and even weeded out front. One day, as he cleaned out the metal shed out back, he couldn't avoid the tarp which sat off to the side of the shed covering the beast that slept beneath it—his chopper, *Marilyn*.

He put down his push broom and pulled back the faded green canvas. *Okay, Jimmy, for you.* The dry rotted canvas tore as he pulled. She was dusty but still enough chrome peeked through the rust to remind him of a time long ago. *Hello, old girl. It's been a while, hasn't it?* He lowered the small lift and wheeled Marilyn into the sunlight to get a better look. *Tires aren't awful. Good thing I had them suspended. Looks like she leaked some.*

He got onto her handstitched saddle and reached for the ape hangers. *Nice to know some things still fit.* As soon as he touched the bars, he felt Jimmy's hand on his back. *I know, man. It's been a while since our last ride.* The brakes seemed to work, the clutch too. He had drained the gas, even fogged the cylinders because he was sure he'd ever ride again.

He drained the oils and made a list before heading into town. He bought spark plugs, wires, a battery, defogger, leaded gas, and oil ... lots of oil. Sully had built Marilyn from scratch—even welded the frame with an angled neck for extended springer forks in front and a rigid rear. *No soft tail for me like the posers ride.* And enough clearance in the back for a forty-four tire. *Now maybe people won't mess with me,* he thought when he sat low to the ground, reached up, and started the panhead motor with shorty pipes for the first time.

Marilyn, yeah, because it seemed like people had always messed with her.

He'd built the bike as a tribute to Stephen. He had loved riding the fields and mountains with his brother on their dirt bikes when they were young. After high school, Sully made himself scarce and found friends in bar rooms and the back of unauthorized Harley shops, putting Marilyn together piece by piece. He hung around long enough to get asked to prospect for a local gang or *club* as they preferred to be known.

With Iraq looming, he went a different direction. He'd felt his uncle and the guys at the Legion calling—especially

Always

Old Joe. After he joined the navy, he and Jimmy rode together, parking their bikes under the same tarp outside their barracks. He even helped start a club within their Marine unit. But after the war, he never rode again.

Sully changed the primary, transmission, and motor oils and used liquid gasket to seal the seams. He changed the plugs, even the wires, and ran a gallon of gas through the tank before connecting the line to the carburetor and the leads to the new battery.

Hope ... a biker's best friend. That and a little luck. He turned the key, turned the petcock, and jumped on the kick-starter. *Nothing.* He kicked, and he kicked again.

Maybe those posers with electric start ain't a bad idea.

But he kept kicking until he was red in the face and sweat dripped from his nose. He took the wet plugs out of the cylinders and realized he hadn't gapped the new ones for his old bike. He put them back in and took in a deep breath.

Hope. He tromped on the kick-starter and heard something. Not much, but he heard hope. Keeping the throttle and the choke in, the next time he tried he heard more hope, then more, and then on the third or fifth time—he really didn't know for sure—Marilyn came to life.

"She's alive!" he yelled with both fists in the air. His laugh was maniacal, reminiscent of Dr. Frankenstein hovering over his monster. "Marilyn lives!" he yelled again.

He rode her around his yard and down the street but didn't get far before Marilyn died. *I never was a mechanic.* He pushed her back home and covered her back up. But this time he didn't bury her.

MaryAnne amazed everyone at the hospital. Sully was amazed, too, but not surprised. In just one week, she had been moved to a general floor with a roommate. Jonesy complained about this, but her doctor said a roommate would help acclimate her back into the world. There was even talk of moving her to the rehab side of the hospital when her last cast was removed.

Sully, thrilled with her success at the hospital and his progress at home, walked a new walk, smiling and even talking to the interns in their short coats and Birkenstocks on his breaks. Sully hated his new white running shoes. He noticed an occasional suit looking in on MaryAnne's sessions which were now downstairs with Sully and the physical therapist.

She used a walker and a balance board with the parallel bars to regain her hip strength and balance. Her ear injury had caused damage to the inner ear. The semicircular canals and the vestibule are the two parts of the inner ear directly involved in helping the body to maintain balance and equilibrium. These were intact, so it was a matter of remapping their pathways in her brain which took time and work—hard, frustrating work. It's one thing for a toddler to learn how to sit up, scoot, crawl, and walk. It's quite another for a fifty-nine-year-old with a litany of injuries.

Dr. C now assigned Sully all the new veteran patients. He'd built quite a reputation, especially because of his work with MaryAnne. He couldn't avoid how the staff room quieted whenever he took his breaks.

He didn't care. When he lay on the mat next to MaryAnne to show her a leg exercise with latex bands, he imagined them in a mound of fresh-cut hay. He saw how the other techs quickly looked away when he helped her to her feet.

He passed the same bulletin board every day he left work and felt free to pause and look at the colorful flyers.

Always

He shook his head when he saw one with Bert and Ernie advertising a Yoga class.

"You should try it." A neatly dressed woman with glasses pointed at the board.

He had seen her before leaving the office at about the same time he walked to Sierra.

"Huh?"

"Yoga, you should try it."

He smirked. "Yeah, right."

"Don't knock it. Even that tough navy SEAL likes it. I'm Dr. Julian, by the way."

Nuts.

"I've noticed you stopping here before. Can I help you with anything?"

Shrinks, never say what they're really thinking.

"No, no. We had a shrink in our regiment. No offense, but we called him the wizard because guys would go see him and disappear."

She smiled. "Uh, I'm not sure what to do with that."

Nothing. Man, they're always analyzing.

"Well, gotta go." Sully had already said too much.

At home he tinkered more with Marilyn. Each time he rode, he got farther down the street and finally got all the way back home without breaking down. There was the usual backfire and stares from onlookers, but he kinda liked it. But more than the looks, he liked the freedom he felt when the wind passed through his hair, the cold against his heart warmed from faith in his machine, his fingers stiffened from the chill, but his thighs warmed pressed against the teardrop gas tank.

A month had passed since MaryAnne was moved to rehab and Sully had taken the tarp off Marilyn. He had the later shift, so he'd ride Marilyn to work. Sully gave himself an extra two hours in case he broke down and avoided the highway. He tied his Harley dew rag on his head and slid on his helmet and favorite amber sunglasses. His gloves had hardened knuckles and his Danner's made for the best riding boots. His leather jacket was cracked from age and a lack of use, much like himself. But it fit good, and when he zipped it up, he felt secure on roads where drivers didn't see him and he could get sideswiped, t-boned, or pushed into the weeds at any turn, intersection, or straightaway. He liked it that way—it was real.

Now, a crotch rocket came up behind him on the two-lane road. Sully couldn't hear him unwinding his gears over his own pipes. The rider didn't signal or slow down when he buzzed by Sully across a double-lined straightaway. A car coming the other way braked, honked long, and even blinked its high beams repeatedly.

"What —?" Sully screamed out loud.

He had always kept his cool while riding, but this unnerved him. A terrible tremble welled up inside him and wouldn't let go. When he looked left, the other rider looked at him through his clear-shielded helmet and laughed. *Jimmy. No, it can't be. Jimmy?* Jimmy had always taken risks, and it would have been just like him to do something this reckless on just this road.

Sully sped up. *I gotta catch him, that little imp. That's Jimmy.* He downshifted into third, a big jump for his old panhead engine, causing the bike to rev. Then he popped the clutch but wasn't ready when his front tire left the pavement. Pulse racing, he pulled the clutch back in, causing the tire to bounce back to earth going at least sixty.

Always

He swerved, skidded, and almost braked, which would have sent him into the woods.

He laid off the levers and straightened out. Jimmy was still ahead. He twisted the throttle and shifted up into fourth again, shooting him forward.

Sully kicked up stones as he followed Jimmy's turn into a tavern's parking lot at the inside corner of the road. His fat, back tire scuffed to a stop. Sully jumped off his bike and ran up to his old friend who had his back to him and his helmet off. He could clearly see his military flat top.

"Jimmy!" he cried as he reached out and pulled on the man's shoulder.

"What, who—?" The biker turned around with a scowl. "You, old man? What? You want a piece of me?"

Sully's expectation turned to bitter rage as his adrenaline boiled over. He quivered uncontrollably but said nothing. This boy was not Jimmy.

"That's what I thought." The biker turned and walked inside.

Tears formed as Sully stumbled back to Marilyn. He started her up on the first kick, and the rest of the ride was a blur. Somehow, he made it to the hospital entrance.

In the past when he got off his bike, he felt like he had already done something, and he hadn't even started work. Now he hardly knew where he was. His vision narrowed, and his senses for the real world grew dim. He felt trapped as if he were the one under the Humvee and not his CO.

"You're here early," Dr. Julian said as she stood changing flyers at the bulletin board.

Sully startled, not realizing he'd entered the building. "Uh-huh ... Where?"

She put a hand on his shoulder. "Sully, are you alright?"

"Huh? Who?"

She frowned, then led him away from the board. "Why don't you come with me?"

Sully didn't argue and followed her through the waiting area and into her office. She handed him bottled water.

"Here, drink this."

Sully sat down and looked at the bottle until she took it back, took off the cap, and returned it to him.

"Drink."

He did as she sat watching him.

Sully noticed her diploma, a picture on her desk with a couple of kids, some sort of military plaque, and a nice seascape painting.

"Did you paint that?" he asked, pointing.

"No."

"Were you in the military?"

She nodded. "Air Force."

"Sorry."

She smiled. "I don't think you're here to kid about service rivalries."

Sully began to feel his familiar defenses rise. "No? Why don't you tell me then? You're the wizard."

"Do you do that a lot?" She sat back against her leather chair and studied him.

"What?"

"Get sarcastic when someone asks a real question?"

Whoa, you're not letting up. But I got nothing. "I dunno. It works for me."

"Does it? It didn't look like it was working just a minute ago. Tell me what was going on out there."

"Nothing." Sully took another sip of the water.

Dr. Julian shifted in her chair but never looked away, never changed her expression.

"So, am I supposed to say something?" he asked.

Always

"Well, tell me what was going on out there."

Sully hated being told to do anything. But when he looked into her eyes, he knew he wasn't being controlled. He knew she was asking because she cared. And she wouldn't go away until she helped. He sipped his water, breathing in and out.

Finally, he said, "I-I saw Jimmy. I rode my bike into work today, and Jimmy passed me. Thing is, Jimmy was the corpsman under me who came home from Iraq in a body bag."

"Sounds awful."

Sully fiddled with the cap to the water bottle. "Last thing I told him when we loaded him on the evac was 'Don't you die on me,' like I was in some John Wayne movie or *Apocalypse Now*. Thing is, he did die, and I brought him home in a box to his parents with full military honors."

"Did you grieve for him?"

Sully scoffed. "If you mean cry, then no. I was in uniform. I didn't need to cry. I grieve for him every day."

"Maybe grief is a good reason to cry."

Sully sighed heavily. "Yeah, maybe."

"I don't know you very well ... is that sarcasm again?"

"I don't even know myself, sometimes. I've been doing it all my life. My family was the best at it. Dinner was a competition. I never won. Then when Stephen got killed, it pretty much sealed things for me." Sully smirked as he looked around the room, anywhere but at her.

"Stephen?"

"Stephen, my brother, Jimmy, my brother-in-arms, and Martha, my wife. Good news, Doc, I cried at her funeral. I wouldn't know where to start with the rest."

"Well-ell, I recommend you start at the beginning."

She drew out her "well" which made Sully smile.

"Okay, Glinda ... you know from the *Wizard of Oz*?"

Dr. Julian sat quietly.

"It's a very good place to start."

When Sully could see his humor wasn't working, he sat quietly too. Together in the silence, he studied the clear globe paperweight on her desk then shifted his focus to the Japanese artwork on a bamboo scroll that reached from eye height to the floor.

"Stephen was a real pain. Not to me, really. Sometimes, but not bad. He liked picking on our sister. He was a few years older, but he really seemed to like picking on Karen. He was stronger and was an athlete, good in school. You know the type—good teeth."

"Teeth?"

Sully looked now at Dr. Julian. "Yeah, good teeth were important in my family. I had crooked ones. Karen had braces. Mom had false teeth. Grandmom too. I hate the dentist. I hate haircuts. And no offense, but I don't like psychologists, either. They all get too close."

"I get that a lot. My supervisor used to say we pick at people's teeth until we find one that hurts, then we pick some more."

"Like *Marathon Man*. You know, Dustin Hoffman?" Again silence. "But Stephen took care of me in his way. I mean he'd pick on me but, like, he'd smother me and try to scare me, but he let me hang around when his friends showed up."

Dr. Julian pulled out a pen and notepad. "Tell me your first memory of him."

"I'm little. I'm so little I'm sitting in the big basket on the front of his bike. He used it for his paper route." Sully shut his eyes. "We're riding down the street, and I feel the

Always

wind. It's warm but it's cold too, in the breeze. I'm free, not a care, not a cause in the world." He opened his eyes again. "Wow." He said the word in a quiet way, not in exclamation, rather in deep reflection.

Something had touched him. Something ... maybe someone ... had reached out and touched his soul.

Sully stared at his water bottle. "When I was a kid, I went camping. We used canvas tents, but in the rain, I touched it on the inside, and water trickled down my hand."

She leaned forward. "That's a pretty good picture of grief."

Sully took a deep breath and continued. "He was so young. I really didn't know it at the time, because I was younger. Wouldn't you know he died on that same bike? He had this round thing about as big as your fist. When you pulled a chain, it rubbed against the tire and sounded like a siren. How cool is that?"

Dr. Julian may have smiled, but Sully couldn't be sure.

"There I was standing on Grover Avenue. The same road we used to ride down together years before. This time, I was standing behind the ambulance, and there was a sheet over his head. Why do they do that? Cover someone's face? He was so close, I could smell him. I reached up and pulled the sheet back. Someone gasped. Someone yanked me by the arm. I didn't know ... I-I didn't know."

The canvas tent burst, and Sully began to cry. Dr. Julian handed him a box of tissues. He started to say something about them being a tool of her trade but stopped short. He took the box and couldn't pull tissues fast enough. He felt himself rocking back and forth on his seat.

"What is it?" Dr. Julian inquired. "What do you see?"

He shook his head from side to side. "I don't know. Not Stephen."

He didn't have the words to describe the image he saw in his mind's eye of what used to be a face with a perfect smile now torn asunder by a three-quarter ton truck's grill, bumper, and front tire.

"Is that the last thing you remember?" Dr. Julian prodded.

"The siren. I mean the one on the ambulance as it drove away. The one on his bike never worked again."

"Tell me about him." Dr. Julian leaned forward.

"He was my protection." Sully wiped a drop of snot from his upper lip. "When I passed by, people would say, 'Leave him alone. He's Stephen's little brother.' I could tell kids about him though. All his accomplishments. Class president. Team captain. I think he even dated the prom queen. People like that don't die. They're not supposed to anyway. And I was to blame."

"How?"

"I know I had nothing directly to do with it, but I just always felt it should have been me. I mean, who am I? Just some skinny little kid with a bad attitude. The world needed Stephen. It sure didn't need me." Sully balled up the tissues in his hand.

"What about your parents? Did they blame you?"

"I really don't know. If I think about it … no. But they never said a thing. Maybe they thought they'd make me feel worse. But nothing? Say *something*." He took the ball of tissues and threw them into the wastebasket beside her desk. "I know they were hurting. We were all hurting. I guess I acted like I was okay, so they let me be. I was so alone. I'd come home from school and hide in my room, the one that used to be Stephen's. I'd come out for dinner and stare across the table at that empty seat. I'd get out of there as fast as I could. I don't think I ate a whole meal at home

Always

until Martha started cooking for me. And at the beginning, some of her cooking, let's say, was a little over-done. But I ate it, every last bit."

Dr. Julian smiled.

"Does that mean we're done, Doc?"

She sat back in her chair, eyebrows raised. "Does it?"

Sully looked at his watch. "It'll soon be time for my shift. Do you think I could come back?"

"Yes."

"I'd like that. Sorry, about all the tissues."

"Danny, it wasn't your fault."

He looked into her eyes. Dr. Julian was half his age and half his size, but he wanted to hug her like he was a kid again.

"It wasn't your fault," she repeated.

He breathed in, nodded, then walked out of the office. He needed to clear his head and begin his work.

After changing into his scrubs, he checked the physical therapy board but noticed MaryAnne was already in the clinic. He walked over to her as she held onto the parallel bars to stretch.

"Hey, MaryAnne with an e."

"Hey, Danny. My room's on the same floor now, the rehab unit, so I came down on my own—on crutches."

She had on a pair of bright sweatpants and a loose, long-sleeved shirt to cover most of her burns. Her hair covered her ear, but the side of her face and neck bore what was left from the accident. The scar across her head remained, but hair had started to grow back.

"You've done wonders, now that your casts and braces are gone," he told her. "Just pace yourself. We don't want you falling. You would have to stay longer."

"That wouldn't be so bad."

Sully thought she was kidding. "Well, let's start you off with your leg strengthening exercises anyway."

"The bands again?"

He nodded and brought over a yellow resistance band, medium strength, demonstrating how to side-step with the band around his ankles. Then he handed the rubber device to MaryAnne.

She complied, speaking as she worked. "They're talking about moving me to a nursing home because of my TBI."

He didn't know what to say. He couldn't picture her with people who couldn't take care of themselves. The worst sights, sounds, and smells seemed unimaginable to him.

"They're saying I could be there for years." She stopped the exercise and looked at him with wide eyes. "Am I that bad?"

"No. Look at me." He stepped closer and rested his hands on her shoulders. "No, you are not. Sure, you don't remember stuff, but you are not a danger to yourself. Look at you now. Sure, you're a gimp, but you're not a helpless gimp."

"Thank you? I think. I'm scared." She sat to take off the band. "I think it's Jonesy. He expects me fully recovered, fully independent, but fully dependent on him. They thought I was ready to talk to him—to help my memory. But things didn't go so well. That man is so possessive. What did I ever see in him? I must have been crazy. Thing is, now that I'm beginning to feel sane, I feel like he is trying to make me crazy. I mean, he's supposed to help me be independent, right? I'm supposed to be dependent on him only, and if I'm not, I'll be banished to a memory unit with people ready to die."

They moved to a balance board supported by a large, half rubber ball. MaryAnne rocked back and forth on the

Always

board. She tried to avoid holding onto the parallel bars but touched them occasionally.

"Remember to look at the horizon, and don't forget to breathe," he reminded her.

"What really scares me is he kept bringing up your name," MaryAnne continued. "He's so jealous, I can't take it. 'Danny is not the issue,' I keep telling him. Last night, I broke down. I told him I knew you from a long time ago when we were just kids. He kept asking if we were lovers. 'I was fifteen!' I screamed. But then I looked at him and said, 'We had something special, and that's the way it will always be.'"

Sully was speechless. MaryAnne got off the balance board, and they stood together as therapists, techs, and patients milled about.

MaryAnne sniffled. "What's next?"

"Let's see." Sully swallowed hard and stared at his clipboard. "The recumbent bicycle."

As MaryAnne stretched her leg over the bike and began to spin, tears formed in her eyes. "Jonesy said to me, 'We will just have to see about your Mr. Sullivan,' and he stormed off. I may not remember him, but I'm pretty sure if he says he's going to do something, he does more."

Sully knew she was right. He put his hand on the back of her seat as she slowly pedaled. "Hey, the most important thing is for you to focus on your health. That's the only thing you have some control over. I'm here, 'K?"

"'K. Side by side?"

"Always."

Sly walked over and handed Danny a slip of paper as MaryAnne finished up. After reading the note, he looked up wide-eyed at Sly.

"Sully, I'll finish up with Ms. Mills."

"What is it?" MaryAnne stretched her neck causing her to wince.

Sully smiled, hoping to alleviate any stress for her. "It's probably nothing, but I have to go."

He handed his clipboard to Sly with the rest of MaryAnne's routine. Sully took her hand and rapidly wrote something in her palm.

He still had the paper crumpled in his hand when he reached the executive suite.

"Mr. Sullivan, they're waiting for you in—"

"I'm aware."

The curtains on the boardroom glass wall shuddered when he closed the door behind him.

"Mr. Sullivan, sit here." The chief surgeon pointed to his left.

"Sir." Sully nodded, sat, then turned to focus on the man sitting across from him. "Mr. Jones."

August 1974

Danny laced up his Adidas on the edge of the stadium steps while teenagers tossed a football around on the field and others jogged around the track. The coach had sent out a summer training routine for getting in shape for lacrosse camp. He knew the workout would be packed with running but that's what he liked. While he may have had some natural talent, mixed with a never quit attitude, he really hadn't done anything aerobic up until now. *This is cake,* he thought as he rounded the third and fourth turns for his first mile. His breathing shortened as did his stride. He passed a couple of kids from the cross-country team at the half-mile, but they overtook him as they headed into the two next turns.

"How you doing?" one of them asked.

"I'm feeling great," he lied. The words took his breath away, but he kept running.

He was hurting. Now his breathing increased even more, and a side stitch began from the mix of talking and running. He stayed with the runners around the final turns, but they left him behind as they lengthened their lead down the home stretch.

His pace slowed to a walk. He managed one more ugly mile before walking home and pouring himself a glass of lemonade ... then another. He had to cut the grass, but he dreaded the old lawn mower with its hard to crank starter cord. This time, it started on the second pull. Cutting a straight swath was boring, so he got creative and cut a big MAB in the grass, but mowed across MaryAnne's initials before anyone else could see his lawn art. After putting away the mower, he got a shower.

Tonight, he had to be at the Anderson House—"Home of Gracious Dining"—by four for his first night. His sister, Karen, was a waitress at the restaurant, and she'd gotten Danny a job as a busboy. "Fifty cents an hour plus tips," she'd told him.

He showed up at three-thirty wearing black pants, a white shirt, and black shoes. The owner, Mr. B, showed him around and explained how and when to clear the tables.

"I'll show you around, but you gotta split your tips with me," Mr. B stated.

Danny looked at the man's white shirt and skinny black tie. What little black hair he had left was slicked back into a short ducktail reminiscent of the fifties. Danny didn't trust someone old with money and short hair.

"I'm kidding, son, I'm kidding." Mr. B slapped him on the shoulder.

Danny just nodded, feeling put off by his odd style.

"Two things ... no, three when it comes to busing tables. First, make sure the customer is done before you pick up anything. Sometimes, they'll go to the bathroom for a long time, or they'll get up and talk to someone—could be me. They don't like to find their dessert gone when they get back. Number two—do not disturb the waitresses' tips.

Always

Don't touch them. Leave the tip on the table, and they will pick it up. And third—the customer comes first."

"Like Gayle Sayers' book," Danny offered.

"Did you read it?" Mr. B. asked.

"Almost."

"Just remember, as far as you're concerned, the customer is always right. Got it?"

"Yessir."

"Did I tell you about the tips?" Mr. B squinted at him.

"Yessir. Leave them on the table."

"Don't touch them. You ever make coffee?" Danny shook his head. "I'll teach you how later. Come on in, and I'll introduce you to the dishwasher, Manny."

They walked through the double doors but almost upended his sister carrying four plates with her hands and forearms.

"Hot plate coming through!" she yelled. "Eighty-six sugar packets and take-out cup lids."

Mr. B pushed Danny against the wall to get out of her way. "Eighty-six means they're all out up front. I'll show you how to restock." He took him to the supply room with boxes stacked on shelves to the ceiling. "The sugar containers at the counters and tables are the waitresses' job at the end of the night, but if you see one low you can earn points by filling them. Remember, all your tips come from the waitresses. That's rule four—don't do anything to upset the wait staff. Got it?"

Danny nodded, and they took the sugar packet box out front and placed it underneath the counter.

"I'll leave you to get acquainted before things pick up. It may seem slow now but don't let that fool you. Keep your bus pans clear. Oh, and don't splash the dishwasher. Is that rule five or six? I lost count." Mr. B looked around his restaurant the entire time he spoke. "Now, what's the most important rule?"

"Rule two ... three ... no two, sir."

Mr. B offered him a quick smile. "Depends who you ask. I say they're all important. But only one will get you fired, maybe two ... or three, depends how bad it is."

Danny was relatively confused at this point, so when Mr. B went to the hostess station to talk to Connie, he drifted to the other side of the restaurant looking for his sister. Instead, he ran into Tony, the other busboy.

"Where's your apron?" the older busboy asked.

"I dunno."

"Go get one from the back."

Danny went through the kitchen and into the supply room again where he found all sorts of linen. He found a white apron, hung in on his neck, and tied the straps around his waist. It draped down below his knees. He noticed the short order cooks laughing as he went back to the dining room.

"Come'ere," Tony called. "Gimme." He motioned for Danny to take off his apron. "That's how a dishwasher wears it. We wear it folded up so we can move quicker and if we need it to soak up a spill at the edge of a table." Tony folded the apron like a tri-fold letter and handed it back to Danny who wrapped the string around his back and made a small bow in the front.

"There, now you at least look like you know what you're doing. Mr. B tell you about your meal?" Danny shook his head. "You can have anything on the menu except steak or lobster."

"All's I want is a club sandwich."

"Good luck with that. The cook'll kill you—too much work. Better stick with a hamburger or a chop steak since you're new."

Always

"What's chop steak?"

"A hamburger without the bun."

Danny frowned. "What's the point?"

"I don't know. Old people order it. Don't ask dumb questions."

Tony looked around the corner and saw customers leaving a table.

"That's you. Oh, and slow is smooth and smooth is fast."

"What's that mean?"

"Just don't break anything, or you bought it. That's my rule, that and don't ask dumb questions—my other rule."

Danny had lost count of the rules he'd been given but went over to the cluttered table with his bus bin and filled it with dirty napkins and crumpled up paper placemats. The pictures of different covered bridges on the placemats caught his attention. *That's neat. Here's one from Monroe County where Auntie and Uncle Vern live.* The mats had almost filled his bin, so he took them out and loaded the glasses. But now he didn't have enough room for the plates, so he took those out too. Finally, he loaded up the plates, then the glasses, and the paper products, and slid the silverware in his bin.

What am I forgetting? The tip. Hmm, funny, no tip.

He hustled his bin to the dishwashing station. He threw the napkins and placemats into the trash can while talking to Mr. B who showed him how to stack. Dottie, a waitress, came up behind Mr. B.

"Did you see my tip?" she asked.

She stood akimbo with her fists clenched against her red apron and bright white uniform bulging at the front buttons.

"No, mum, there was none."

"Mum?" She glared at him. "Are you sure? I thought I saw one."

Mr. B looked over his black horned-rim glasses.

"No, mum." Danny rubbed his neck.

Dottie peered into the trash bin where a five-dollar bill stuck out from one of the mats. "Then, what do you call this?"

Danny was dumbstruck. He looked at the waitress, at the owner, and at the covered bridge near where his uncle lived.

"Better not let that happen again." Dottie stormed off with her five-dollar bill clutched in her hand.

Mr. B held up two fingers. "Like I said Danny, rule number two—most important. But I know it was an honest mistake."

Mr. B went on to show him how to load the silverware without splashing Manny before heading back to his office. Danny hung his head as he dropped the knives, forks, and spoons into a large round tin of soapy water.

"Don't let Dottie get to you, kid. We've all been there," Manny said.

Danny went back out front but tried to avoid Dottie for the rest of the dinner shift which was difficult to do at the busy, narrow counter. He thought she had forgiven him until the end of the night when the other waitress tipped him five dollars, but Dottie stiffed him.

Karen had been working the dining room side of the restaurant and gave him a ride home.

"So, what are you going to do with all that money?"

"You mean my five dollars? Hey, can you pull into the pharmacy?"

"Why? You want an ice-cream soda? I could have made you one at the restaurant after Mr. B left."

"No, I need something."

Always

The pharmacist dispensed drugs perched on one side of the store. In the back, a long counter and stools stood where older kids scooped ice cream or sodas or both. *I bet I could work here someday and make great tips.*

Danny strode down the middle aisle and found some stationery with matching envelopes. *Light brown ... beige, I think it's called. Guess this is okay for a guy.* He took his selection to the front. The stationery was just short of five dollars, so he bought some Good & Plenty candy and baseball cards with some stale gum inside.

"Why'd you buy stationery?"

"No reason."

"MaryAnne?"

Danny reluctantly nodded. "Her father doesn't like me."

"Dads are like that sometimes. Just be nice."

"I am."

"Danny, look at me. I mean it. *Be nice.*"

"Geeze, already. I am, I am. It's just that I haven't heard from her, and I'm pretty sure it's because of her dad. Don't tell anyone, okay?"

Karen pulled back out onto the main road home. "That's tough. One thing I know about you, you're not a quitter. I'd drive you on a date if you want sometime."

The idea of going on a real date with MaryAnne seemed next to impossible—after all she lived hours away. Danny still worried about what his friends and family would think. He was too easily embarrassed, too self-conscious. He couldn't even talk about a girl to anyone, including his friends. He wished he were Catholic so he could go to confession and talk to the priest. But what did he know about girls?

In the fifth grade, he had planned on meeting a girl at the movie theater. They were going to sit together at the nickel matinee, but when he saw his buddies, he left the girl alone on the sidewalk and walked home. In some ways, he was still in fifth grade.

"Remember, don't tell anyone," he said to Karen as he shut the car door and headed for his room.

His parents sat in the living room as he entered, Dad reading a magazine and Mom knitting.

"How was your first day?" his mother asked.

"Good," Danny called over his shoulder on his way to his room.

He tore off his white shirt stained with gravy, spaghetti sauce, and something called tapioca. Even his pants smelled like the dishwasher. He had washed his hands at the restaurant, but he couldn't wash off five hours of other people's garbage.

After throwing his restaurant clothes into the hamper and putting on his worn jeans, he sat down with his new stationery.

Dear MaryAnne,

Guess what? I'm a working man! I have a job at a restaurant as a busboy. I get tips, and they said next week I'll get a paycheck, but it's only fifty cents an hour. I'm going to save for a ten-speed, but tonight I bought stationery and Good & Plenty. Oh, and baseball cards. I don't even collect them anymore, but I had ten cents left. I'll do better next time.

I work with all sorts of people at the restaurant, and I call them by their first names even if they're older than my parents. Except Mr. B. He knows my sister who works there, and he knows my father because they go to Rotary Club together. He's a little weird, but he acts like he likes me, and he's my boss, so I smile and try not to say anything dumb.

Always

Tonight, I had a bunch of tables to bus at once. The waitress wanted me to make more coffee, and both of my bus bins were full. Coffee is in these huge urns, so tall I can't even see in them. I just fill these big strainers with coffee, then turn on the water, and make sure the burners are lit. Before long, blackwater comes out the bottom. Here's the weird thing—people drink it and tell me how good it is. Who knew I could make coffee? My mom drinks tea, but that's another story. Old men sit at the counter smoking cigarettes and eating pie. I was so hungry surrounded by all that food and not a drop to eat. "Water, water everywhere and not a drop to drink." I don't know where that's from, but it almost fits, right?

So, can you tell I'm happy? People counted on me, I learned new stuff and met so many different people. I met Herman, the short-order cook who works in Wildwood during the summer and makes more money there than he makes all fall, winter, and spring at the restaurant. I met Connie, who everybody says has a crush on Mr. B. But Mr. B is married and he's rich. I mean he must be, he drives a Cadillac and owns a big restaurant with a huge parking lot.

Tonight, before it got busy, I had to go outside and sweep cigarette butts into a little dust bin with a long handle. Boring. But then Manny told me I had to empty the trash can in the trash room. You have to go outside, then into this dark room with one lightbulb. I hit the switch when I opened the door and huge rats tried to climb the walls to run from the light. Sounds like a sermon, right? I hate rats, so I shut the door. Then I opened it and dumped my trash and ran. Manny came up behind me and locked me in the walk-in fridge! They do it to all the new workers, even the waitresses. But some of them quit. Imagine that.

Tips are everything to waitresses. Some even have kids at home that depend on them. I know because I almost threw away Dottie's kid's college tuition. Let's just say

Dottie's keeping a close eye on me these days. Boy, I can't believe I've written so much. It's almost eleven-thirty, and I'm not even tired. I can't wait till next week—lacrosse starts soon, so I'll be plenty busy.

But hey, don't be fooled. No matter what, I can't wait until I see you again—next week or next year or a hundred years from now.

Danny took out the other lined page he had already started and folded it into his new stationery. He looked at his last line and the space left on the paper before signing his name at the bottom and folding everything into the matching envelope. He raised the envelope to his lips but put it down and took out the last page, staring at his signature.

Danny took his pen and in the space above his name he wrote "*Love.*" He took a moment to remember what he had done for eternity, what line he had crossed, and how his life would never be the same since the moment she thrust out her hand, giggled, and remarked to her sister she thought the awkward boy on the bluff was cute. The only difference now was he wrote it down, recorded for history. He meant for it to always be.

The hopeful, young athlete stayed faithful to his workout regimen and MaryAnne. He learned to pace himself better while running. He still left everything he had on the track and drank as much lemonade or iced tea as he could and watched every summer rerun on TV. He had all but given up hope of ever getting a letter from MaryAnne. Two months had gone by already.

"Guess who got a letter?" Karen teased him one day. "Guess who got a letter?"

Always

Danny tore into the dining room where all the mail lay on the table. He sifted through it but saw no letter addressed to him. Just when he thought his sister had played a mean trick, he turned to see his mother.

"I put it on your desk so no one would bother you."

Danny tore into his room, grabbed his letter, and tore it open before flopping onto his bed. While lying on his back with both arms stretched to the ceiling, he began to read.

> Dear Danny,
>
> I've written to you since I got home, but I never heard back. I can't believe you would have forgotten me and thought maybe you have the wrong address. Maybe I wrote it down wrong, and some other girl is getting your letters and is writing back to you. I'm sad to think that could be true, but at least you would be happy. I just don't know what else to think. I put my letter to you in our mailbox before going to school and I always check it when I come home but again no letter from you. ~~I will keep writing for a hundred years.~~

Danny stopped when he saw the crossed-out sentence. *That's weird,* he thought, before reading on.

> I hope you made the lacrosse team and love it. I think lacrosse is better than football. Around here, kids play it all the time, so I'm glad your school finally got a team. For me, homework is enough. I'm studying hard because I want to be a nurse. Biology is hard and Chemistry is even harder, but I just have to try harder, right?
>
> Anyway, I got a job sitting with old people in my neighborhood. It doesn't pay very much, but they told me it's good experience that colleges like to see. I give them their meals, even give them their medication, and help them do things. Other people might think it's gross, but I think it's an honor.

Mrs. Sheila lived on the corner and owned a cat that kept her company. She called it Kat. She had bedsores that I had to clean. But I was fine with it. She hardly ever talked, but she looked up at me and whispered, "Thank you, Angel." Yesterday, she died. She's in a better place, I know, but I hope she knows someone here still misses her. I realize now how important that is, especially now that everyone has someone that misses them, even if it's their cat. (I know you are a dog person.)

I should get back to my studies. Sorry I'm not a good writer.

Danny rolled over, propped himself up on his elbows, and read the letter again.

Funny, the paper is torn and there's no signature. I wonder if it's because I signed Love on my last letter? No, she said she never got any letters.

Then he saw a tiny, curved arrow at the bottom of the torn page. On the other side was a message in block letters.

MY DAD FOUND ME WRITING THIS LETTER. HE TOLD ME IF I PROMISED NEVER TO WRITE TO YOU AGAIN, I COULD READ YOUR LAST LETTER. IT WAS TORN AT THE BOTTOM. HE SAID IT'S NO USE TRYING ANYMORE. HE SAID HE BURNED ALL OUR OTHER LETTERS AND INSISTED WE STOP BECAUSE HE KNEW I WAS CRYING AND SAID THIS IS FOR THE BEST. *Always* I AM SO SORRY. THAT'S WHY I CROSSED OUT THE LINE IN THE BEGINNING.

Danny sat motionless, reading the back print over and over again. *Her signature was torn away. Why is Always stuck in the middle in cursive?* He was certain it would be the last time he would ever hear from her for a hundred years. But he knew just what *Always* meant.

May 2021

Sully took the same seat as before in the glass conference room, and Jonesy sat across from him. This time three new suits sat next to Jonesy, each with a stack of papers in front of them. Again, Dr. Armstrong, the chief surgeon, was the first to speak, but his tone was much different.

"Several things have changed since our last meeting, I think we can all agree. First, I want an update from our neurologist." He nodded at his colleague.

"Gentlemen, ladies, after two months of multiple surgeries and therapies, Ms. Mills has vastly improved physically," the neurologist began. "She can walk unassisted, and she is capable of using the facilities, shall we say, and feeding herself. Her balance is still problematic. Her skin is still healing, but as far as the hospital is concerned, she meets the criteria for outpatient services."

"Yes, yes," the chief said excitedly, waving his hand. "We all know that. What about her mental facilities? Can she care for herself?"

The neurologist looked at the neuropsychologist. "Dr. Podd can best answer that question."

Dr. Podd looked at her notes, swallowed hard and began. "Ms. Mills's short-term memory is questionable.

Her ability to take in new information, retain it, and recall it, continues to be poor. While she has learned through repetition, like how to find her way around the hospital, verbal information is difficult for her to retain, and abstraction is exceptionally poor. On the positive side, she is a visual learner, her procedural memory is strong, and her long-term memory has improved with the obvious exception."

Jonesy jumped out of his chair. "Sure, it is! The obvious exception is the last forty years."

"Sit down," the chief surgeon said, his voice authoritative, his eye contact firm. "And this time keep those rings off my table."

Wow, Boss, I'm beginning to like you.

"Please continue, Dr. Podd, and explain what you mean. Put it in a picture for those of us less psychologically minded."

Pretty sure he's not just talking about me this time.

"Yes, Mr. Jones, she doesn't recall most of the last forty years. She does know your name. As far as her relationship with you, she knows she was involved with you, but at the same time remains in denial. It's like she cannot see what is right in front of her because in her mind it's still an impossibility. Yet, her childhood, her developmental years, family of origin, all good."

Dr. Armstrong shifted in his chair. "What about this procedural memory you mentioned?"

"She remembers how to do things she has learned in the past forty years, but she still cannot retain most new procedures without repetition. She is vulnerable. She could get lost, not know her way back, and would have difficulty recognizing danger. Lastly, sir, she's scared—really scared."

"Scared?"

Always

"She's afraid she's going crazy. She's afraid of regressing, and ... and she's afraid of ... of Mr. Jones."

Now no one said a thing. Jonesy stared straight ahead, straight past Sully.

The chief looked at the neurologist and Dr. Podd. "Can one of you tell me how long?"

Dr. Kay, the neurologist spoke up. "I wish I knew. It's not unprecedented. It could be years." Kay looked at Podd and back to Armstrong. "It could be never."

"Never?" Jonesy fell back into his chair.

The neuropsychologist shrugged.

Dr. Armstrong nodded. "Okay, got it. So, this is where we are. We have a patient who meets outpatient criteria but is likely unsafe at home because she will not know where she is. This by itself wouldn't be insurmountable. She could learn through, as you say, repetition. She could receive in-home nursing care, but she's a flight risk. The problem is her fear, whether real or imagined. I suspect some of it's real. I'm a little afraid of Mr. Jones also." He smiled.

No one laughed. Jonesy squinted at Sully as the three suits began shuffling their papers.

"Solution, people, present a viable solution." Dr. Armstrong now rapped the table.

Sully hadn't noticed the older woman sitting at the end of the table until she smiled and spoke softly. "As the assigned case worker, I've investigated a number of very nice long-term care facilities that specialize with memory units. They're costly, for sure. The problem is Ms. Mills has refused any of these options for fear they would become permanent. Frankly, I don't blame her. The units won't take her unless she is voluntary and well, they are costly. Only certain hospitals, the state hospital for example, will take—"

"What?" asked the chief, leaning in. "Please speak up."

The social worker collected herself, then spoke more loudly. "Commitments. The state hospital will take commitments to their geriatric building. It's a complicated process for those who are otherwise healthy, but incompetent to manage their own affairs. It's not something I endorse. The courts look unfavorably upon it. The law has safeguards to assure we no longer warehouse people, which I believe is what we would be doing if we pursued commitment."

Mr. Jones stood again. "Well, something needs to be done."

"Mr. Jones." The firm rebuke was all that was needed from the surgeon. Jonesy sat down. "Sir, you brought your team from your law firm. The floor is yours, but please take full advantage of the chairs we have provided you. This is not *Perry Mason*."

The first lawyer spoke up. "Mr. Joel Atborough, lead counsel for Mr. Jones. For the past month, we've managed to clear the hurdles, or I should say the state's safeguards. While it's true the process is lengthy and complicated for most, we've managed to expedite the process. Before me are the documents legally obtaining guardianship of Ms. Mills. You may know this type of arrangement as a conservancy."

"Power of attorney?" Dr. Armstrong's voice went higher.

"No, sir. Mr. Jones has had POA since before the accident. This is much more. This basically states her care is now entirely within his purview." The lawyer nodded toward his boss Jonesy.

"You can't do that." Sully had shown incredible restraint but could no longer contain himself.

"But we can, sir, and we did," the second lawyer said. "County Protective Service, CPS, was petitioned and

Always

guardian ad litem within the legal system was appointed to take care of all Ms. Mills's decisions for her."

"Who ... who is her guardian?" Sully asked.

"That would be me, Mr. Brian Smythe," the third suit spoke up.

"And who might you be, Mr. Smythe?" asked the chief.

"Junior counsel at Jones, Jones & Tate."

"What judge in his right mind appointed independent counsel from the fiancé's own law firm?" The chief's voice had gone even higher.

"Old golf partner." Jonesy just smiled and gestured like he'd just made a putt. "My connections run deep, and I'll do anything to protect my world."

Sully felt sick. *He gets an old golfing buddy from the club to hear his fiancée's case and actually thinks he's protecting her?*

"I see," said Dr. Armstrong. "If you've covered all your bases, then I'm assuming the appropriate specialists, psychiatrists, forensic psychologists, et al., have already conducted their examinations and filed their reports?"

"That's what you see in front of me," stated Smythe.

The social worker cried out, "You've just done an endrun and made a mockery out of the entire health care. You managed to turn back the clock forty years."

"Ironic, ain't it, Doc? 'Cause it's like the forty years Mary can't remember." Jonesy sat back and crossed his arms.

Sully could see from the looks on the faces around the table that Jonesy's words disgusted everyone. Even Gucci's own lawyers looked embarrassed. Sully's insides burned.

The chief surgeon knew when the battle was over. He'd probably made a career of fighting battles that were worthy and winnable, something Sully had never mastered. But this one couldn't be won.

Dr. Armstrong looked at his team. "W-when can she be moved?"

One of Gucci's suits spoke up. "We've arranged for transportation to Boughton State Hospital. An ambulance should be arriving this afternoon."

Sully snarled, his fists clenched. *Box ambulance. I hate those.*

Armstrong shook his head. "Seems like you've thought of everything."

"Not quite," stated Jonesy. "What about him?" He pointed at Sully.

"Mr. Sullivan is our concern, not yours." Now Armstrong's voice grew in volume.

"Not exactly," the lead counsel stated. "In front of me is a petition for a civil lawsuit against this facility for unethical treatment leading to delayed care. Because of a duplicity of roles—a clear conflict of interest—Mr. Sullivan managed, in our opinion, to deny proper care that could have restored Ms. Mills's memory. If his continued presence hadn't complicated her therapy, she may have been going home today, instead of the unfortunate condition of being committed for the unforeseeable future. Furthermore, his lack of formal training goes against standard of care protocol for which the hospital is negligent."

"Now hold on a dang minute! You were the one who insisted I be involved in her care." Sully pitched forward in his seat.

"Ironic, eh, old man?" Jonesy never flinched. The only thing that changed was his sardonic smile.

"You're saying I'm the cause? Me?" Sully pointed now at the best dressed man in the room. "It's you, you're the one that ran off the road and almost killed MaryAnne. You're the one that caused her to regress every time you forced

Always

yourself on her, and now, you're the one that's throwing her away." Sully pounded the table, punctuating every time he said "one" with a rap on the polished mahogany.

Armstrong placed a hand on Sully's forearm, and he leaned back slightly, breathing heavily. Jonesy sat back with his hands folded across his Armani silk tie decorated with a gold chain.

"What are you seeking?" the chief asked.

"We will be looking for compensatory damages in the neighborhood of—"

The lead lawyer stopped when Jonesy stretched his hand across the lawyer's chest. "Dismiss Mr. Sullivan today, and we will drop the matter."

The chief turned to Sully.

Sully looked him in the eye. "Sir, I have worked here quietly for the last ten years. I kept my head down and the water in my bucket clean. I've never set foot in this room, not with people in it, anyway, until all this was laid in my lap. But I'm glad it was. I have no regrets for my behavior with the patient. I am resigning immediately, and while I apologize for withholding information from this hospital, I acted alone. No one else knew about my prior relationship with MaryAnne. I resign."

Sully stood and opened the door to leave. He was met by hospital security who held a box containing some official papers, his jacket, his helmet, even his tuna fish sandwich and one napkin. *They already planned to fire me. The chief surgeon lost nothing to that idiot. The brass always come out on top.*

Sully grabbed the box away from security and walked through the closest exterior door into the parking lot. His cell phone lit up as he walked to his bike.

"Danny, it's me," said MaryAnne through the phone. "I called your number you wrote on my palm. They're packing up my things. I overheard Sly and Dr. C talking. An ambulance is coming to take me away. I'm getting committed to a state hospital."

"I know, Angel. I just found out myself." Sully extended his stride and picked up his pace.

"What should I do? I can't go there, I won't. The last time I gave in, it was to my dad, and I never saw you again." She sounded just like she'd sounded over forty years ago. "We have to do something."

Sully stopped by his bike, thinking on his feet. "Remember where the housekeeping locker rooms are?"

"No, not really."

"Think now, just breathe. We walked down there, and I showed you my locker and my old cleaning cart with the flags?"

"I think so."

"It's just down your hall to the right. Go in there. There's a tall laundry basket with housekeeping uniforms."

"Okay."

"Put on a custodial smock and hat. Then get a cart, not mine, out of the janitor's closet and push it down the hall to the first fire exit you see. You'll see lots of people at the intersection, but no one will bother you. I'll be waiting outside."

He hung up the phone, worried he was asking too much of her. Sully knew they would be watching him from the door. He dropped his box in a dumpster, then put on his jacket, helmet, shades, and gloves. He straddled his bike, reached down to turn the key, and turned on the gas line, making sure the bike was in neutral.

Don't fail me now, Marilyn.

He jumped on the kick-starter. Nothing.

Always

Nuts. Come on, baby. Just one, give me just one, old girl.

He pulled out the choke, jumped a second time, and the sweet sound of his '72 Panhead roared and readied itself. He put her in first and headed around the building toward the rear exit, but instead of turning left, he ducked in behind a second set of dumpsters across from the exit door. Sully kept his bike idling in neutral with the kickstand down to rest his legs.

He imagined MaryAnne limping down the hall, using the patient hall railings for support. He could see her reading the sign and going into the locker room, no problem.

Maybe she fumbled. Maybe she tried several times, but just maybe, just maybe she got there. She may have even smiled when she put a uniform on over her clothes. I hope she finds a hat. She'll forget to close the door, so what? Now just grab a cart, use it for balance, and head out again, past the busy hall, your hair tucked under the cap, with everyone going on their break to the cafeteria. After all, no one notices housekeeping. And keep on walking to the door.

Outside the loudspeaker barked, "Code Silver, Code Silver, female, long brown hair, fifty-nine years old. I repeat, Code Silver, Code Silver."

Nuts. Now everyone is looking for you.

Sully started to sweat. His heart pounded fiercely, and his head pounded with every beat. He took off his helmet.

Come on, come on. Where could you be?

As he stared at the door, he saw it move, and he waved. An alarm blared. MaryAnne came out and limped toward him, holding a backpack with her things.

He put on his helmet without buckling it, kicked up the stand and shifted into first. But someone else came through the door as he moved closer.

Hurry, MaryAnne, hurry.

"Sully, no! MaryAnne, wait," his friend John yelled.

Other people came through the door, but now MaryAnne was next to him.

"I like your motorcycle."

"It's not a motorcycle, baby, it's a chopper." He smiled at her through his helmet. "I always wanted to say that."

John hustled across the parking lot with others following.

Putting her leg across the low bike proved difficult. Sully pulled on her pant leg to help her on and handed her his helmet. He popped the clutch and took off just as John grabbed for his handlebars. Sully split the group that had come through the door.

"No! Don't do it!" John yelled, but it was too late.

He'd done it. They'd done it ... together. As Sully approached the exit of the parking lot, the ambulance for the state hospital came through the gate, occupying the guard's attention.

The two teenage kids careened out of the parking lot, ducked under the security gate coming down on them and never looked back. Sully was no Steve McQueen—he didn't have to jump barbed wire—but they had broken free from their own Stalag Luft III. He drove the back roads back toward his place while MaryAnne held on tight. He was sixteen again, in the mountains, saving the one person who'd saved him.

He pulled over at the tavern to give MaryAnne a chance to get a jacket out of her backpack and helped her buckle the helmet. He gave her his extra gloves from his bike's front bag, then he hugged her. Like two teens unaware of anyone else, they held tight to each other in the middle of the stone parking lot while cars filed past.

"I guess we should get going," he said.

"I guess," replied MaryAnne. "So now what?"

September 1974

A hundred years revolved in his head. Danny lay on his bed for some time and looked at his lacrosse stick in the corner. He stood, grabbed the piece of equipment, and walked outside to his makeshift goal in front of the garage wall. Next to him sat a bucket of balls he spilled across the cinder-flaked driveway. Danny scooped a ball into the basket at the end of his stick and tossed it into the net. When he missed, he ran to where it bounced and shot again. He shot, scooped, cradled, missed, and caught to near exhaustion. Lacrosse was the only thing that stopped his endless circle of thinking.

A hundred years.

"Dinner, Danny!" his mother yelled.

He waved but kept playing until all the balls were in the net. Then he pulled at the netting until all the balls spilled down the driveway, and he started all over again. He saw his father on the edge of the grass and his mother at the kitchen window. Danny's T-shirt and even his pants were soaked with sweat, and he could barely see the balls when he fired again. He figured there'd be times when he wouldn't see the net in a game either. He lurched at the last second for a rebound and fell to his knees depleted.

Danny.

He tried to ignore it.

Fred.

"What?" he asked out loud.

You're scaring your mom.

Danny didn't question the voice. He collected what lacrosse balls he could find and went inside.

"Get yourself a shower," his mom told him. "Your dinner is in the fridge. Do you have homework?"

"Not really."

They both knew he did but said nothing as he went into the bathroom and showered until he nearly drowned in hot soapy water.

He worked hard that year and eventually got to start in a few games. Danny even made a few friends on the team. He learned to hang out and do stuff without ever really saying anything about himself. He and his friends ate pizza and drove around on the weekends. They had their own jokes and laughed at most people they didn't know but clammed up when a pretty girl walked by. A friend set him up with a date for the prom at the end of the year. He slow danced, listened to her talk about college, but spent most of the time joking with his friends.

During the last dance, his date, in a long, purple gown and contrasting boa asked him, "So what about you? You going to college?"

"I dunno." It had been his longest sentence the whole night.

So, what about you? The thought repeated itself to him again and again.

The next day, he applied to a small school that had just started a lacrosse team. College went by quickly. He played

Always

freshman lacrosse, but the next year he put away his stick when he knew he would never get much playing time. A week away from graduating, he found himself on one knee proposing to his college sweetheart, Martha.

She's really nice. He heard inside his head. *You don't want to lose her too, do you?*

He graduated, married, then worked. Danny worked hard and harder. He took an entry level job crunching numbers for an accounting firm. He had no windows, no walls, but he decorated his cubicle with pictures of his sister's babies, trout caught on the end of a fly, and chopper motorcycles.

Everyone said he was crazy when he joined the navy after the US decided to defend Kuwait in '91, but all he could think about was Old Joe at the end of the Legion bar. Martha didn't understand, either, but she didn't object.

"Maybe this will make you happy," she said.

But Danny wasn't looking for happiness. He'd enlisted for his uncle Vern, to make a difference.

He thought he was doing both until he ended up in Iraq, trying to decide if he should have used his med kit on locals who were on the wrong end of IEDs or conserve his supplies for his men. He never guessed right even when he tried to save a kid in the middle of a gun fight. But when he knelt over an Iraqi farmer, the dying man reached for Danny's 9-mil and would have shot him if Jimmy hadn't stepped on his hand before he bled out.

But it wasn't the blood or even the dying that disturbed him most. It was the *why*. As soon as he landed in Al Assad, the largest mobile trucking depot in the world, he couldn't ignore the containers filled with supplies. When he ran around the base for PT, physical exercise, he'd read the names out loud, "KBR, IAP, Environmental

Chemical Corporation. Look, there's Blackwater USA." And the alphabet continued, "AMEC, AECOM, Lockheed Martin. Triple Canopy, I've heard of them. Spooky. CACI International, Tyco International, Boeing Company. This is corporate America on wheels, everyone including Zenith is here."

But when he saw the Oshkosh Truck, he thought of the Oshkosh B'Gosh overalls his nephew wore and felt dirty.

Back at his tent, he asked Jimmy, "Why, man? Why are we here?"

"Because we got on a C-130, and this is where it ran out of gas." Jimmy rolled over on his cot. "Man, this isn't about freedom. What's it about? Oil."

Danny sighed. "I guess it's about money. All those rich contractors, getting richer while we keep dying."

"Dude, you think too much."

"Yeah, I've heard that before," Danny said, and returned to cleaning his kit, readying himself for the next day, the day after, and the day he got on a bird for the last time with his only buddy in a box.

After he'd walked off his last C-130, Martha tried, his world distracted him, and work hounded him. The dreams didn't start right away, but the anger did. His temper flared, and he shrank. He collected emergency supplies and kept them behind his truck seat. His go-bag had everything he needed except a firearm. Other than his uncle's pre-'64 Model 70 and his Browning shotgun, he swore-off weapons. He went hunting, but when he shot a doe and saw her yearling run into the snowy woods, he put away his gun.

At home, he remodeled their house, but what he was really doing was fortifying his FOB, Forward Operations Base, like they did downrange. He built a six-foot wood fence around their yard. At night, he'd walk the perimeter,

Always

sometimes with his Browning, before he could sleep. But sleep proved fitful at best and often ended with Martha shaking him awake and holding him until dawn.

When he was at work, he kept his head low, his nose clean, laughed at office clichés but knew he had become one. No one got his dark humor. Gallows humor connected him to his boys in the combat zone but made him a pariah back home. People dispersed at the coffee machine when he approached. People grew quiet in the breakroom when he sat down. Nowhere could he find peace. The satisfaction of a job well-done eluded him. He managed a nice pension, people said nice things, but he knew he'd never see his coworkers again, even before the retirement cake with too much frosting was gone.

He cried like a baby when he got the news about Martha. He had no tears left when they handed him a box of green ashes and told him to pick out a suitable urn. *One that Martha would like.* He didn't know what *suitable* meant so he spread her ashes amongst her flowers and butterflies instead, then went inside, turned over the house to family, got in Sierra, and found a trailer no one could see from the road.

He made the usual excuses at the holidays, got a certain enjoyment from Dickens's *The Christmas Carol* in black and white, but as a strict rule, never watched *It's a Wonderful Life*. For some unknown reason, his only satisfaction came from the saddest of Bluegrass music from the rural pre electrification era and the only thing of interest was when Hurricane Florence came through and took part of his roof. He built a new one with the insurance check and gave the rest to a little boy in Africa who didn't have a roof or walls.

Boredom took over. Kat wasn't giving him much feedback. Even introverts need some contact, so he took the part-time custodial job at the hospital and assumed he would live out what was left of his miserable life in desperate anonymity. He filled his spare time cursing at people who didn't know any better from the inside of his truck, making fun of most everyone on TV, and picking apart plot lines of the latest *NY Times* bestseller. "How do they print such drivel?" And he'd throw the book in the corner before he finished.

Kat hid, and the books piled up. After a while, he stopped noticing inside as well as outside and did what he had to do to get one day closer to Martha, Jimmy, and Stephen.

Thoughts of suicide became so commonplace—he didn't even think of them as suicide. They were simply another stage of life, a means to an end. Driving into a tractor trailer was a nightly thought, but then, he'd remember that Kat needed to be fed. *And what about the poor sucker in the truck who'd feel like it was his fault or something? Maybe jump from that overpass instead.* But then the deed still ended with a truck running over him, so he gave up on that idea too.

He came upon the old bridge when he'd driven across the new bridge one day. It was the same bridge he'd driven across countless times in the dark, but in the dark, he never saw the old stone abutment fifty feet down the hill.

I could fly down the road, maybe in bad weather, so no one would suspect. Lock the cruise control, unbuckle my belt, even move to the middle so the airbag would miss me. In the winter, the ground would be hard, so it wouldn't slow me down. No one would know.

Danny figured they'd assume he was trying to get to work because he had never been late. *Sure, I'm an experienced driver, but hey, I'm not getting any younger, and everyone*

Always

knows my reactions aren't what they used to be. He could hear the conversations at work. John would be bothered, but there were plenty of other dying people to occupy his head.

He thought about writing a note for weeks, but he really wanted people to think it was an accident and figured that was better than a note. But he found himself writing one anyway, then tore it up.

Danny left the ripped-up note on the counter for days. Then he heard the forecast, saw the sleet coming down, and knew his shift started in a few hours. *It has to be tonight. Tonight, I end the madness, the lies. Tonight, I stop being the poser I accused everyone else of being.*

He gave Kat her canned food, made sure her litterbox was clean, and put out extra helpings of dry cat food. She wouldn't eat dry food unless she got really hungry, but it would keep until someone finally came. On his desk, he placed the unlocked metal box with insurance and retirement papers ... even the name and envelope for his prepaid burial plot. The idea of being cremated was a nonstarter since Iraq. Before he walked out of his house for the last time, he grabbed the note and burned it in a metal trash can. Then he left an inside light on for Kat, left his front door unlocked, and climbed into Sierra.

Sully came to when slush pellets smacked across his windshield, and his plans were thwarted when the line of cars had slowed to a crawl. He knew his plan was over when he saw the Humvee's front end crumpled against the stone abutment where he was supposed to die. His eyes focused when he saw the woman with brown hair being loaded onto the ambulance and his heart beat once more when he first saw her in the hospital.

But hope awoke when she called out, "Fred."

May 2021

After winding through the back roads, slowing down at each little town, even passing a cop snoozing at a speed trap, Sully pulled into his lane, down over the hill and between the trees. He put down the kickstand, shut off the engine, looked at this trailer, and sighed. He helped MaryAnne avoid burning her leg as she got off and pushed Marilyn into the storage shed. He pulled out a cooler, shut and locked the door tight, and headed toward his home.

He turned back to MaryAnne and opened his front door. "It ain't much, I gotta warn you."

She smiled then said, "Oh, who is this?"

"Kat."

"That's what an old person on my street used to call her cat."

"I know. You wrote about her."

She looked up at him. "And you remembered."

"I remember everything."

Kat pressed against MaryAnne's leg and rubbed her ears against her pants. "How come she has two food bowls?"

Sully had never put away the extra bowl. It was a painful reminder that both he and Kat hadn't touched. "Oh that? That's a long story for some other time."

MaryAnne straightened and walked over to a wall of pictures. "Is this Martha?"

"Yup." He pointed to several. "That was our wedding day. There's my nephew."

"You must be proud. Half the wall is him."

Sully didn't answer but got busy filling the cooler with what little food he had. He went to the bedroom and found his navy duffle tucked high and in the back of an over-stuffed closet. He jammed all sorts of coats, insulated overalls, hats, mittens, and most of his clothes and a few toiletries.

When he reappeared, he wore a navy peacoat he'd bought at a yard sale and the duffle strapped over his shoulder. MaryAnne had changed out of her hospital garb into a pair of jeans and a top.

"My sailor." MaryAnne smiled, and he saluted sheepishly.

"I've been thinking as I packed. It won't be long before they find this place. I only gave a PO box when I took the job at the hospital. I like to stay off the grid. But knowing Jonesy, I'm sure he'll find some way of finding this place, so we have to leave."

"We didn't do anything wrong."

"Not unless kidnapping is no longer a crime."

"I came willingly."

"But, MaryAnne ... how can I put this? You were declared ... incompetent. No judge is going to see any decision you make as independent. Jonesy was given the authority to make all your decisions, and he's going to use the full extent of his power to get you back. From what I saw, he's not afraid to bend the law for his means."

Sully pulled down the steps to his attic and reemerged carrying a square tin box.

Always

"We have plenty of cash. I can't use my credit card again. Come to think of it, we can't use our cell phones either, so leave it here."

"Won't your nephew be worried?"

"Not for a while."

He loaded Sierra with his duffle, the cooler, a bunch of tools, and old camping gear. He noticed MaryAnne had come out of the house holding Kat.

"Can't leave her behind—" She stopped when she saw Sully holding his rifle and shotgun. Her mouth gaped open.

He hastened to reassure her. "For hunting, honest. I wouldn't do anything crazy."

MaryAnne nodded, then the three got in the truck and left the mildewed single-wide trailer without looking back.

"You haven't told me where we're going," MaryAnne said from the passenger seat. She was bundled up, still cold from her bike ride.

"The heat will take some time to warm up."

They drove in silence for a spell. He knew she was waiting for an answer.

"I got an idea. It came to me when I pulled out the camping gear."

"It's been a while since I went camping," she said. "Maybe forty years or more. Maybe I was under a rock with a cute teenager."

Sully looked over at her smile. *My angel.*

"Don't worry about that. I just thought there might be stuff in there we might need—stove, lantern, stick matches, maybe even the plates and sandwich press for over a fire. I'm thinking the farm."

"Your aunt and uncle's place?"

"It's mine now. I haven't been back since Martha died, but I locked it up and gave your uncle the key."

"Uncle Bill?" MaryAnne put her hand to her mouth. "How do you know he's still alive?"

"You remember Uncle Bill. That's good."

MaryAnne held her head. "I remember being there once. You were there."

Danny now held her hand. "He was alive at Christmas. He sends me a Christmas card every year, telling me he misses me and that the farm is still there. I couldn't call him tonight in case they trace my call history, so I don't know if he'll be there or not."

"Danny, I'm feeling pretty worn out."

MaryAnne slid against him and lay her head on his shoulder and fell asleep.

"I'll bet you are, I'll bet you are."

Pangs of guilt shot between his head and his heart, and the war between his ears kicked up another volume.

I shouldn't have brought you out here. I'm crazy thinking a rich woman used to all the finest things for the last forty years now wants to give all that up to be with me.

He heard her voice again.

Don't worry about me. This is what I want. Wherever we end up, I'll be with you and that's always better. Always.

"But you're still so frail. I could see the exertion in your face just after a short ride."

I'm getting stronger, remember, I'm a medical miracle!

"There you go with those exclamations again." Sully smiled.

Well, we did it, no sense thinking about it now.

He could still hear Uncle Vern saying, "You really did it now, boy, you really did it now."

He stopped the truck for gas, and MaryAnne stirred but shut her eyes again. When he got back in, he carried two cups of coffee on top of a case of bottled water and a box of Cheez-Its.

"Cheez-Its, my favorite! You remembered."

"And so did you, MaryAnne with an e."

Sully put the water in the back, brought a few forward, and put the coffee cups in the center console. He also had bread and lunchmeat from the cooler. MaryAnne made sandwiches as he drove.

"Are you ready to tell me about Kat?"

The cat hadn't stirred since getting in the cab and lay on MaryAnne's lap.

"That ... yeah ..." He looked over at her. "Before you came back in my life, I was completely alone—isolated, depressed, angry. Really angry—out of my mind angry. I mean I wouldn't hurt anyone, not like that, but I'd let them know it."

He tightened his lips and looked away. "I yelled at the TV every night, and once, I yelled at Kat for being on the counter and knocked her off. She didn't come near me for a week. I knew I had a problem. The Sand Box, the war, screwed with my mind. I was a corpsman, sent to save lives, but I lost too many."

He glanced at his passenger again. MaryAnne was sitting up straight, turned to keep her eyes on his every expression. Sully blew on the hole in the lid of his coffee and sipped. "Don't you want yours?"

"Well, to be honest, I'm a tea drinker, but I really appreciate the thought."

"Oh, I'm sorry. I guess there's a lot I don't know about you."

She smiled. "Yeah, me too. It's okay. Please, finish your story."

"So anyway, I was at my lowest and came up with a plan—a bad one. And I waited. I waited for cold, but also for sleet and ice. I planned ... an accident. On March 11, it rained all day. I just walked around and around in my little trailer. I wore a hole in the carpet."

"I think I saw it."

He laughed, thinking she was making a joke, but he realized her brain was still having difficulty with abstractions.

"Anyway, that night, the roads started to freeze, and the rain turned to slush. 'Perfect,' I remember thinking. I was going to drive as fast as I could down this hill and head Sierra ... my truck off the road, right into an old bridge abutment. So, I loaded Kat up with dry food in two bowls knowing if she got hungry enough, she'd have to eat it before anyone found her." He waited for his angel to speak.

MaryAnne rubbed her hands against her hot coffee cup. "You were going to take your own life, and the only thing you could think to care about was Kat?"

"Yeah, well, it felt like she was all I had."

"What about family?"

"I've pushed any family I had away. I'm not a nice man, I'm not. This way, I figured, would be a whole lot easier than sticking me in some smelly nursing home and feeling even more guilty for not visiting and worrying if there would be an inheritance left after I was gone."

"Danny."

Sully let out a sigh. "I know, I just wasn't thinking right. I haven't been since Martha."

"So, what happened?"

They drove in silence until tears fell on his cheeks. They were two people so connected, so in tune with each other's hurt, they could hear each other's tears fall. MaryAnne pulled a Kleenex from her purse and raised it up to his face before he took it.

"You. You are what happened. A bunch of slush from your Humvee pounded my truck the night of your accident.

Always

That woke me up. I had to stop behind a line of cars going down the hill. And when I got to the bottom, I saw you being carried into the ambulance. I saw your wrecked Humvee wrapped around the very abutment I was going to hit." He turned to look at her. "You took my place."

MaryAnne gasped and held her hand to her mouth. He reached over for her hand and brought it to his lips.

"You made the difference, and I am here because of it."

"Not me, Danny, it wasn't me that made the difference. So much has happened to me too. I'm not the good little girl you once knew. I don't know who I am, but I'm not her."

He held her hand in silence until they turned into Mr. Bill's driveway.

"But it's God, Danny. God is all that matters. Jesus took your place, not me."

Nighttime in the mountains is a darkness like no other. Danny could barely see his hand as he left the cab of the truck.

When he knocked on Bill's door, Mr. Bill called out in a raspy voice. "Who's out there? I got my Remington trained square on your chest."

"Mr. Bill, Mr. Bill," Sully replied in his falsetto *Saturday Night Live* impersonation.

"Shoot, Danny, is that you, boy?"

Mr. Bill turned on the porch light and opened the door. He hugged Danny before noticing a second person.

"Who's that there?"

"It's me, Uncle Bill, MaryAnne." Her voice trembled.

"Come here, darling, come into the light so your uncle Bill can take a look at ya."

MaryAnne stepped forward and reached out.

"Well, I'll be, it is you, girl, you're all grown up. It's you, all right."

They went inside and sat at the table where MaryAnne's mother had celebrated her birthday so many years before. Danny noticed the watercolor he had given to her, faded but hanging in the same place.

"Never moved it, Danny. They never came back, but I left it there hoping they would," Mr. Bill said. "Figured someone's going to see it someday. I don't have much but let me fix you something."

"Mr. Bill, I'm sorry I didn't call, and so sorry it's later than I expected, but can you give me the keys to the farm—we need to be moving on."

"Of course, of course. I have them right here hanging up in the kitchen." The old man rose to fetch the keys. "Been taking real good care of the place. Thank you for the checks, but you know I'd do it for free. Here they are." Mr. Bill handed Danny the keys and they walked back outside. "Wait until I tell the boys at the Legion about this one."

MaryAnne was already in the truck, and Sully's hand was on his door. "No, Mr. Bill. Please, we need some time to settle in."

Mr. Bill nodded but looked perplexed. Sully left him standing on the porch and climbed back into Sierra and drove down the lane. The dusk-till-dawn light on the weathered telephone pole shone brightly, guiding them into the drive and then into the farmhouse.

Danny needed a flashlight to find the breaker box and turn everything on. Next, he had to prime the well pump to get water flowing through the pipes. They wouldn't have hot water until the morning. But after lighting the pilot in the old furnace, he was surprised to find some oil still in the tank. Soon, the place began to warm up.

There was scattered firewood outside, so he built a fire in the stone hearth. MaryAnne unloaded the food and wiped down the countertops and kitchen table before sitting in front of the fire with Kat.

When Danny took his place next to her, the adrenaline from their great escape had long worn off. The initial worry of getting caught had subsided and the excitement of seeing Mr. Bill now died down. In its place was a certain awkwardness that hadn't been present since they were teenagers. They wrapped themselves in one of Aunt Clare's crocheted afghans and stared into the fire, hoping to find the answer to the question yet to be asked. Neither knew what to say now, and they sat silent, transfixed by the flames. All that was done or undone filtered back. Danny thought *What now?*

MaryAnne nodded off in his arms before he started to blink, and his head started to bob. Watching the flames and feeling the mixture of warmth and cold brought back his memory of the night so long ago, so fresh in his mind. He could feel the roughness of the stone and smell the damp burnt wood. He could feel the pine straw underneath them. And he could smell her hair.

If age is just a number, tonight, I'm ageless.

He nudged her gently. "Hey, hey. I have a room for you upstairs. It should be warm by now."

The two walked up the stairs holding onto the old banister and each other.

When he rounded the corner at the top of the stairs, Danny pointed. "You can take my aunt and uncle's old room. I'll be next door."

"Oh, I thought ... ah, okay." MaryAnne reached up and kissed him on the cheek. "My gentleman. Thank you."

"No, ma'am, thank you—for saving my life."

"Danny, like I said, it wasn't me."

The old farm plaster and lathe walls were cracked with age. The yellow pine floors were only partially covered with braided rugs, and the double sash windows rattled in the breeze. Danny could hear every movement as MaryAnne settled herself in the bedroom next to his. He pictured her brushing her hair then climbing under the cold sheets and comforter. He thought he heard the bed squeak a moment later. He lay in his own bed for the longest time staring at the ceiling wide awake with questions.

He had been tossing back and forth for a while when he heard his door creak open and saw a sliver of light cross his bed. The light evaporated again as the door closed. He heard her quiet steps move closer to his bed, then felt the quilt and sheet being pulled down. His bed sagged to one side. He could smell her hair when she pulled his arm across her chest.

"I'm scared, Danny."

"Yup, me too." He pulled her closer, and they fell asleep together once again.

May 2021

The next morning, Sully looked out the kitchen window and across the meadow where hints of light broke through the trees. He dried off the dishes and set them on the table. Bacon sizzled, eggs cooked, and the kettle steamed on the stove. He turned to see MaryAnne standing in the morning sun with light streaming through her hair.

She looks like ... what's the word? Oh, right. Sully smiled.

"Hey."

"Hey. Have a seat." Sully dropped bread into the toaster, slid the eggs onto MaryAnne's plate, and poured boiling water into her cup. "I brought the eggs in the cooler and found a canister of tea bags—hope they still work." Sully fried two more eggs before sitting down as MaryAnne steeped her tea.

But he sprang back up and went out the back door. He returned in a minute, breathing out the cold air. He went to the sink and returned with a tiny vase and one tulip.

"First one of spring."

"Must be a sign," she said.

He could get lost in her smile.

After the toast popped, the dippy eggs were sopped up, and the bacon disappeared, she asked, "What shall we do today?"

She sounded as if she hadn't a care in the world and had every option available to her. She made him smile.

"Anything we want. Drive to the lake, walk in the woods, sit down by the dock, or clean the dirt out of this place."

MaryAnne laughed. "Normally, I'd say the latter, but lately, I don't want to waste another moment. We spent too many hours in the car already, so how about a walk?"

Sully rose. "Let's go." When he returned with their coats, he said, "I found one of Aunt Clare's canes if you want it."

MaryAnne had rinsed off the plates and started filling the sink with hot water. "I couldn't help myself. This egg will cake on the plates and the pan, well, you know."

He sighed. "I'll wash, you dry."

Washing up the few dishes, cups, pans, and utensils took but a few minutes. The hot soapy water felt good on his cold hands, and seeing clean plates stacked in the plastic dish rack felt better. At his trailer, he would have just put them in the dishwasher until the end of the week, washed them, and taken them out as he needed throughout the week. The routine had been simple but left him so unsatisfied.

They left their clean dishes behind, put on their coats, and walked together to the mountain. Sully turned up the collar of his peacoat and kept his hands warm inside the deep pockets. MaryAnne carried her cane in one hand and slipped her other hand into his coat pocket. The old sailor was a kid again.

They walked to the edge of the field and squeezed between a rusty, barbed wire fence.

"Stop." MaryAnne pointed with her cane to a doe and two spotted fawns. The mother chewed on pasture grass while the two little ones danced around in a game of tag.

"They're early," he whispered.

Always

"They're so innocent."

The deer grazed as the new couple moved on up the first hill and into the woods. Climbing proved harder than either had bargained, and both were shortly out of breath. They stopped by a fallen tree, and Sully took out a canteen from his knapsack.

"Drink."

MaryAnne pushed the water away. "I'm not thirsty."

"Drink, your muscles need it."

MaryAnne complied but looked sternly at him.

"You sound like Jonesy. He used to tell me when to drink and when to eat."

Sully cocked his head. "I'm sorry. I didn't mean it that way. I was just trying to show, you know, I care."

They started walking higher and the terrain grew steeper and familiar. They came to a rock outcropping that looked over the valley. The sun beat on the stone and the stone blocked the breeze.

"Bedrock." MaryAnne looked up at him. "Fred."

"My Wilma." He slipped his hand in hers and dropped carefully to his knee.

MaryAnne's hand went to her mouth. "Danny."

He reached into his pocket and pulled out his class ring. 1975. "I ain't much, and this is all I got, but what I got is yours. Please, MaryAnne, will you—"

She slowly shook her head from side to side as tears welled. "I'm so sorry, it's just—"

"Jonesy?"

She shook her head more. "Yes, but no. I'm so confused." MaryAnne took his hand and placed the ring in his palm. He squeezed his ring until it hurt. "I just can't. Not now."

Sully whispered, "I never let you go."

"I know. You were always there."

"Always."

He couldn't help touching her face. "You are so soft."

The two walked to the edge of the bluff. Sully got cheese and apples out of the backpack and pulled out his pocketknife he had found in the kitchen drawer.

"Your Boy Scout knife."

"You remember that?"

He sat a while looking over the valley, then began cutting slices of apple and cheese and putting them on one napkin.

"MaryAnne, I've been thinking. You said you remembered my knife."

"Yeah."

"Earlier, you said you remembered Jonesy telling you what to eat and drink."

"Oh right, dinner was always at six sharp, and a glass of water had to be next to his plate." She pushed a breath hard out through her nose. "It didn't matter if there wasn't anything on the table. If his water was there, it seemed to assure him he was important."

He stopped slicing apples and cheese. "Don't you see? Think about it. You remembered something."

"Well, it's just—"

"Not just. It's important. It's like someone who's paralyzed but after a long time moves a finger. It's not much, but it's a finger."

She frowned at him. "So?"

"So, MaryAnne, you just moved a finger."

Her face lit up with a smile. "Yeah ... yeah, I did. I moved a finger!"

They sat on the rock soaking in the sunshine, not talking, just thinking—as much as Sully tried not to.

"Maybe being up here, just seeing Uncle Bill," she said after a time, "seeing the house, the pond, even these rocks are reminders. Maybe it's helping me get my memory back."

Always

"Maybe. Maybe we should get back to the house."

Sully wanted MaryAnne whole, but he also wanted all of her. And now he feared he could lose both.

The two packed their things, retied their shoes, and made their way down the trail. The pines gave way to the hardwoods now with leaves sprouting and the beginnings of acorns showing. The trail was littered with winter's branches and leaves. Sully no longer took in the flora—his mind stuck spinning. He thought he'd never feel the angst, anger, or helplessness again, but those emotions were coming back with every mental revolution.

MaryAnne stepped ahead on the narrowing trail, and her shoe slipped down the muddy side of a rock. Before he could reach her, she fell backwards, hitting the back of her head on the trail at his feet.

He went down on one knee while MaryAnne struggled to get up. "Stay down, stay down, just catch your breath first. Let's make sure you're okay."

MaryAnne moved her feet and hands, legs and arms as Sully felt her head where she'd smacked it. He didn't find anything unusual. *I need to pay better attention.* He scanned her limbs like he'd been taught at his corpsman school.

"I'm okay. Just help me up." She sat up, turned on all fours, and rose with him holding her under her arms. "Wow, that was close, huh?"

They walked farther until they arrived back at the rusty, barbed wire fence.

"Oh," gasped MaryAnne and pointed.

A fawn lay bawling in the grass with its leg tangled in some fencing. In the distance, Sully could see his mother pawing at the ground with every step. As Sully kneeled, he could see the fawn's underbelly panting and blood oozing from her hind leg. He unwound the wire and pulled her leg free. The mother moved closer. She dropped her head and snorted when he cradled the doe in both arms. Then he lowered her to the ground. The fawn ran off with her mother and never looked back. *I guess that's what we gotta do too.*

"Sir Lancelot."

"Yeah." Sully shook his head, and the two walked through the field and around the pond with the old dock now listing to one side. Cropping up through the weeds were the remnants of the old rowboat, green with lichens, no longer seaworthy.

As they walked past the old swing and headed up the back porch steps, MaryAnne squeezed his hand. "That was special."

He nodded.

"You're really quiet."

"I get that way," he told her. "I'm sorry."

He opened the door, and the two sat again at the old oak table. Thoughts of Uncle Vern and Aunt Clare flitted through his mind.

"I have something I need to tell you." MaryAnne got up to look out the window. "Ever since this morning, my mind has been spinning."

He nodded. "Mine too."

"But mine are old memories. They're coming back in little pieces, and sometimes I put them together, and sometimes I'm so confused. After I slipped, they started coming faster. Danny, I-I think I'm engaged to Jonesy. He told me before, but now I feel it here." She held her hand over her heart. "I have friends. I have a life. I really don't know who I am or was, but I-I have to figure it out somehow."

Now Sully stood. "You have to go back."

"No." She shook her head. "I can't."

Always

"You have to. I've been thinking about it too." He stared at his feet while she propped herself against the porcelain sink. "Ever since you said that about Jonesy and his water on the table ... and then when I freed the fawn, I knew it then. I have to let you go. It's why I've been so quiet."

She frowned. "What are we going to do?"

"I'll take you back."

MaryAnne pushed herself away from the sink. "No, you can't. Jonesy will shoot you on site."

"That's funny. You *are* getting better."

"Take me to Uncle Bill's. I can make calls from there. There's a few numbers rolling around in my head. One of them has to work."

MaryAnne went upstairs while tears streamed down Sully's cheeks. He stared out the window to where his grandparents had sat every evening.

When MaryAnne returned, she carried her backpack and handed him his custodial uniform. They held each other, neither ready to let go.

"I can't do this, I can't," she cried.

"Me neither. I can't let you go. I will always—"

A moment later, she pulled away. "What's this? I never saw this one before." She pointed at a watercolor on the wall.

"That's Aunt Clare and Uncle Vern sitting on their swing out back. They did that every evening at sundown."

"I think that's your best one." MaryAnne ran her finger across the frame.

She kissed him, and he kissed her back. Together, they walked out to Sierra and drove down the lane. He drove slowly, but Bill's house came into view too soon.

The old man was already on the porch when they parked the truck. "Didn't expect to see you twice in two days already."

"Mr. Bill, may I use your phone? It's long distance."

"Sure, sure, young lady, just leave your quarter on the table."

On her third try, she got Jonesy on the phone. Sully walked into the other room, and Mr. Bill started talking about the farm and the Legion.

"Well, it's done," she said when she returned. "He's sending a limo of all things. It will be here in a few hours. He didn't even offer to come. Maybe he's worried about me changing my mind. Or maybe he's afraid of you, but I told him you were nowhere around. Guess a limo is better than listening to him all the way back."

"How'd he sound?" Sully asked.

She shrugged. "Large and in charge. But he calmed down and was pretty businesslike. 'Just so you're okay,' he said, but I don't think he really cared, not really."

"I don't think I can stay here," Sully said then made for the door. "This hurts so bad. I can't lose you, not again."

"You're not losing me." MaryAnne touched his chest. "You never did, right? I was always here with you."

"You can stay here, Danny. I was just making lunch," said Mr. Bill.

"I can't. I'm sorry."

He turned to leave, but Mr. Bill stopped him and turned to MaryAnne.

"This morning, I went into my attic and found this box. Your father brought this up here some time ago, and after seeing you two together, I got to thinking about it. Anyway, here it is."

He set down a rusty box the size of an old bread box.

MaryAnne opened the dusty lid. Inside were two large packets of letters, bound and stained with age.

"Look, Danny, they're our letters. He never burned them."

Always

Sully moved closer and picked up the other packet.

"There's some paper in the bottom," Mr. Bill said, pointing.

Sully picked up the torn bits. On one was written, *Love always, MaryAnne.* The second he handed to MaryAnne. *Love always, Danny.*

He could feel his eyes filling fast with tears.

"Danny?"

He drew in a breath and sniffed. "MaryAnne, I couldn't say it back at the farm, but I will always love you. It's just the way I'll always be."

He hated himself for not looking up at her. Anyone else might have grabbed her and not let go, but he knew what he needed to do. He took the one packet of letters and her torn page, went out to Sierra, and didn't look back. He just couldn't.

May 2021

Sully drove back to the farm, tossed the packet of letters on the table, and opened a can for Kat. He didn't do much for the next few days. He figured the county sheriff would be by with an arrest warrant, but one never came. He worked on the house, patched the roof, dug the gardens, and gathered up any barbed wire he could find. He ventured into town a few times but said little and never stopped at Mr. Bill's on the way home. *Next time,* he told himself.

In town while shopping, he noticed a flyer on the bulletin board. *Canadensis Counseling Center. Call for an appointment.* He saw the notice every time he pushed his cart through the automatic sliding doors. After a particularly fitful night, he called the listed number. The next day, he shaved, put on a collared shirt, and drove into town.

The jeans-clad receptionist handed him a clipboard, and he filled out all the typical information. He stared at the last question. *Why are you here today?* He wrote *Life.*

"Mr. Sullivan?" a man with small, round glasses said, holding out his hand. "I'm Martin." The therapist shook his hand weakly.

Sully worked up a smile. *My gosh, he's young.* "Hello, Marty."

"It's Martin."

After going through introductions, informed consent, duty to warn, and insurance, Martin looked down at the clipboard.

"Life?"

"Yeah, well, there's a lot, and you only had a few lines, and I never was much for words. Well, maybe a long time ago, but that was a long time ago."

"Pick just one," Martin said, handing him back the clipboard. "It doesn't have to be the biggest, but maybe the thing that made you to decide to visit today."

"Now?"

"Yes. Why did you decide to come in today?"

"That's a good question."

Martin looked at him. *Do they all get staring lessons in school?* Sully looked around the room. A master's degree from East Stroudsburg University and a couple of certificates hung on the wall. A coffee mug, no pictures, sat on the desk.

"I guess because of the other night ... I-I couldn't sleep and when I did, I had the dream."

"The dream?" Martin pushed his glasses up his nose.

"Yeah, it's always the same theme. I'm down range, guys are dying, and I can't get to them like I'm in quicksand, or I miss something stupid. Last night, I lost my stethoscope, and when they were carrying Jimmy away, I saw it sticking out of his sucking chest wound."

"Jimmy?"

"A buddy of mine from Iraq. I've been over this a million times in my mind. It was a long, long time ago in a far distant land."

Sully rubbed his thighs and stared at the certificates on the wall.

Always

"Have you ever told anyone about what you've been through?"

"Lots of times, parts anyway."

"Never the whole story, from beginning to end?"

Sully frowned. "No, why?"

"Memory is a funny thing."

No kidding, Doc.

"We tend to skip over things unpleasing or distasteful, and we fill in the gaps. Before long, we can have a made-up memory that doesn't look like the real thing."

"So, you saying I'm making stuff up? That it really didn't happen?" He reached for his keys inside his pocket.

Martin held out a hand to stop him. "Not at all, sir. I'm just saying if you've never told the whole story from beginning to end with your thoughts, your emotions, your behavior, then you never got the relief you are seeking. And maybe it spills over into your dreams."

"Okay, Doc. What would Freud say about my dream?"

The therapist laughed. "How about a Coke before we dig in? Some coffee?"

"Sure, coffee, black."

After retrieving two mugs of coffee, black, Martin sat back down while Sully sipped.

"I'm more into a type of therapy that's been shown to be effective for PTSD," the therapist said. "You pick the story, and we go through it from beginning to end. I ask certain questions, but we go at your pace."

Sully blew across the top of his mug. "Then what?"

Martin smiled. "Then we do it again."

"Again. That's it?"

"That's enough for now, isn't it? I mean sometimes I might ask you to write it down, or you could use your phone and record it, then replay it or reread it through the week."

"Dude, I want to forget this stuff."

"Sorry, *dude*, that ship has sailed. But what you can do is recall it without the fear, without the guilt."

"Man, how did you know? I mean about the guilt?"

"Hey, you're good at doing what you do—holding this stuff in—I'm good at what I do—getting it out."

Now Sully smiled.

"Is this where I begin ... at the beginning?"

Martin pressed his lips together, looked over his horn-rimmed glasses, and nodded. "Just record your voice on your phone."

Sully fumbled with his phone before he found the right app. "I was thirty-two, so I could only join the reserves in '90. If I was a corpsman, I could train as a radiology tech at a military hospital each month and stay home. But when Bush thought we should liberate Kuwait, things changed for me, and I found myself with the Marines fighting through to Iraq."

Martin nodded as he jotted some notes. "I think I remember that."

"Anyway, we weren't supposed to get much resistance. There were some Republican Guard, and some Ba'athists and Fedayeen Saddam militia, and we needed to take two bridges. Easy day, right? The first bridge was easy. I was in Charlie Company, in the back of an AAV."

Martin seldom looked up as he scribbled feverishly on a yellow legal pad, but this made him squint at Sully. "Huh?"

"Oh, Amphibious Assault Vehicle. Bravo got bogged down in mud, but we continued up Ambush Alley, which was a street bordered by tall buildings. We were taking small arms and RPGs, rocket propelled grenades."

Martin nodded and returned his gaze to his notepad.

Always

"We got across the second bridge and set up a herringbone formation of vehicles that stretched along this canal—fully exposed."

Sully stopped when Martin held up his hand. "That's a good start, but I want you to tell me your story just as you are there, right now, not like an after-action report. First-person, present. Start with 'I am' and take it from there. Shut your eyes for a moment, and one picture will come to mind."

Sully took a deep breath. *Combat breathing they call it.* "I'm kneeling on this concrete pad wrapping a grunt's head who's got shrapnel embedded like a human pin cushion. Blood is pouring out faster than I can wrap. Hell is raining down on us."

"Better. Now say 'hell is raining down on me' and continue."

"Hell is raining down on me. I climb out of our vehicle through a port because the back ramp is jammed. Hell is raining down on me from enemy mortar fire that's walking in closer. I hear the roar of A-10s flying overhead. 'We're saved,' I scream. Then our Air Force Wart Hogs direct their massive guns at me—at us. Our vehicles are getting lit up. There's a Marine, Hobbs, running to me. Now he's chopped in half. There's nowhere to hide." Sully looked up. "You know my last therapist was air force." He tried to smile.

Martin looked past him. "Stay in the story, Sully."

Tears ran down Sully's cheeks as he continued. "The second, then the third air strikes. 'Make it stop!' I scream, 'MAKE IT STOP!' My sergeant shoots flares but they come again. Someone raises an American flag, and they finally leave us alone, but now mortars are exploding in the soft mud all around us. Dead Marines, moaning from the wounded. I'm working so fast. Wrapping bandages, T-shirts, anything to stop the bleeding, but I never could."

He opened his eyes and wiped sweat from his face. Martin handed him a box of tissues.

"Sergeant yells, 'Load up.' We go back down the same alley we came up. The gauntlet, someone says. Old men, women, even kids shoot everything they have at us. Snipers are crouched on rooftops behind walls. Our grenade launchers and 50-call machine guns can't keep up. We break down and break for cover inside a house. A man and woman run out of the back, but minutes later, he runs back in screaming at us until someone shoots him dead."

Sully shook his head and took a sip of his coffee but choked. His shirt was wet with sweat, his stare fixed, a thousand miles away.

"I'm giving morphine shots like it's flu season. I run IV bags, tie two tourniquets on mangled legs. No Blackhawk can land, but the gunships give us hope. Someone says the other vehicle turned around, and I load the wounded, then the two dead. I'm the last to leave, right in front of the staff sergeant, and we head south to the first bridge."

Sweat poured now from Sully's head and neck. His collared shirt, limp.

"Okay, good, Mr. Sullivan. You're doing good. Take a deep breath. Combat breathing, is it? Now, let another picture come to mind. This one may not be the first or the last, just one that haunts you."

Sully cocked his head then slumped in the chair with his eyes shut, his hands and his face both clenched tight. Only his breathing was heard.

A minute, maybe two, passed.

He slowly shook his head. "We evac back to the first bridge, and I hear some gunfire in the distance. Everything is over, except for the fat lady singing. Corny, I know.

Always

Blackhawks are evacuating our casualties. Jimmy had been taking care of the other vehicle but now he gets pulled out by four Marines. I kneel in the bloody sand on both knees. Jimmy's spit is gurgling. I hear nothing but wheezing, so I yank on Jimmy's MOLLE pack and harness to get to his armor. 'You left your armor plate behind, so you could carry more supplies and you got yourself shot,' I yell at him. I cut apart his BDUs—his uniform. This is bad."

Sully rubbed his now empty coffee mug between his hands. "A Marine asks, 'Doc, what do want me to do?' 'Do you remember your BLS—basic life support,' I shout. Then I hand him a tourniquet to tie right above Jimmy's knee. 'Which one?' he asks. Instantly, I'm furious. 'The one that isn't there anymore!' I scream at him."

Sully took a deep breath before continuing.

"Marine does what I say while I work on Jimmy's chest. I throw a packet at the Marine's face. 'Cut this open ... Gimme ... now.' I tape a three-sided bandage over the hole in his chest.

"'Way to go, Doc,' he tells me. 'You did it!' No, paradoxical breathing. I grab Jimmy's stethoscope. It's got a stupid smiley face sticker on it. Plural effusion ... pneumothorax. 'He's got a collapsed lung ... Gimme.' I snap my fingers. The dude freezes and I yell, 'My med pack! Bring it closer.' When he does, I order him to tear apart some bandages and keep the wound clean.

"Blood and fluid are flowing from the tube. Dang it, where's the 60?" Sully opened his eyes wide and stared at Martin. "I think of my uncle Vern then. He used to say 'dang it.'"

When Marty nods, he closed his eyes again.

"'On its way, Doc,' the Marine says. 'On its way.' We carry Jimmy back to the bird. I keep two fingers on Jimmy's throat and feel his breath. 'Drop him, drop him here,' I say. Someone runs from the helo with a defibrillator. 'We got him from here, Doc.' 'Clear.' The PA shoots him with electricity. 'Don't die on me, don't you dare,'" I scream.

Sully opened his eyes.

"What's the last thing you see?" Martin asked.

"His stethoscope. I left his stethoscope on his chest. I used to steal it, now I give it back."

Sully sat staring into Martin's caring eyes. "You did good, you did real good."

"I thought I'd be a blithering mass of tears."

"You're dealing with a lot. Tears may come later. It's important to know you didn't fall apart. Is this the first time you've told your story to anyone?"

"Yeah." Sully nodded. "I forgot about the stethoscope until now. Jimmy had a smiley face on it because I always borrowed it."

"Take your phone with you," Martin suggested. "Every day, at least once, sit down by yourself, use your earphones and replay it with no outside distractions."

Sully looked at him, expecting his look of disgust would unsettle Martin and he'd recant.

But the therapist simply smiled. "You can do this. You've been doing it for the last fifteen years, but you never saw it through to the end. Leaving the memory unfinished kept it alive. Now you'll finish, and it will make a difference. Just do it for one week. Come back then, and if you are not sleeping better, I will buy you a new phone."

"Yeah, that's funny. I just got this one."

Sully left after paying a nominal fee. As he drove down the road, he noticed the Legion sign still with one lightbulb and decided to go see Mr. Bill.

Always

Sully sat beside Mr. Bill at the Legion several hours later. Gone was the smoke, Old Joe, Melvin, and Marge. While the two old vets sipped their beers, Sully started to talk.

"The thing that still gets me isn't the A-10s or our aluminum AMTRACs, and it isn't even the lousy intel." Sully took a big gulp of his beer.

"I got angry when I saw all those CONEX boxes with all those contractors' names. I wanted to paint Jimmy's name across one of them. And you wonder why I'm angry? I lost Jimmy, my only friend." He shook his head. "He used to call me 'Pops' because I was almost old enough to be his dad. At our missing Marine memorial, in this case a navy corpsman, we hung his stethoscope around his M-16, his boots on the ground and his helmet on top—the same stethoscope I used to *requisition* from him. That smiley face kept staring up at me."

Mr. Bill stood and raised his beer. Sully followed.

"To Jimmy," Mr. Bill said, "and to all the boys of Charlie Company."

They toasted, but Sully started to cry.

Bill pulled him close with both arms and whispered, "If I were down range again, I'd want you standing over me when someone yells, 'Corpsman up,' 'cause I know you'd answer the call."

Sully might have seen Old Joe in the mirror tip his hat after they settled up with the barmaid and headed out the door.

A month later, Sully saw a "William Becker" listed in the obituaries. The obit said he'd been a Korean War veteran.

Sully found a clean shirt, arrived late to the funeral, and sat in the back of the church packed with old vets, old ladies, and an old minister. When everyone stood at the end, he thought he saw an angel, but his eyes were filled with tears. He started shaking, got some fresh air, and cursed at himself for not going back in.

Sully returned home in time for the sunset.

He had sat on the old oak swing suspended by two chains every night since she left. And every night before the sun went down, he'd read one of her letters. On this night, he pulled out his last envelope. He gently sliced the short end with his pocketknife. His fingers trembled as he held the paper before he held the letter to his nose as if he sensed her fragrance. Then he read her words.

> Dear Fred,
>
> One of the best things about my week is writing to you. It brings me joy. I've gotten to the point where I no longer expect a reply. I really don't think it's not fair. I'm not owed a letter or even deserve it. If one comes, I will be ecstatic! If it doesn't, I will still be happy! Sorry about so many!! But when I think about you, I can't help myself!!! Anyway, I will never forget our promise, and my only hope is I will see you in a hundred years, but maybe a little sooner would be nice. I don't know what this world has in store for us, what we will do, where we will be, but no matter the changes, no matter the times, or how old we get, I know we will always share our love. It's the way we'll always be side by side.
>
> Always,
>
> Wilma

Sully cried most evenings, and this one was no different, just maybe more. But he had started painting again, sunsets mostly. He picked up his watercolor paper already

Always

taped to a board and started sketching in some trees on the perimeter, a doe and two fawns, and the horizon. He worked with reds, oranges, and purples with dark trees surrounding the edges. His work took on darker tones, giving them a mysterious, almost ominous look.

He tossed his watercolor to the side after a while and fiddled with something inside his pocket.

"Why, MaryAnne? Why do other people grow old together surrounded by the one they love but not us?"

Maybe there's something better in store.

"I tell you it isn't fair. I can't accept it, and I can't understand it. I know you went back to a tough situation. I hate to think of you being abused, but that's what it is."

Not anymore. I won't put up with how I was treated ever again.

"I can't imagine a man like Jonesy ever changing."

He didn't.

"Then you need to get out of there."

"I did."

Sully turned. "MaryAnne?"

"Danny, I'm here."

An old man stood, but two kids reached for each other and kissed each other—warm, sweet, and soft. *Oh, so soft.* They wiped tears from each other's cheeks and laughed briefly, before the two kids gently eased down onto their swing.

Danny dropped to one knee beside the swing. He reached inside his front pocket, took her hand in his, and slipped his class ring from 1975 onto her finger. He whispered the words, "Will you—"

"Yes."

MaryAnne took his hand in hers, and they held onto each other as the sun went down on their sunset together.

The day had been set just a month before. Not much to plan, really. The preacher, a few old friends, and the fellas from the legion. Even Martin showed up. Danny—as he preferred to be called again—had built a little white trellis on the dock at the pond which needed shoring up. MaryAnne wore a light blue dress that went below her knees and a matching floppy hat that dipped below one eye. In her hands, she held a bouquet of tulips and baby's breath.

And after the I do's, the group had set up a small catered lunch on the lawn. The fellas from the Legion slapped Danny on the back, someone elbowed him in the ribs, and just as quickly, everyone left the newlyweds to themselves.

"Well." Danny's thumbs were in his pockets as he looked at the ground.

"Well." MaryAnne giggled.

"Suppose you're pretty tired," he said.

"I guess I could lie down."

"Oh okay, I mean if you really are tired."

"Well, I have another idea. Wait here." MaryAnne went upstairs and after a few minutes returned in a pair of jeans, carrying a backpack over her shoulder.

Danny reached to zip it up and saw the blanket inside. "Oh."

She didn't say a thing but grabbed his hand and led her husband out the screen door. They climbed once again up their mountain until they reached Bedrock.

MaryAnne took a blanket out of her backpack and lay it on the soft bed of pine needles. With her large soft brown eyes, she looked into his.

Always

"Mr. Sullivan, I ... I always—"

"I know, Mrs. Sullivan. I always knew."

About the Author

As a twin in a family of five children, **Andy M Davidson** grew up sitting at a crowded kitchen table in DelCo, the suburbs of Philly. After Messiah College, I went on to graduate school at Indiana State to pursue my doctorate in Psychology. This was followed by a twenty-year career, retiring as an O6/Captain in the navy. The navy took me as far away as Iraq and Afghanistan but dropped me off in Georgia. I'm alive and well in my little cabin in the woods where I work from home, helping veterans who are struggling with their past. It's demanding at times, but my message is one of hope that can only come from God who is gracious. And I get far more than I give.

I hope you get a chance to read *When Sunday Smiled*, the memoir of my pilgrimage on the Appalachian Trail after my son's life was taken in a motorcycle accident. I'm also excited about *All that Matters*, my first novel about Carol who heroically searches for her missing daughter.

After working on the next great American novel, I love to paint—watercolor is my medium. And when moved, I make a mean batch of homemade ice cream. My children live in different time zones—Texas, Colorado, and Heaven—with children and grown-up lives of their own. But I count it all joy. I am loved, blessed, and no longer seeking greatness, just goodness.

I choose real,

I chose gratitude,

I chose Jesus.

Discontentment's Twin

I am discovering
The beauty left
layered within
beneath soulful
yearnings are
discontentment's twin
Folded over, a
seedling buried
now stretched to the sun
is glowing
I gave up great
and found only
Good
'Tis good is better
'cause great is
only great.
But Good is
Always good

AD

Other Andy M Davidson Books

WHEN SUNDAY SMILED

walking through life and loss

ANDY M DAVIDSON

ALL THAT MATTERS

Saving Becca

ANDY M DAVIDSON

Always

Made in the USA
Columbia, SC
20 May 2025